The Lone Sentry

Michael Conwell

The Lone Sentry

Michael Conwell

Miguelgran41@gmail.com

A soldier from a northern industrial city is redirected into the Military Police at the end of World War II. He falls in love just as he is leaving Missouri and has a romance in New York City before embarking on his adventures in Europe.

The cover photograph is courtesy of the Military Police Corps Museum, Fort Leonard Wood, Missouri, U.S. Army.

The original photograph appeared on a pamphlet, "The Story of the Corps of Military Police" later changed to Military Police Corps.

Dedication

This book is dedicated to the men and women who served during World War II and its aftermath, especially my brothers, Chuck, Joe and Jim and our uncle, William Conwell, who fought in the Normandy invasion.

Michael Conwell

Contents

Forward

This novel is inspired by, but not about my brother, Joseph Conwell. There are some similarities between Joe Conrad and himself. I put together a few stories told by my brother about his service in Germany and my imagination got the best of me. Joe Conrad is from Erie, PA, ninety miles from Buffalo, NY. Our family lived in Erie before the Depression but moved to Buffalo, NY in the years prior to World War II. Our brothers Chuck and Jim both served in the Navy during and immediately after World War II. Our sister, Patsy, was the model of a 1940's bobbysoxer. Several historical entertainers appear in the story in plausible situations. Some incidents are based on the author's personal experience.

Never write anything that does not give you great pleasure. Emotion is easily transferred from the writer to the reader. ~ *Joseph Joubert*

Better to write for yourself and have no public, than to write for the public and have no self. ~ *Cyril Connolly*

Write in recollection and amazement for yourself. ~ *Jack Kerouac*

Acknowledgements

I am thankful to my wonderful wife, Patricia. She is my closest friend, advisor and supporter. Her encouragement has helped move my projects along. She is my editor and proofreader.

I thank my friends in the Marketing and Publication Group at the Helen Hall Library in League City, Texas for their willingness to teach newbies like myself how to progress, once the writing bug has attached itself.

I made liberal use of Google, Wikipedia and the *Life Magazine* Archive especially the VE Day issue. My French and German phrase books were most helpful.

The primary inspirations were the stories of my brother, Joe. He was redirected from the Army Air Corps to the Military Police. He arrived at the port of LeHavre and travelled to Nuremburg in the old French 40 and 8 boxcars. I inspected an example at the Holocaust Museum in Houston Texas. He contracted an internal infection and remained in a bombed-out hospital in Nuremburg for several weeks. I didn't know how to deal with that illness but I know how to treat pneumonia.

I thank my daughter, Jennifer Stief, for editing portions of the story and wading through my military jargon and attempted foreign phrases. I also thank René Armstrong for her assistance in polishing my work.

Michael Conwell

Chapter 1 – Fort Leonard Wood

"How come you decided to be an MP, Joe? Were you a cop before you were drafted?" Bill had been a security guard in the Humble Refinery in Baytown, Texas. They were sitting on their plywood footlockers in their two-story, wooden barracks. The Military Police training school was located at Fort Leonard Wood, Missouri. They were polishing their brass buckles and insignia, sharing a can of Brasso. The brick-red linoleum shined from waxing it in the morning. The windows were clear with no nose prints.

Joe Conrad said, "I wasn't drafted and I really wanted to fly. I enlisted to be a radio operator in a bomber. I was qualified to be a navigator or bombardier but I wanted the electronics training. The training was minimal but I know my way around a radio receiver. Trouble is that there wasn't much left to bomb in Germany and my specialty was no longer needed. I was given the choice of going to the Pacific for the invasion of the Japanese mainland or I could become an MP." The Military Police were in high demand in Europe with the war rapidly coming to a close.

Joe's family came to St. Louis in February to his graduation from radio school at Scott Field. They travelled by train from their home in Erie, Pennsylvania. His dad was an engineer on the Pennsy. Joe got the news after they left that he would have to change directions. There was a class available the following week at the MP School at Fort Leonard Wood. It was just west of St. Louis. He was almost there. He had dreamed of flying since grammar school and even took a class in aircraft design in high school. He delayed his enlistment until he graduated and hooked up with an Air Corps Cadet program near Erie. He received a uniform and reported every other weekend for a couple days of on the job training. This was mostly marching drill and classes. There was also busy work. They did any unskilled, menial task that needed doing.

"I enlisted in June but couldn't begin basic until July. I took the train to Fort Dix, New Jersey. It was the farthest I had ever been away from home."

He hadn't counted on all the spit and polish that went with the MP training. Then again, it was better than being shot out of the sky to wind up in a German POW camp. The Allies had the Krauts on the run and they would soon be in Berlin. They were racing the Soviets for territory. Fort Leonard Wood was in the foothills of the Ozarks. Joe and Bill were preparing to go to St. Robert's in the evening after inspection. There was a spaghetti dinner for the troops at St. Robert Bellarmine Church on Route 66. First, they had to get through this inspection. He had his footlocker laid out with the six rolled pair of boxer shorts, and six pair of socks that he never wore. They were just for inspection. The clean double-edged Gillette razor rested on the white washcloth. MP School was expensive. Joe and his buddies had to buy extra uniforms since they had to be laundered daily if not twice a day. That's why a free dinner at church was better than a pass in St. Lou.

Bill Wallace really got into this training. His work as a security guard at Humble Oil Company was like playing at being a cop. He told Joe that he just manned the gate and checked lunch boxes of the men on their way out of work. It was crazy that they didn't care what you brought in the refinery as long as it wasn't matches. Don't get caught taking a tool out in your box. Soldiers manned machine gun posts around the perimeter of the refinery. They weren't that far from Galveston and German saboteurs had been apprehended there. Submarines can go anywhere. Bill's uncle was a mule wrangler at the Red Barn in the refinery and got Bill the job. Humble favored the mules for pulling equipment because they didn't make sparks or use precious gasoline. Most of the output was aviation gasoline and that's why the Army was there to protect the plant.

They could use Bill's uncle tonight. The church was sending a hay wagon and a couple of Missouri mules to pick up the boys at the front gate. If the stars were right, a few of the girls would come along to welcome the soldiers. There would be a dance later in the evening.

"Bill, why are they always Missouri mules? Why not Texas mules or Rhode Island mules? Just askin'." Felix said, "Rhode Island's got chickens. You've heard of Rhode Island Reds." Felix Jackson knew of what he spoke. He was from Quincy, Massachusetts and that is near Rhode Island. He worked in a stone quarry before the draft board began making noises and he decided to enlist to get some training. If you want to blow something up, Felix was your man. He was too young to be an explosives expert. That came with years of experience. He just knew how to drill the holes and tamp the charges. Experience as a Military Police officer could lead to a job on the Boston Police Force after the war.

That just left Mike Schneider, the quiet one. With a name like Schneider, he learned to keep a low profile with anti-

German sentiment being what it was. He actually had law enforcement experience as a sheriff deputy in Jackson, Mississippi. He had little training, just experience. It was time to go now. They had to go by the Orderly Room to sign out and pick up their passes. There'd be another quick inspection by the Officer of the Day to make sure they weren't bringing discredit on their service. Shoes shined? Check! Brass shined? Check! Ties tied? Gig line straight? Check! Check! The wagon was waiting at the gate and it was half-full. Four girls came along to act as hostesses. Any more and there wouldn't be room for the GI's. The early birds got the girls. There were half a dozen animated conversations going already. The girls were dressed pretty much alike, fluffy sweaters, plaid wool skirts below their knees, Bobbie socks and saddle shoes. It was spring but it was still cool. There were three brunettes and one was kind of blonde. Her hair was short with a bit of a curl in front of her ears. A few more guys came along, and the wagon was on its way.

The two mules plodded slowly along Missouri Avenue to the church. Some young kids on the sidewalk yelled, "Get a horse!" Felix said, "Look at these guys. A couple more years and they'll be joining us in the Army." Most folks just waved or said, "Hi." The three-mile ride took about a half hour and they arrived around 18:30 hours. The church ladies welcomed them to the church hall. On Sundays, this hall magically turned into a church as they set up the altar for Mass. Tonight, it sported eight tables and plenty of chairs. The wagon hostesses joined about sixteen of their friends giving them a numerical superiority of two over the sharply dressed soldiers. The girls gathered together and the men did the same in spite of their bravado about what they would do with these chicks tonight. One of the church ladies talked to the girls and a couple of them broke off and walked over to Joe and Bill. One was the somewhat blonde girl from the wagon.

She said, "She told us we're supposed to mix and I'm mixin'. My name is Margaret. What's yours and where are you from. I don't suspect you're from around here."

"Hi Darlin." Joe said, "My name is Joe, Joe Conrad and I'm from Erie in the Great Commonwealth of Pennsylvania."

"Why you callin me Darlin? I don't even know you."

"Don't know me! Why we just met and Margaret seems kind of long," said Joe.

"Well, you can call me Daisy, Daisy Watson from the Great State of Missouri."

Joe introduced his buddy, Bill Wallace, to Daisy and her friend, Hazel. "Howdy ladies," said Bill in his best Texas drawl. "Now when does the food come out? We're all starving from a hard day of working."

Hazel spoke up, "Yeah! Your hard work is all about writing speeding tickets and standing in front of a gatehouse looking like a tin soldier. No! I'm just being unpleasant. I've had a long day putting up jars of pickles in boxes at the cannery."

"We are tin soldiers. Aren't we Bill? From our tin helmets to our brass buckles and our shiny boots," said Joe as he nudged Bill with his elbow. "I joined this Army to fly planes but here I am in police training but it's where the Army says they need me and I have to do something for the next couple of years."

"Japan still has things to bomb. Why not go over there and end this damn war?" said Hazel.

Daisy piped up, "Slow down Hazel. We just met these two fellas and you're getting all hot under the collar. Give them a break, girl."

Hazel returned with, "All right guys. We know what you do and you know now that I work in a canning factory. Last week it was peas. This week pickles. One goes into cans and the other into jars. That's what my three and a half years of high school taught me. I quit in January to help out my family. Margaret here will be graduating in June."

Daisy said, "I can't wait! Two more months and I'll be out of school and I'm going to find a fella and get married. Should I have said that?"

Joe said, "So you're not a career girl. You don't want to be a teacher, secretary or a nurse. What are you going to do until Mr. Right comes along?"

"I can be a checkout clerk at the A&P. They're always hiring and I'm good with numbers."

One of the ladies called, "Come on ladies, gentlemen. Everyone take a seat. We'd like to see boy, girl, boy, girl. We will serve you at the table when you're seated. You boys get enough of chow lines. We want this to be family style."

Joe and Bill grabbed a table along with Daisy and Hazel. Another couple filled in the last couple of seats. The men from the kitchen brought bowls of spaghetti noodles and the women brought out the red sauce and meatballs that they cooked all afternoon. The meatballs had a secret ingredient. They used

Kellogg's Corn Flakes to make the meat stretch. The sauce was rich and spicy. They also put out loaves of crusty French bread that were split and slathered with margarine, garlic, parsley and paprika. This was new to most of the guys.

One of the men spoke up. "Let us pray for this bountiful meal. Bless us O Lord and these, your gifts, which we are about to receive from your bounty through Christ, our Lord."

"Amen" everyone said together. "Now chow down!" They would find it hard to believe that the cook who prayed was the pastor. He wore a plaid shirt and denim trousers under his sauce stained white apron. He was Father Richard St. John and he had been building up this parish for only a short time. St. Robert was canonized in 1930. Fr. St. John liked to bring the church members together for activities like this. He was helped by the local merchants to buy the food. They weren't all tattoo parlors and pawnshops. The A&P let him buy the ground meat at cost. "Let's see, fifteen pounds of meat at a quarter a pound. That was his biggest expense."

Joe picked up the spaghetti plate and passed it to Daisy. He would serve himself last and then he could fill his plate without being polite. He did the same with the sauce but he grabbed a piece of bread to chew on in the meantime. The food made its way around the table and Joe filled his plate and topped it off with Parmesan cheese, imported from Wisconsin.

"Hey! This is good!" said the new guy. His name was Bob Martin and he was in his first week of training. He had seen the announcement of the dinner on the bulletin board today. Shirley Jones just sat down at the table as she asked, "Is this seat taken?"

Bob said, "No! Not at all. Please sit down." He stood and pulled her chair out for her.

Shirley liked that and said, "Wow! A real gentleman. Thank you. Now if you'd please pass the spaghetti."

Bob asked the two guys how long they'd been at the fort.

Bill said, "It's been eight weeks."

Hazel asked, "Have any of you boys encountered the Bloodland Ghosts?"

Bob bit on it and asked, "Ghosts! What ghosts? Where?"

Hazel narrated the story, "Back before the war, the powers to be wanted to expand the fort to the south but the hamlet of Bloodland was in the way with its one hundred German residents. It wasn't much of a town but it was an old town. They had been there since 1830. The government condemned it and bought the residents property. The Bloodland Cemetery is still back by the shooting ranges. A couple years later, some of the former residents hatched a plan after a day of drinking. They couldn't attack the whole government but they could go after that lone sentry by the back gate. They snuck up near the back gate and made some hooting noises that attracted the guard. They grabbed him when he came near the brush and forced him to drink the hard cider they carried with them. Can you imagine having to force a soldier to drink? Well, he was on duty. He was discovered to be drunk on duty and spent a year in the stockade. His defense was that he was abducted by ghosts and forced to drink their liquor. There are still several of those people around and they are still pissed at being moved."

Bob said, "That is a scary story even if they aren't real ghosts. Has it ever happened again?"

Daisy said that they tried it again a year later but the Army smartened up and simply made the area Off Limits at night. "It didn't help poor Jim Klown though."

Bob asked who Jim Klown was.

Daisy said, "He was the MP on duty that night who spent his next year behind the fence."

Joe asked Bob if he had taken self-defense yet and Bob said that he completed that class and did pretty well for himself. Joe said, "Good, because we'll be walking home tonight and we don't want any trouble from the Bloodland guys."

With that, one of the women announced, "Dessert is served and please bring your plates to the kitchen when you pick out your dessert." Several parishioners contributed cakes and pies to the celebration tonight. The soldiers and their ladies went up to the long table to choose among the delicious confections. The music arrived and the disc jockey for the night put on a couple ballads to set the mood. Bing Crosby sang "Moonlight Becomes You" and then "Don't Fence Me In" with the Andrew Sisters. Daisy said that the disc jockey managed the local five-and-dime and has a big collection of records that he can buy at cost for his new RCA Victor player. "It's electric. You don't need to crank it." They had a hand crank player with a big horn at their last affair. The hand crank model doesn't need tubes, which are critical war goods. The disc jockey's name was

Larry Ferguson. He was wounded at Guadalcanal and walked with a cane.

Bob ate a forkful of berry pie and announced, "This is really good."

Shirley said, "Our mother made that dewberry pie. She puts honey in it to stretch our sugar ration. Dewberries are the first berries to come out in the spring. They can be a little tart."

Hazel quipped, "Who are you calling a little tart?" and they all laughed. Shirley began to blush. The girls took the dessert plates back while the boys moved the chairs to the sides of the room and folded up the tables. Larry changed the mood a little by putting on "Over the Rainbow" followed by "Mission to Moscow." He had several Glenn Miller records. The country was still mourning the loss of the bandleader since his plane disappeared last December. Shirley grabbed Bob and said, "Let's dance!"

The other two couples joined them along with most of the others. A few of the guys along with two girls stepped outside for a smoke. The rhythm changed a bit with "Blueberry Hill." Bill and Joe exchanged partners so that Joe and Hazel were together. Larry put on "Blue Orchids" making it easy to talk.

Joe said, "It sounds like Daisy is really out to get married."

"She talks like that but I'm not sure she's ready to leave Mama. Her mother guards her pretty close. You watch. She'll be here at nine to walk her baby home. She needs another year or two to mature. What am I saying? She's my age. I just feel older being out of school these past few months."

"Did you really have to leave school early?"

"It's not always happy on the day that the Army gets its pay. Mom gets my dad's allotment but it doesn't stretch to take care of Shirley, our brother and me so I had to help out. Maybe I can use that GI Bill to finish high school. Fat chance."

"I plan to use it. I'd like to go to Cornell and study aeronautics. I always wanted to work on the railroad but my dad said that's no future. Go to school. Be an engineer. I guess he's right." "Elmer's Tune" was Larry's next selection.

Larry announced, "The Next song is for our British friends," and he played "The White Cliffs of Dover."

The couples got back together for the last song. Daisy danced with Joe and Hazel with Bill. Bob and Shirley were together most of the evening. They seemed stuck on each other. Larry ended the evening with "The Story of a Starry Night."

Joe and Bill decided they could afford a cab ride back to the gate if Bob would go along and chip in. Bob found that agreeable. They asked the girls if they could drop them off.

Daisy said that her mother would be here to walk her home.

Hazel said, "See. What did I tell you? But Shirley and I would be on your way."

Daisy said, "You know mom doesn't like me walking alone at night and it gets her out of the house."

Bill used the parish phone to call a cab. Several soldiers were teaming up for rides. A few of the heartier ones began the walk back to base. They could take the jitney bus once they were on the base.

The cab arrived and the boys gave their thanks to Father St. John, Larry and the kitchen ladies for the night of fun. They got in the cab. Hazel sat between the two boys and Bob and Shirley sat in the jump seats.

Hazel said, "I know you guys just want to avoid those Bloodland devils."

"Whatever do you mean? I haven't thought of that story all night with your charming company at hand."

They were at the Jones house all too soon and Mrs. Jones left the porch light on for them. "Goodnight fellows. We had a lovely evening."

"Goodnight ladies. It's time to leave you now."

They were at the fort in about ten minutes and paid the cabby 40¢ each. They saw the jitney bus coming toward the gate. That would be another 10¢.

Chapter 2 – Picnic

Since it was Sunday, they were able to sleep in, except for the poor saps on KP. Joe got up early enough for breakfast and then went to the base chapel for the nine o'clock Catholic service. He considered going to St. Robert Church but that would have been too much of a hassle and might have looked like he was too eager to have a relationship with Daisy. She is looking for a husband and he is going overseas for a couple of years. He just took it easy after Mass. He wrote a letter home to his family and one to his brother who was somewhere in the Pacific. He wound up the day with the Army cold cut supper and a movie at the base theater. The movie was *Meet Me In St. Louis* with Judy Garland. The movie *St. Louis* looked a lot better than the one he had seen. He got to bed early.

"Reveille! Reveille! Reveille! Time to wake up boys." Ernie Economo was Charge of Quarters (CQ) today and this was his favorite part of his night's duties.

"Go back to the orderly room, Ernie, the phone's ringing. "

"Leave us alone, Ernie. We had a late night!"

In spite of their jibes at the CQ, they were on their feet in seconds and getting their shaving gear together. Shit, shine, shower and shave and they were out the door to reveille. It was Monday and time for school. After roll call, they broke for the mess hall for bacon and eggs, pancakes and syrup. Sorghum syrup was available in this part of the country and several of them were used to it by now. It tasted somewhat like motor oil and molasses. Joe and Bill were comparing notes with Felix and Mike. They hadn't seen much of each other after that dinner. Felix had gotten crosswise with one of the girls that night. He wanted to go outside and make out but she said that wasn't permitted. A chaperone would have followed them out anyway. He grabbed Mike and said, "Let's blow this joint" and they walked back to base. Mike was just getting the nerve up to ask a girl to dance but he was relieved to be on his way. The girls were mad about being left like that. There were still plenty of boys left, just more competition for the girls.

"Felix, if you're going to a church dinner and dance, you have got to play by their rules. These aren't some dance hall floozies that will do whatever you want." Joe was angry.

"I know. Next time, I'll just go to St. Louie. Those women know how to play."

"Yeah and you'll come back with an empty wallet and the clap besides. Don't talk to me about big cities. I grew up in one," said Joe. Felix knew big cities also. He had often taken the streetcar to the War Zone in Boston to go to the burlesque show.

Bill broke in, "Come on guys. We've got to line up for class." They assembled in platoons and companies to march across the fort to the classrooms. They passed the training fields where the combat engineers played with their bulldozers and earthmovers. Felix would have made a good engineer. He liked to blow stuff up. They also passed the chemical corps training facility and wished they could pick up the pace while they marched by the foreboding building. They arrived at their classrooms, a group of one-story wooden buildings built in the same fashion of their two-story barracks. They broke up into their classes. The four of them were in the same class. They were training to secure a crime scene and protect evidence until Criminal Investigation became involved. This was a lot more interesting than their law classes and even finger printing. They had other practice on traffic control but Joe did that in eighth grade when he was a patrol boy. That is all he could think of when he was standing in an intersection with one truck rolling by every five minutes. When he was thirteen, he felt he was taking his life in his hands standing in the street holding up four lanes of traffic with drivers shaking their fists at him while a child crossed the street.

Crime scene was all about roping off the area and keeping the curious out. The curious included reporters with their 4 by 5 inch Graflex press cameras and blinding flashbulbs. You are supposed to note the obvious and unusual physical evidence like spent cartridges, bloody knives and bullet holes. The instructors provide fabricated tableaus with dummies and room settings depicting a possible crime scene. The first scene was an alley with GI cans full of trash, a bloody manikin with a Kabar knife in the back and an empty wallet. The scene was reminiscent of the death of his uncle, Clement, outside a boarding house in Brooklyn on New Year's Day, 1939. No one ever talked about what Clem did in New York but he had lived there for several years. The weapon in his case was a double-sided dagger that was never found. His body had been sent back and was buried in the cemetery in Erie near the reservoir. That story always intrigued Joe. Clem must have been partying with some bad fellows that New Year's Eve. Who could have hated him that much? A friend sent the gory photograph from the New York Herald Tribune to his father who kept it safely filed away. The photo was gory even in black and white.

Back to the issue at hand. Joe and his team of three roped off the alley. There was no crowd to keep back so they made notes of everything they saw. The knife was of a type favored by American Marines. Someone put that in as a jibe at the other Corps. There were ten clues that they were supposed to pick up on and Joe had nine recorded. He finally noticed a button made of woven leather with a patch of blue wool cloth sewn to it. That did it for the morning and they formed up with their companies to march back to the barracks for lunch. They checked the bulletin board to keep abreast of company activities. Sure enough! His platoon was scheduled for a night firing class at the rifle range. This training had been rotating through each of the four platoons over the past couple of days. They would be the last in their company to go to the training field.

The class after lunch was more of the same, more death, more mayhem, and more grief. The scene was a front parlor with a blood stained sofa, a dead woman, and a dead man holding a German Lugar. It was thought that this may be a common scene in the next couple of months as Germans despair of having lost the war that their leaders had sold them. The woman was shot in the forehead and the man holding the gun was shot in the chest. Was it murder/suicide or just plain murder? There was plenty of retribution to go along with despair. The instructor, Captain Laurence, gave them plenty to think about and items to consider. A war that has been going on for six years will not end in a day with everyone welcoming the conquering heroes.

They formed up again and marched to the barracks to eat and put on their field gear. They would be marching back again past their school to the rifle ranges in the far end of the fort. Why couldn't they drive them out in a couple of trucks? That's right! Gas is not plentiful. They shouldered there M-1 carbines and marched along with their ponchos hanging behind their pistol belts and their helmet liners on their heads. There was no MP on their helmet liners or a black band on their arm. That wouldn't come until graduation. It was dark already and they had attached red lenses to their gooseneck flashlights that hung from their pistol belts. These belts would probably not see a pistol because most of these new MP's were carrying the carbine and not an automatic one at that. The Army didn't trust these fellows with firing off a twenty-round magazine into a crowd. "Go to your left, your right, your left. I got a girl in Abilene. She's a Peach but her father's mean. Honey! Oh Baby mine.

A few Jodi songs and they arrived at the firing range. It was all about night vision and protecting it. That's the reason for the red lens. The red prolongs your night vision but lets you see to adjust your sights or reload your magazine, which you should be able to do in the dark.

Earlier in the afternoon, an Army sergeant pulled up to a nearby farmer's house and left two cases of Budweiser beer on the back porch. He never saw anyone. He just left the beer and drove off in his jeep.

The firing range used small automotive lamps for targets. They would light for half a second to simulate the muzzle flash of a weapon. There was an 18-inch square of heavy paper behind the bulb and any hole in the paper would score as a hit. They weren't too worried about the light bulbs because the possibility of hitting one was so remote. They would replace a few the next day. They were more concerned about a bullet cutting a wire. The troops enjoyed it and took it for the challenge that it was. You tried to look off to the side instead of straight down the barrel because you peripheral vision is more sensitive to movement. They each fired 20 rounds of ammo. Policing up their brass was a chore with the dim red glow of their flashlights. It was ten o'clock and time to march back. There was less singing and more tripping because they were tired.

Suddenly there was a sound, "bonk," followed by, "What the hell?" Then bonk...bonk...bonk, bonk, bonk. Someone was throwing stuff at them. A few guys recognized them as horse chestnuts. Are they kids? They heard shouts of "Feingruppen" and "Auslander." Others called "Abartige," "Dekadente" and "Schwine." Who the hell is throwing chestnuts at soldiers? The sergeant ordered them to fall out and take cover. A few troopers shined their lights on their assailants and got bombarded with nuts and something else. They were green, the size of grapefruit and looked like brains. Some guys called them hedge apples. Several troops unslung their carbines. They didn't know what to do with them. They had no ammo and they sure weren't going to shoot any locals. They tried to use their carbines as shields, ineffectively at best. Suddenly they were gone. Their attackers had just disappeared into the woods. Or did they? They may have just gone silent. Who could tell? The sergeant laughed and ordered them to fall in. "Forward march!" They recovered their senses and some of their dignity. A little farther on, the sergeant shined his light in the bushes. An old battered wooden sign proclaimed, "Bloodland Cemetery."

The other three platoons had gone through this rite of passage and kept the secret. They laughed about it as they returned to the barracks. They were exhausted though and earned an extra hour of sleep in the morning. They learned as much from the sudden violence of the local farmers as they did from their weapons training. The local farmers were able to channel some of their resentment into some fun and two cases of Budweiser beer.

The latrine was a madhouse when they got to the barracks as everyone tried to get into the shower at once. Several took their carbines into the shower with them. They were full of mud and grit from their night of shooting. They were a sight though; a dozen at a time, well-armed, naked bodies soaking wet. They toweled off and wiped their weapon dry before cleaning the bore and oiling the piece. The inventor of the carbine, a man named David "Marsh" Williams, provided a compartment in the butt plate for the cleaning kit and Lubriplate grease. The oiler was a cylinder that held one end of the sling in the stock. David developed the handy firearm while in Federal Prison. He was sentenced to 30 years for shooting a revenue agent involved in a raid to shut down his moonshine still.

The rest of the company had to wake up at the regular time and with the noise of reveille, most of Joe's platoon woke up also. They just had an extra hour to get themselves together before roll call. The sergeant called out their names: "Conrad", Joe answered, "Joseph F. Sir"…"Jackson", "Felix M. Sir"…"Schneider", "Michael T. Sir"…"Wallace", "William W. Sir". The sergeant turned to the platoon leader and said, "All present and accounted for. Sir."

"Today is Field Day, men. Report back here at 08:30 with your helmet liners, pistol belts and leather gloves. Fall out." They did and headed for breakfast.

Field day is usually busy work, trimming the grass, pulling weeds and painting rocks. The Army liked their rocks painted white and arranged in pretty rows. They fell in at the appointed time and stretched out in a single line to police up the area, picking up matches and toothpicks and other detritus left behind by the careless. Every now and then, someone would find a discarded cigarette butt with a filter on it that someone brought back from Europe. This was especially maddening since any soldier worth his stripe, would field strip his cigarette butt, cast the tobacco to the wind and stick the paper in his pocket. They returned to the company area for the next assignment. The sergeant told them they were to check out shovels, hammers and crowbars from battalion supply and they were going to demolish the burned out remains of a two-story barracks. The barracks had caught fire last month when a coal furnace exploded and caught the furnace room on fire. The fire spread to the first floor but an alert fireguard woke the residents and they all got out safely. Most had time to grab their boots and a blanket and lined up outside in the cold March night in their skivvies. The fire department put the fire out which was rare in these tinderbox buildings but the barracks was a total loss.

The troops shouldered their tools and marched to the burn site looking like a gang of WPA workers. Half the men climbed to the roof and began stripping shingles with their shovels and crowbars. There was nothing to hold them on the roof and the quicker they got a few boards loose the better so they could wrap a leg around a rafter. The work was slow with the long roofing nails passing through the deck. Some nails were even clinched underneath. Joe said, “They didn’t want these shingles to come off.”

"They should have just let the whole thing burn and then we wouldn't have to be doing this," said Felix. Bill and Mike were pulling the plumbing out of the latrine. The whole place smelled smoky.

"If we weren't doing this, they'd have us on some other dirty job."

"At least we wouldn't be twenty five feet off the ground. I don't know what use this lumber will be. You'll never get the smell out.

Joe said. "Maybe they could use it to build more crime scenes for us to investigate. They could build some more smoking shelters for us to enjoy a cigarette. There'd be no conflict there."

"I could use a cigarette now. Do you think we earned a break, Joe?"

"Sounds good to me!" They made their way back down the ladder. "Let me try one of your Chesterfields, Joe. My Camels have tasted a little harsh lately."

Joe said, "Sorry Felix. I decided to try to quit. If I had them with me, you could have them. My Pa has been smoking Camels since he was a kid. He says that doctors recommend them. Oh! Oh! The sergeant."

Felix asked a rhetorical question. "I wonder what makes these things blow up? We all have coal furnaces up north and I can't think of one blowing up unless it was a boiler or a gas-fired furnace."

"Oh! I know that one. I fired furnaces at Scott Field when I was waiting for radio school. We all use anthracite coal in our homes but the military uses this cheap soft coal. If you put in too much coal, it covers the flame. That way the new coal just cooks and fills the firebox with combustible gas. When the flame breaks through, the whole thing goes thump and blows the door open. That's usually all, unless there is something flammable nearby like someone was drying their laundry."

"Okay, you goldbrickers! Get back up that ladder!"

"Yes Sarge!"

They climbed back up the shaky ladder and pulled shingles and nails until the KP's brought lunch out at noon. They had sack lunches in the back of the truck so as not to waste time marching back and forth. The bags contained sandwiches, a bag of potato chips and an apple or banana. There was boloney, pressed ham or liverwurst with a slice of cheese and plenty of mayonnaise. Joe picked boloney but traded it with Felix for his liverwurst. Joe's family all liked liverwurst, even the smoked stuff that came in a ring like sausage. He would have preferred mustard on it but he was hungry enough to eat pig snouts.

They got back up the ladder and managed to tear the roof off, and a good start on the second floor over the afternoon. The rest could wait for someone else's field day or the base carpenters could probably knock it down in a morning. They lined up in platoon formation and marched back to the company area. They still had to turn in their tools at battalion and clean-up for supper. They were filthy from the dust and charred wood. They were ready for a hot meal after a hard day's work. Tonight was spaghetti. They usually had that on Wednesday but maybe the mess sergeant thought they earned it today. The meal reminded them of the girls they met last week. "Joe, remember those girls we met last Saturday?"

"You're darn right. I've had Margaret on my mind all week."

"Joe, it hasn't been that long."

"I think I will make my way to St. Roberts next Sunday and see what develops. We don't have that much time left but I'd like to see her again."

Chapter 3 – Death of a President

Ernie Economo barged into the classroom at the end of the afternoon all excited. "The president's dead, you guys! I just heard it on the radio! "

"Aw, Ernie, are you sure that's not some Nazi propaganda? I'd more expect the Fuhrer to be dead as close as we are to Berlin."

"No! I heard it! He was at that place of his in Georgia getting his portrait painted when he keeled over from a stroke."

"Does that mean that what's his name, Harry Truman, is president now?"

"The Missouri Man himself. I wonder what he'll be like?" said Bill. The classroom went quiet. No one knew what to say.

Joe said, "He was a fine man. He got my old man back to work on the Pennsy."

"He put us all to work one way or another. Some of us are fighting this damn war."

Ernie said, "Now don't put that on the president. If you remember, the Japs had a lot to do with that and then Hitler declared war on us."

Their school day was finished and they went outside to line up for their march to the company area. The base flag was already at half-mast and a bugler played taps.

Supper was a somber affair that evening. They had that indeterminate steak that always smells like liver. No one said much as they walked through the chow line and the conversation at the tables was kept low.

They plodded through their training on Friday without much enthusiasm. There was a commemorative service at the base chapel that evening with all of the base chaplains participating. The commander of the fort spoke and the chaplains offered up some prayers. They concluded by singing Amazing Grace and God Bless America. The 2nd consolidated mess offered coffee and donuts afterward for the attendees.

They completed their inspection the following morning with no major discrepancies. Bill had an accident a short time before the company commander entered the barracks. He was trying to light one last cigarette when a puff of wind blew back the flame on his Zippo lighter and ignited half of his mustache. He quick slapped it and it didn't hurt him but the burning hair smell was awful. He brushed away the little balls of hair when the commander walked in. The commander, platoon leader and platoon sergeant walked up to each soldier. The commander looked him over carefully and asked him some inane question like, "What is your fourth general order soldier?" "To repeat all calls from posts more distant from the guardhouse than my own...Sir!"

"Soldier, what is wrong with your mustache?"

"I just burned it with my lighter...Sir!"

"Well, shave it off and start over or better yet leave it off." And they moved on.

With the inspection completed, they were free to pursue their own interests. Many of them went directly to the orderly room to pick up their passes from the company clerk. Joe and many others went to the mess hall for lunch. In the afternoon, Joe walked to the craft shop to reserve a bicycle for the next day. He stopped at a workbench where there was some scrap leather in a basket and fooled around with the tools until he had a very decorative and unique coffee coaster. He didn't have room for much more. He tooled a wide belt with a basket-weave pattern and twenty loops for .30-30 cartridges. He mailed that home because he wouldn't have occasion to wear it for a few more years. The craft shop had a lot of stuff to do like ceramics and woodworking. They even had sewing machines, which helped for sewing on patches.

Half a dozen guys were working on their cars. A couple were working on a '32 Ford three window coupe with the original flathead V8 engine in it. The other bunch was pulling the engine from a Hudson *Terraplane*. It was a 1933 model KT that had a straight 8-cylinder engine. This was a big engine in a light car and that's why the gangsters liked it. John Dillinger and Baby Face Nelson were said to drive this car. They liked the lightness, acceleration, handling, and discreet appearance of the car. It wasn't flashy but sport drivers liked it for casual competition like hill climbs. The vent doors on each side of the hood made it look like it could go fast.

He caught the jitney bus and took it to the main gate. From there it was a short walk to the businesses that served the base. He picked up his class A uniform from the cleaners. The Chinese ladies there did a better job than the cleaners on base did. They didn't break so many buttons. They would also point out small tears or separated seams and repair them for pennies.

He walked into the saloon a couple doors down and hung his suit on the coat rack. He ordered a Budweiser draft and changed a quarter into nickels for the pinball machine. He was good at it and could occasionally make that quarter last a half hour. Today, he got twenty minutes out of it. Two more stops and he'd be done. He picked up his uniform from the rack and went across the street. He bought twenty 3¢ stamps at the post office in the back of the five-and-dime store and picked up two pads of writing paper and a pack of envelopes. No telling when he would have the opportunity to buy stationary again. Joe remembered Larry Ferguson from the other night and wrapped on the window of his little office to say hello.

"Yes? Can I help you?" said Larry.

"Oh! Nothing, I remember you from the dance the other night and I just wanted to say hi and thanks for the music."

"I remember you now. I don't know your name but I remember you spent your time with Margaret. She is a nice girl and a good customer. Stocking up on writing supplies I see."

"Yeah. I'm getting ready to ship out in a week and I will have plenty of time on my hands and I want to be prepared. My name is Joe Conrad."

"What do you think of our new president?"

"Frankly, I liked the old president just fine. I'm really sorry that he couldn't have seen the end of this war. I'm sure that Harry will be up to the task. He's from Missouri, isn't he?"

"Have you seen Daisy since the dance?"

"No, but I was going to come to town tomorrow morning and go to Mass instead of going to the base chapel. What time are the Masses anyway?"

"I'm afraid there is only one and it's at 10:30."

"That's a long time to fast but I can do it. I'll see you there tomorrow, Larry."

"So long, Joe. Thanks for stopping by."

Joe paid for his stationary and headed back to the fort. It was almost time for supper. He went to his barracks and put his uniform and purchases in his locker. Bill and Felix were there and the three of them walked to the mess hall. They had stuffed pork chops tonight with corn bread dressing, sweet potatoes and green beans. They also had okra but he was a little slow on them. He took two just to be polite. They sat down and dug in. Joe said, "You know these okras are kind of good once you get pass the slimy, fuzzy part." Felix didn't even try. He turned down the grits in the morning also.

Bill said, "You guys don't know what's good. You need to try some of that good gumbo from Louisiana."

Bill asked Joe what he'd been doing all day. Joe related his errands to them, the beer he had, his less than stellar performance at pinball and reserving a bike for tomorrow.

Felix asked, "Where are you going riding?"

"Oh! Just into Mass at St. Roberts."

"Not me, man. Sunday is my day to sleep in and that's what I'm doing tomorrow. Why don't you go to the base chapel? Oh! You're looking for that girl you met the other night. What's her name?"

"Daisy and yes, I would like to see her again. You didn't really hang around for the dance. Did you?"

"Well me and one of those chicks had a difference of opinion about a little petting."

Bill said, "I'm going back for another coffee and see if there is some of that cake left. Can I get you anything?"

"I'm good," said Joe.

"Grab me a piece of that cake," said Felix. The beauty of eating weekends in the mess hall was that half the troops were on pass so you could eat at your leisure and maybe get seconds. Half of the guys on KP were getting paid for their duty. It was common practice for well-heeled soldiers to pay someone to take their place on KP for five bucks or so.

They went to the base movie theater after dessert to see *Cover Girl* with Rita Hayworth and Gene Kelly. Joe wanted to see it and so did Bill. Felix said he saw it and it wasn't bad. That is a big recommendation coming from Felix. "A lot of singing and dancing though but the broads look good."

They stopped by the PX snack bar for a beer and then back to the barracks.

Morning came early but Joe could let reveille play and roll over for another hour. There was no use hurrying to chow since he couldn't eat until after Mass. He propped himself up and picked up the *Field and Stream* magazine that he bought last night at the PX. He began reading about Steelhead fishing in

Maine. Soon it was time to get ready. He showered and shaved and put on his freshly cleaned uniform and walked to the craft shop. He had the key to a fairly good-looking Schwinn but the tires looked a little soft. He fastened a clip around his pants leg to keep his trousers out of the greasy chain. He struggled to get to the base gas station and fill the tires. "Please don't get a flat!"

He was on his way headed to the main gate and then it was three miles up Missouri Avenue. He left at nine and the time seemed to be going fast. He finally saw Saint Robert's in the distance and knew he would make it. He locked the bike outside. "Who would steal a bike from a church but it's better to be safe. I'd hate to have to pay for that bike." One of the two ushers greeted him and he took a seat in the rear. It was true. The dining and dance hall was now a church. The altar was set up on the wall away from the kitchen. A couple decorative banners were hung to soften the pine paneling. Everyone looked to be in his or her Sunday best. He saw Daisy sitting in the fourth row with her mother and father and he guessed it was her brother. A few whispers began near him and worked their way forward. Eventually Daisy turned around and said, "Come on up!" with her arm. He made his way out of his row and walked down the aisle while people in the fourth row moved left or right to make room for him.

"Good morning, soldier." she said. "Mom and Dad, this is Joe. And this is Marty my brother." "Shh."

"Introibo ad altare Dei" said Father St. John.

"Ad deum qui laetificat juventutem meam. To God, who gives joy to my youth." Joe whispered.

"Pardon," whispered Daisy.

"I was an altar boy. Just remembering."

Fr. St. John spoke of the president and his accomplishments and asked for President Truman to receive God's own wisdom to help us through the war and the recovery. Mass ended and Fr. St. John went to the rear of the hall to greet people as they left. Daisy introduced Joe to her mother, Ann, and Charles, her father. Her brother, Martin, introduced himself as Marty. They made their way to the rear and Daisy began to introduce Joseph but the priest said that he remembered Joe from the dinner last week and said, "He was a good dancer and had a good appetite." They laughed.

Ann said, "That reminds me, Joe. We have a pot roast on the stove slow cooking and you're welcome to come and join us."

"Thank you ma'am, if it's not putting you out."

"You're not putting me out! If you were, I wouldn't have asked you."

Joe said, "I rode a bike to get here. Just tell me where you live and I'll meet you there."

Daisy said, "I can do better than that. If you ride me on your handlebars, I'll get you there. I do it all the time."

"That's no way for a young lady to ride. What about your skirt."

"Oh, mother!"

They went out and Joe unlocked his bike and fastened the clip on his cuff. He mounted the bike, uncertain what to do, and Daisy jumped up on the cross bar right in front of Joe. He couldn't have hoped for more. He smelled the fragrance of her hair and neck. He wobbled a bit at first but it soon smoothed out. It was only five blocks to her house and they were there in no time. Dinner was really cooked by the time they got there. The family was already in the house. Marty ran out with a model of a P-38. It was made of balsa wood and paper. "Daisy told me you're in the Air Corps. That's what I'm going to join when I'm old enough."

"I'm afraid your sister has it mixed up. I joined the Air Corps but now they need military police more, so that's why I am here."

"Well, I'm still gonna join the Air Corps when I'm older."

"I pray that you won't have to," said Joe.

"It's time to eat, everyone," called mother.

They took their seats. Charles led them in prayer.

"Bless us O Lord and these, your gifts, which we are about to receive from Your bounty, through Christ our Lord."

"Amen"

They passed around the chuck roast, slow cooked with potatoes, carrots, turnips and peas in savory gravy. Afterward, mother brought out slices of her dewberry pie and Daisy served cups of strong coffee to all who desired it. She also passed around a brick of cheddar cheese for each person to serve himself.

Daisy and her mother cleared the dishes and retreated to the kitchen to wash them. Charles said that the president is supposed to address Congress in twenty minutes. He asked Joe if he cared to listen. Joe said that his life is in the president's hands and that he would appreciate hearing what he had to say.

The Speaker of the House introduced the President of the United States.

"Mr. Speaker, Mr. President, Members of the Congress:

It is with a heavy heart that I stand before you, my friends and colleagues, in the Congress of the United States.

Only yesterday, we lay to rest the mortal remains of our beloved President, Franklin Delano Roosevelt. At a time like this, words are inadequate. The most eloquent tribute would be a reverent silence.

Yet, in this decisive hour, when world events are moving so rapidly, our silence might be misunderstood and might give comfort to our enemies.

In His infinite wisdom, Almighty God has seen fit to take from us a great man who loved, and was beloved by, all humanity...

At this moment, I have in my heart a prayer. As I have assumed my heavy duties, I humbly pray Almighty God, in the words of King Solomon:

"Give therefore thy servant an understanding heart to judge thy people, that I may discern between good and bad; for who is able to judge this thy so great a people?"

I ask only to be a good and faithful servant of my Lord and my people."

Margaret was confused when Truman greeted "Mr. President" but Charles told her that would be the president of the Senate and he couldn't think of who that would be now. She had come in with her mother to hear the speech. Ann said that she was sure Mr. Truman would do a fine job of being president. Daisy piped in with, "Hear! Hear! To the President of the United States."

Ann said, "Let's lighten up a bit. How about a game like Monopoly? We can all play."

"You'll have to excuse me ma'am. I rode a bike here and I need to be back before dark so I don't wind up as somebody's hood ornament."

Charles spoke up, "Joe, I think we can afford the half gallon of gas to get you safely home this evening."

"Oh! Thank you Dad. I mean if that's alright with you Joe."

"Count out the money! I'll take the old shoe. Thank you sir," said Joe.

Marty got out the game and began setting it up on the table. "I'll be the banker." Marty always wanted to be the banker. The arithmetic was good experience for him. Joe could not believe how aggressive everyone in the family played but he quickly upped his game buying everything he could afford and raking in the rent. He seemed to wind up in jail more than he thought he ought to but he played in good humor.

Charles asked about Joe's future. "I don't know, Sir. I am nearly certain to be going to Europe. I think my whole class will. Once we get to Berlin, there's a whole continent to put back together. There'll be German POW's to be sent home and hundreds of thousands of displaced persons to return home. Many won't have any homes to return to."

Ann asked, "How long do you think you'll be staying overseas?"

"I don't rightly know, Mrs. Watson. They're talking about a two-year tour but they're in uncharted territory. I'll have to see what comes of it. Now, I want to buy Marvin Garden."

Daisy said, "I wanted that. It would go well with my Boardwalk."

"I can't have you owning both. You'd kill us with the rent. You've got all of the railroads."

"I understand that you come from a railroad family, Joe. What railroad does your father work on?" asked Charles.

"The Pennsylvania, Sir. He works on the extra list, lines west."

"I don't follow you."

"The extra list gives him sixteen hours off and then the dispatcher calls him to drive the next train. Lines West are everything west of Erie to Chicago, western Illinois and even north to the iron range of Michigan. He mostly hauls coal and iron ore."

Ann asked, "Did you work before you joined the Army, Joe?"

"No, ma'am. I joined right out of school." He told them about the cadet program and his love of planes, "Just like Marty, right Champ."

"Yes sir! I'm gonna fly!"

Joe said that he set pins in a bowling alley and did some construction work for a friend of his older brother. The contractor is a German but he has no love of the Third Reich.

Ann said, "We've been playing and talking for nearly three hours. We need to get some supper on and send you home, son." Daisy nearly choked when she said son. "Mother!"

"What?"

"Well, who had the most money since we didn't finish the game?"

"Margaret won as always," said Marty.

Mrs. Watson made a soup from the left over beef from dinner and added some additional vegetables from their garden and elbow macaroni. There were enough biscuits leftover from morning for everyone to have one with a bit of jam. They finished with a small glass of sherry wine for dessert. It was dark by then and Charles said, "It's probably a good idea to get Joe back to his company and I said I would. Joe, If you'll put your bike in the back of the pickup truck. Daisy, you come along too." Marty asked if he could tag along but his dad said there wasn't room.

"Aw, gee. I wanted to see some tanks," said Marty.

"I'm afraid you would be disappointed Marty. The combat engineers have the only tanks around and they are in a shed.."

"Well! I'd still like to go."

Joe said goodbye to Marty and his mon and thanked her for the two meals. Margaret got in the truck and Joe entered after her. Dad pulled out the choke and started the engine with a slow and then a fast putt-putt. He pushed in the choke and they left.

Charles asked him if he could drive him to the company area.

"Yes. If I show the guard my pass, he will let you in. I need to turn the bike in at the craft shop and I can walk back to my company from there."

"Nonsense! You take care of the bike and I will drive you to your company."

"Thank you sir."

They pulled up to the guard shack.

"Let me see your ID please" said the guard. Charles showed him his driver's license and Joe handed him his ID and pass. The guard handed them back and gave them a pass to put in the windshield. "Drop this off on the way out."

They drove through the fort to the craft shop and Joe got the bike out of the truck. When he took it in, Charles said to his daughter, "He's a nice fellow, very polite. Too bad he has to go now."

"Yeah Dad, I'll miss him even though I hardly know him."

They drove to his company and Joe started to leave. Daisy kissed him softly on the cheek and said, "I'd like to write you."

Joe said that would be swell. "I've got your address. I'll write and let you know where I am at."

"Goodbye Mr. Watson. Goodbye Daisy."

"Goodbye Joe."

Chapter 4 – PFC and Graduation

Joe found his name on the bulletin board when he returned from class. There were four other names on the list. He decided that he better get it over with. He reported to the company clerk who asked him to take a seat in case someone else shows up. Two of the other fellows arrived and the clerk entered the commander's office.

"He will see you now."

They walked in stiffly and gave the captain the snappiest salute they could muster. The captain returned their salute and said, "At ease, gentlemen."

"I guess you are aware that you've been in the Army now for eight months."

"Yes, Sir!"

"It is my pleasure to promote each of you to Private First Class. You are now officially PFC's. As you progress through your career in the Army, you will be promoted and more will be expected of you. Newer troops will look up to you, so you must endeavor to be a model in both appearance and your actions." He passed out a pair of single stripes to each of the men.

"Thank you, Sir!"

"That's all. You're dismissed."

"That was easy. I thought we'd screwed up something."

"Now we are models and people will look up to us."

They laughed...nervously. Joe went immediately to the supply room where he was issued six sets of PFC stripes. Now he wouldn't have to travel across the country with no stripes. He checked his mail and there was a letter from his mother.

April 14, 1945
Dear Joseph,

Isn't it awful about our poor president? I was talking with Mrs. Meredith next door when the paperboy told us. He said his friend, Franklin, was dead. Aunt Liza said she has a friend who lives in the South, Maryland I believe. She said that Mr. Roosevelt's girlfriend was with him at the end and she had to hurry and get out of the house before his family got there. He was having his portrait painted at the time. Does that sound right to you? I hope Mr. Truman can do as good a job as Franklin did. They say he was a haberdasher. They're usually Jewish, aren't they? They are here in Erie.

We had such a good time visiting you in St. Louis. You looked so nice in your Air Corps uniform. I know that's what you wanted to do but I'll feel better with you a policeman rather than flying in a bomber over Germany. Jim and Pat still talk about the train ride back from Missouri. Patsy had a good time with all those soldiers and sailors that wanted to get on her good side. Your father put his foot down and told them to leave his fourteen-year-old daughter alone.

Grandma Fitzy is selling her home on Pleasant Street. Keeping up with the chickens and hogs has gotten to be too much for her. Uncle Don is quitting the railroad, and he and Kate are buying a saloon in Sherman. It's called the Café Española. It is very Spanish looking. Grandma is investing in the restaurant and she will be moving in with them and baking pies.

That's all the news I have from here.

Sincerely Yours,
Mother

Joe read the letter over again. He figured that Don and Kate needed Grandma's money to buy the saloon and she'd probably wind up slinging hamburgers on the grill as well as baking pies. She did make a fine pie though. It's been twenty years since Mr. Truman owned a clothing store with Eddie Jacobson.

He decided to write a short letter home and mail it when he went to supper.

April 17, 1945
Dear Mom and Dad,

This is my last week here in school and I should be getting my orders for overseas. I got good news yesterday and I am now a private first class so I don't have to travel again with no stripes on my arms. I need to go to the craft shop and sew them on. I could let the Chinese ladies sew them but I'm trying to make my pay stretch. This week is mostly exams and an oral exam or interview where three officers decide if I have what it takes to carry a nightstick.

I met a real swell girl named Daisy last week. We met at a church supper and dance and then I went to her house for dinner on Sunday. I wasn't invited but I just sort of showed up at church and they asked me to come over. Her real name is Margaret but everyone calls her Daisy since she has an Aunt Margaret that comes over all the time. Her last name is Watson and her dad owns an insurance office in St. Robert. That's the name of the church too. The priest's name is Father St. John just like Aunt Liza's neighbor. I've got to go now so I can post this letter on the way to chow. Much love.

Sincerely,
Joe

He sealed the letter and put on a 3¢ stamp. He dropped it off at the mail slot on the way to the mess hall. He filled his tray and joined Bill and the other fellows at their table. "Nice stripes," said Felix.

"Thank you" said Joe. He had the advantage on the other fellows having already gone through a tech school before he was reassigned to the MP's. He would be the only MP around that can understand Morse code. "I don't feel any different. Just as long as they pay me for it." He sewed the first pair of stripes on last night but still had the rest to sew.

They were headed back to the barracks when he heard, "PFC Conrad, report to the orderly room."

"I wonder what that's all about. I hope they don't want their stripes back. I better go see.

He walked into the orderly room. Ernie was CQ again tonight. They rotated it among the permanent staff so they got the duty fairly often. "Hey Joe. I see you got some stripes. Congratulations. I just got a phone call from Charles Watson. Do you know this guy? His number is Crocker 9964. I'd like to let you use this phone but I can't."

"I know the drill. I must call him from the PX pay phone. Yes, I know him. I hope there's nothing wrong."

Joe walked to the PX where there was a bank of pay phones in white oak booths just inside the door. "Good, there is no line," he thought.

He chose an empty booth and dialed CR9964. The operator's voice came on the line and said, "Deposit 10¢ for three minutes." He put in a dime and heard the characteristic ding.

The phone rang three times and a girl answered, "Hello."

"Hi, is this Daisy? The CQ said your father called. Is there anything wrong?"

"No. Daddy thought that if a man called, he might get faster action than if I called. I guess he was wrong about that. We were wondering if we could come to your graduation ceremony on Saturday. Daddy thought the public could come. He has to work until one but he could drop us off earlier. Marty wants to come and see the soldiers march and I'd like you to know there is someone there cheering for you."

"Gee, I'd love to have you there. Would your mom be with you?"

"Yes. It's just that Daddy's office is open on Saturday mornings and he gets quite a bit of business when others aren't working. Hazel would like to come also. Will Bill be there also? I don't remember his last name."

"Wallace, Bill Wallace. Yes. He'll be there."

"Mom and Dad would like you to come here afterward and cook some hamburgers outside if the weather is nice. Could you come?"

"You bet I will or we will. I'll ask Bill."

"Deposit 10¢ for an additional three minutes," said the operator.

"Gotta go now, Daisy. See you Saturday."

"Bye Joe" and he hung up.

"Darn, I should have put in another dime," but all he had was a quarter.

He walked back to the barracks and Bill was listening to Dick Haymes on the radio as he was reading the *Life Magazine* with General Eisenhower on the cover. "I can't figure it Joe. They mention Lloyd George dying in this magazine but there's nothing about the president."

"They had probably gone to press when Roosevelt died and had to get their magazine out. Enough of that! You got a date for Saturday."

"What?"

"Hazel wants to see you. She's coming to our graduation on Saturday with Daisy and her brother. Mrs. Watson will be there too but her dad can't come until later. He will pick us up after work and we'll go to their house for hamburgers."

"Well, thanks for asking me."

"I had to give her an answer and didn't have time to run back here to ask you. Are you going?"

"Sure, I'm going. Who'd pass up hamburgers?"

"What does *Life* have to say about the war?"

"It says the Nazis are running scared. The Allies are trying to figure out what to do with all of their prisoners and slaves. These people are starving, Joe."

"We'll be there in the thick of it shortly."

Ginny Simms program came on next. Bill said, "Now here is a Texas gal. Not like that draft dodger that was on before." Bill didn't much like entertainers that avoided the draft because of their nationality or got classified as 4F.

"What's happening Saturday?"

Joe explained it as he heard it. He picked up his *Field & Stream* and read about the hottest new rifle cartridge. He drifted off to sleep.

"Reveille! Reveille! Time to get up," the CQ vocalized.

"Yeah, we hear you. Go back to your orderly room."

The guys got up though and began their morning routine culminating with breakfast. Today is an important day since they would have their orals today. They formed up in front of the barracks and marched to school in their class A uniforms, a preview of Saturday.

It was mid-morning when Joe's name was called. He had been reading *The Magnificent Ambersons*, a pocket book he picked up in the day room. He set it down and walked in. "Private First Class Joseph Conrad, Sirs."

"At ease Private," there were two officers and the company first sergeant. These men were legends. The first shirt had directed traffic on Omaha Beach when he was shot in the shoulder. He carried on for three hours until he was finally evacuated.

The other two men were executive officers from Battalion and the other training company. Major Conover made the amphibious landing and was also wounded. He was a 1st Lieutenant at the time but received two promotions and a Silver Star and Purple Heart since then. He didn't know Lieutenant

Kelly's story but he saw his Purple Heart in his ribbons and knew it was hairy. The questions weren't all that difficult. They were mostly looking at his bearing. One asked him how he would feel about working with German police if it ever came to that.

"Sir, I would do my duty whatever it came to be. Do you think we would actually be working with Germans?"

"Soldier, you never know where this war will lead."

"Dismissed!"

Joe returned to the waiting room and the next fellow went in. "That was kind of weird," he said to no one in particular. He got out early and went to the craft shop with the remainder of his shirts to sew on his stripes. He returned his shirts to his locker and went to the mess hall with Felix and Mike. Bill was already there but just finishing his dinner with some other guys. It was spaghetti but it seemed a lot plainer than St. Robert's spaghetti, not as much spices. More like catsup but with big meatballs. They had time to go to the base theater to see *The Curse of the Cat People*. The Movietone News was mostly about the new president and the war in Germany. The one article that caught Joe's attention was a picture of an enormous Pennsylvania locomotive. The narrator spoke excitedly about, "this 500 ton behemoth is the future of the steam locomotive industry and possibly the coal industry." He went on to describe, "The 6-8-6 steam turbine locomotive measures 123 feet long and carries 37-1/2 tons of coal in the tender, enough coal to pull a passenger or freight train 225 miles. The locomotive shown here in front of the roundhouse in Harrisburg, Pa. was built by Baldwin Locomotive Works with steam turbines supplied by Westinghouse Electric. Power from the steam turbine is applied through a reduction gear to the center two-drive wheels. These power the outer wheels via the connecting rods." Joe thought, "my dad would really go for that."

This was followed by a Donald Duck cartoon about Commando Duck. It was really nuts. He was fighting Japs but with German subtitles. Where is that come from? The Curse really was a curse. At least it wasn't a long movie. They stopped by the PX on the way to barracks to have a beer.

The next two days were taken up with training films including the infamous VD film. There were lectures about what to expect in France and Germany when they got there but no one really knew. The situation was so fluid that it was changing daily. Their orders appeared on the bulletin board. The four of them were going to Company C of the 713th MP Battalion somewhere in Germany. The headquarters kept moving east along with the advance of the Allied Armies. The individual soldiers were spread out all over western Europe guarding every intersection from Normandy to Berlin. They would not get their travel orders until next week.

Saturday morning began with reveille followed by breakfast but this day would be different. They checked their carbines out of the armory and used a toothbrush and rag to remove any dust. Joe sighted through the barrel to make sure it was bright and shiny. They had traded in their helmet liners for new shiny ones with a big "MP" emblazoned on the front and received their "MP" armbands. They wore their class A uniforms with the pants bloused inside of white spats or leggings. They were sharp. Now to make the CO believe they looked sharp.

"Fall in men!" The sergeants shouted the roll call for their platoons and turned to the platoon leaders, mostly second lieutenants, "All present and accounted for, Sir." For the next half hour, the company commander inspected his troops. He didn't have time to be too nit pickin'. He didn't need to be. These men knew what was expected of them and they did it. They were off to the parade field.

"Left face!" called the first sergeant.

"Forward, harch!"

"Why do they always say 'harch'?"

"Shut up Conroy!" said Joe.

They marched to the parade field and fell in behind the 5th Army Field Band. The 22nd Armored Engineer Battalion arrived and joined in behind their MP battalion. Finally, the men of the 164th Chemical Training Company of the 3rd Chemical Brigade brought up the rear. Those poor guys would be taking their flamethrowers to Japan soon. Joe tried to look around as they made their turns to see if he could see Daisy. There she was in a wide brim hat, next to her mother in a scarf and Hazel with her red hair waving in the breeze. He didn't see Marty at first but he was at the end of the row.

They lined up in ranks to listen to the remarks of the base commander. He welcomed the visitors and parents especially of the young men who would be graduating this morning. Fortunately, he kept his remarks short. The war in Europe was coming to an end but there was still a massive amount of reconstruction to accomplish. No one knew when the war in the Pacific would end. It might be a year away and Japan would be only a pile of burned out sticks by then… He told them to go do their jobs to the best of their ability. "Pass in review."

"P-a-s-s in review!" called the sergeant major.

The band struck up *The Army Song*.

"Forward...harch!"

"We never go rolling along. We always harch."

"Shut up, Conroy!" said Joe.

On the second trip around the parade field, the companies split off and marched to their barracks area. A mass dismissal would have been chaos on the parade field. The Army Band remained on the field playing *Colonel Bogies' March*. The civilian crowd trailed off to follow their soldiers. The MP Battalion marched to their area and the companies broke up. Marty found Joe first and brought him back to his family. Joe grabbed Bill and dragged him along.

"Hi, Joe," said Daisy and Hazel said, "Hi" to Joe and Bill. "You boys were looking good out there. I didn't imagine there would be all of those troops out there," said Mrs. Watson.

"Oh! All of those engineers and chemical guys out there were just extras to fill up the field. We were the important ones," said Bill.

Joe said, "Hi Daisy. Hi Hazel. Mrs. Watson. We have to go change into something lighter and we'll hurry right back. First, we gotta get rid of our shooting irons. How about if you wait here at the PX and we'll be back in a jiffy?"

Joe and Bill lined up at the armory to turn in their weapons, “Maybe it won’t be a jiffy.”

They got their carbines turned in. They would come back on Monday to clean them. They ran to the barracks and changed to their khaki uniform and low quarter shoes and no MP armband. They went back to the PX to meet the family. They were sitting at the lunch counter enjoying a coke and sharing some pretzels.

“Can we take that little bus back out to the gate? Charles is going to meet us there a little after one and then we can go have lunch.”

“Thank you, Mrs. Watson for inviting me along,” said Bill.

“Me too,” said Hazel.

“Oh Hazel! You know you’re always welcome.”

Bill said, “So Hazel? What have you been packing this week, more pickles?”

“I’m not even sure whether I’m supposed to talk about it. We have been packing K Rations that are going to the Pacific.”

“Well, I don’t think it’s any secret we’re building up to attack Japan.”

"You know how you sometimes forget about a chocolate bar and find it in your sock drawer two years later and it’s got that white stuff all over it?”

Bill said, “Hazel, I think I know where you’re going.”

"Well that's what that jungle chocolate tastes like. We tried it. Some of the packs have Charms in them. They're like fruit Life Savers but softer."

"Sounds appetizing."

"Well, here's the bus. Everyone get your dimes out." They boarded the bus and Joe took a seat next to Daisy and Bill sat next to Hazel for the short ride to the gate.

Daisy said, "I hope you don't think I am too forward by asking to come here today. I read in *Life Magazine* where it is sometimes all right for a girl to ask a boy out. It was actually an ad for Etiquet Deodorant Cream but I decided to run with it."

"It is fine with me. I just didn't think you would want to be there. I mean it is such a routine thing to happen here. A class graduates nearly every week."

"But it's not your class that graduates every week. I mean, it's not often that I actually know someone who is graduating. In fact, you're the first fellow I've met here at the fort. We're not encouraged to hang around with soldiers. Mom and Dad think you're really nice and I do too. I wish we could have met sooner."

"Gosh! You're full of it, Daisy. I remember you saying you were in a hurry to get married."

"Oh! I know that's not possible and it wouldn't be wise either. I don't want to tie you down or anything but, I'd like to get to know you more. That's why I asked you to write me."

"I will definitely write to you and try to make our time together meaningful."

In the meantime, Bill asked Hazel how she'd been doing and she said she'd been doing fine.

They approached the front gate and saw Mr. Watson parked by the side of the road. They all walked by the guardhouse and Bill and Joe showed their passes to the MP. They all piled into the 1940 Blue Dodge sedan. Marty and his mom got into the front seat. The others jumped in the back. Hazel sat in the middle with the men on either side. That left Daisy to sit on Joe's lap but she didn't mind. Neither did he. She took off her hat and passed it up to her mom.

"You comfy back there, kids?" said Ann.

"Oh yes, Mom," Daisy said with a grin.

Charles said, "I could have been here a little sooner but I closed up early and started the fire in the barbecue. There should be some good hot coals by the time we get there. I bought some chuck steaks and had them grind it for beef patties. I also have fresh Kaiser rolls from the bakery. I'm surprised they still call them Kaiser rolls and not freedom rolls or liberty rolls."

"I also called Father St. John and invited him over."

Bill said, "That's good. I liked him when we met the other night and I'm not even Catholic. Gosh! That was two weeks ago.

Hazel asked, "What are you, Bill?"

"I was brought up Baptist in Goose Creek, but we started going to the Methodist church when we moved to Baytown."

"Was that a very long move?"

"Heck no. Shoot, they're all attached to one another, Baytown, Goose Creek and Pelly. They'll probably all be one town when I get back. Mr. Sterling never did like the name, Goose Creek and nobody likes Pelly. You know they come over from Pelly one night during a football game and everyone was at the stadium. They threw a rope around the jail in Goose Creek and two horses dragged it to Pelly."

Charles asked, "Who is Mr. Sterling?"

"Oh, that's Mr. Ross Sterling. He organized Humble Oil & Refining Company and went on to be road commissioner and even governor for two years. He calls the shots around there.

"Sounds like a pretty powerful man."

"Yes and everyone around has a family member working at that refinery turning valves and reading gauges. My uncle is a muleskinner. He tipped me off when there was a spot open for a security guard in the refinery."

"Do you wear cowboy boots and carry a six gun?" asked Marty.

"Why, I certainly do wear boots. They're made by a feller down in Laredo that's got a bunch of Mexicans working for him. I don't know whether my pistol had five or six chambers in it. Never paid much attention since it belongs to Humble. We don't need it much to check lunchboxes. The real firepower are the GI's that manned the machine guns around the perimeter fence."

"It would be too hot for me to live down there. I'd melt," said Hazel fanning herself with her hand.

"It's not that much different than around here but it doesn't get as cold in the winter. And then we get a couple hurricanes in the summer to cool us down."

"Those hurricanes must be neat. We have tornados and they're not much fun at all," said Marty.

"Here we are," said everybody to nobody in particular.

Charles said, "You boys grab yourself a cold Bud while I check the fire."

"You want a beer, Hazel, Daisy?" said Bill.

Hazel said she would love one but Daisy declined. She'd rather have a Coke or a Nehi. Bill had a church key in his pocket and popped the tops off the three bottles.

"Ah, it doesn't get any better than this."

About that time, a 1938 Black Plymouth coupe pulled up and Father St. John got out. He was wearing brown saddle shoes, grey flannel trousers and an Argyle sleeveless sweater over a pink shirt. He topped it with a working man's wool cap, not very priestly at all.

Charles called, "Hi Dick, go get a beer on the porch. They're cold."

"Gee," said Bill, "This is changing my opinion of priests. All of the ones I've seen, wear a black dress looking thing and a square beanie with a puffball on top."

Ann said, "Fr. Richard is a different kind of guy. He served as chaplain in the North Atlantic for two years before he came here to build St. Roberts. He was kind of shaky when he first arrived and the first thing he had to do was build a church. We made do buying the building from the Fraternal Order of something or other and it serves as a church and meeting hall. Well, you've seen it."

Father St. John came by to say hi and went to join Charles at the grill. He carried an extra beer for Charles. The hamburgers were doing fine. Ann went back inside for the potato salad and Daisy brought out the coleslaw. Hazel asked if she could help and brought out the plates and dinnerware. Marty brought out a big pitcher of lemonade. The boys didn't know which way to go so they went in to see what they could carry. The table was extra-long and would easily seat the eight of them. It was an old harvest table that the Watsons kept covered most of the time. Charles brought over the burgers and everyone took their seats.

Ann asked, "Father, would you lead us in grace, please?"

Father St. John raised his head up and said,

"Good bread,
Good meat,
Good God
Let's eat."

Everyone said, "Amen."

"I know I met you fellows at the spaghetti dinner. Are you nearly finished with your training here at Fort Wood?" asked Fr. Richard.

"Yes sir. We've got our orders to go 'somewhere in Germany'," said Bill. "We have the unit and company but we won't know where they are until we get there. "

"Well, I hope the conflict is over by the time you arrive but you're going to have your hands full restoring order to Europe after the war. Where are your families?"

Bill said, "I'm from Baytown, which is near Houston, Texas. He said that it's an oil town with a refinery as its primary employer. The bay is full of oil wells. You travel up north of there and it is woodland and paper mills. My father's a millwright. He is works for a contractor that does work in Baytown. My mother stays home with my younger sister, Evelyn. "They go to the First Methodist Church of Baytown."

"Joseph comes from Erie, Pennsylvania, "said Ann.

"Yes my dad is a locomotive engineer on the Pennsylvania. He hauls coal and iron ore all over the place. He was too young for the first war and too old and critical for this one. My brother Chuck is in the Navy in the South Pacific messing around with Lord knows what. He began his Navy career in the North Atlantic guiding convoys to Iceland and Murmansk, Russia. Then he picked up his armed cargo ship in Rhode Island and sailed through the Panama Canal. I have a young brother, Jim, who is probably joining the Navy by now and my sister, Patsy is fourteen and is in high school."

Father Richard said, "I'll bet your brother was glad to get out of that convoy duty. That's where I served and it takes a toll on a man. The South Pacific is no picnic either."

"The last time we were together, the girls were telling you about the Bloodland ghosts. Those fellows didn't give you any trouble. Did they?" asked Father Richard.

Bill said, "If ghosts can pelt you with chestnuts and hedge apples then I would say yes. Yes, they gave us trouble."

Everyone laughed.

"What? Are you all in on it?" asked Joe.

"No, Joe," said Ann. "We just hear about things."

Marty said, "I wanna see a ghost," and they all laughed.

Daisy and her mother brought out a peach and a dewberry pie for dessert. "These are about the last of the dewberries."

They played horseshoes and croquet after dinner. The girls hatched a plan with Charles that if they could talk the boys into taking them to an early movie, he would take them back to the gate afterward. The movie was *State Fair*. They might like it.

Hazel approached Bill about the movie. It sounded like a perfect evening.

"Is that the one with Will Rogers in it?"

"No, this is a new production with Jeanne Crain and Dick Haymes."

"No," said Bill. "I'm not going to see that draft dodger in a movie. It was bad enough hearing him on the radio the other night."

Joe pulled Bill aside and said, "Bill, could you stop waving your flag for a little while? This is my chance to sit with my arm around Daisy for a couple hours in a dark theater and you're screwing it up."

"Are you sure Will Rogers isn't in it?"

"Definitely!"

"Okay, let's go."

"We're going Daisy!" called Hazel.

The movie began at five and the two couples walked the four blocks to the theater. The Movietone News began the program. It showed films of the 9th US Army crossing the Rhine and also views of Iwo Jima after the deadly battle that brought American bombers that much closer to Tokyo. Next was a cartoon called *The Three Caballeros* with Donald Duck.

Bill said, "I think that parrot on the left is a draft dodger. He looks Argentinian. "

"Shut up Bill," they all said.

The movie began and soon Jeanne Crain was singing "It Might As Well Be Spring." Joe had his arm around Daisy's shoulders. He lightly touched her breast with his thumb. It felt warm and wonderful. Soon Dick Haymes was singing "It's a Grand Night For Singing" and Joe moved his finger a little closer to Daisy's breast.

"Back off, Big Boy. I know you're a gentleman. Now prove it to me," and Joe skittered away. Hazel whispered,

"Bill, you know you haven't kissed me yet. Come on, Tex, give me some sugar."

Chapter 5 – Base Dance

Joe had been dreading this day all month. He had KP on Sunday. He had it back in March but that was different. He was doing it for Felix and Felix paid him for it. It just felt different when you were getting five dollars for your day of work. He tied a towel to his bunk and the CQ woke him up at 04:00. He was actually awake a few minutes before the CQ arrived. He got to bed at 22:00 last night even after going to the movies. He wanted to see Daisy again before he shipped out next Sunday. They didn't make a date though. He said he'd call her. The movie was wonderful with his arm around her shoulders. They held hands on the way home in spite of the jibes from Bill and Hazel.

He skipped a shower and just shaved before going to the mess hall. It only took him a half-hour. The servers had already been selected so he got the cutter room with the dishwasher. At least it wasn't pots and pans. The last man in the door got that job. He helped the others set up the dining room; taking the chairs off the table. Their breakfast was ready so he loaded up his tray with fried eggs on top of pancakes and sausage links on the side. A glass of orange juice and a cup of coffee completed it with some Log Cabin syrup. They had big cans of syrup that they normally used but sometimes they had name brand items available in small quantities.

Mike Schneider also had KP today so they sat together with two other guys from their company.

Mike asked, "What did you do yesterday after the big parade, Joe?"

"We had a big day of it. Bill and I went to Daisy's house for a picnic lunch and later on we went to the show."

"What did you see?"

"It was *State Fair.*"

"Oh, that draft dodger's movie? "

"You've been talking to Bill? He was going on about Dick Haymes all the way to the show. What did you do Mike?"

"Felix and I went to a cock fight in Devil's Elbow."

"Where's that and how'd you find it?"

"We met some guys playing pool at the Silver Slipper. They told us it was at a barn about five miles east on route 66. It was a bunch of hayseeds gathered around a pit with a couple of pissed off chickens. They had great refreshments that came out of a Mason jar. Whewee! I can still feel it. I made enough on side bets to get me through the end of the month and send a little home. "

"You'll go blind drinking that stuff, Mike."

"Naw. These folks are brought up on that hooch."

"Come on you yard birds. Let's get to work," said the second chef. The mess sergeant was already at work planning tomorrow's meals and drinking his third coffee.

Joe rinsed off the eight trays, eight cups and eight goblets and put them in the dish machine. Only 160 more to go. Breakfast was finished. He scrubbed the stainless steel surfaces bright and shiny, mopped the floor and dragged the garbage can of slops outside. They would go to a nearby hog farmer who contracted to take the edible garbage from the fort. The other can was nonedible paper trash and there was darn little of that. The sergeant told him to scrub two other GI cans with a toilet brush and a cake of all-purpose yellow soap. That finished, they paused for a coffee break and a smoke. Joe didn't smoke any longer but was glad for the breaks it provided.

Soon it was time for lunch. There was salad, tomato soup, grilled cheese sandwiches and fruit. This was just like mother used to make. They had either fruit drink or milk out of five-gallon cans to drink. When he was done cleaning up the cutter room, there were 170 potatoes to peel. There was minimal garbage from the meal except apple cores, orange skins and banana peels. He wondered what the hogs would think of that. Peeling potatoes was relaxing, as well as time to shoot the bull. You'd catch hell though if you took too much potato off with the skin. The other two guys were new to the company and just beginning their training.

"You're Joe aren't you? We met at the dance at the church two weeks ago."

"Yeah and you're Bob from, where are you from?"

"Westfield, New York. My family has an orchard and vineyard there."

"Westfield! That makes us practically neighbors. I'm from Erie, just across the line. We used to drive to Westfield because you can drink at 18 there and Pennsy is still 21. Heck, I was sixteen and I could still get a beer in New York. Now we're back up to 21 again here in Missouri."

Joe asked if he'd seen that girl, Shirley Jones, again.

"No. I've been hanging around here at the fort since then. Not enough money to go anywhere else. I don't have PFC pay like you do."

"I haven't seen Shirley but I've been around her sister once or twice and I have hit it off well with her friend, Daisy."

"I don't remember Daisy. You spent time with Margaret. What happened to her?"

"One in the same, Champ! I don't know why they have different names like that but I've called her Daisy ever since. Let's get this pot of spuds in to the cook."

The cook added water to cover the potatoes and they lifted the heavy pot onto the stove. Mike had just finished snapping 50 pounds of green beans and the meat loaf was in the oven. The mess sergeant baked a big sheet cake and was frosting it. They took a break. Joe couldn't tolerate another coffee so he had a glass of the fruit drink. He couldn't tell exactly what fruit it was but it was sweet and cool...like Daisy.

The cook asked Joe to come help him take the pot of spuds off the stove so Joe grabbed a hold of the handle with a potholder. One, two, three and they lifted the heavy pot. Some of the boiling water splashed on Joe's hand as they got to the edge of the stove. Joe yelled, "I can't hang on," and they lowered the pot quickly to the floor.

"You clumsy fool. Can't you even lift a pot?"

Joe responded with, "Why did you have to fill it so high?" His hand felt numb at first but now really hurt.

"Go put some ice on it."

The mess sergeant called Joe to his desk. "Do you need to go to the infirmary?"

"I think I'll be alright if I can just ice it down for a few minutes. I can hold ice on it while I eat."

"Just the same. You should probably go to sick call tomorrow and let them check it out."

"I'm processing out tomorrow and I have to go by the infirmary, so I can have them look at it then. It just seems to be red and there is no blister."

"Just be safe," said the sergeant.

Joe and the rest had their dinner, meatloaf with plenty of gravy, green beans, carrots and mashed potatoes. He felt like a little bit of himself was in the potatoes. Mike said that he thought Joe might be interested in the dance at the club next Friday. "Woody Herman is appearing in St. Louis with his First Herd on Saturday. They're going to swing by here on Friday for a dance at the EM club. They're just putting it together. I thought maybe Margaret and you would want to go."

"That sounds swell, Mike. Do you know how much it is going to cost?"

"What do you care? You'll be rolling in cash come Friday with your travel pay. Me too."

Back to work. His hand bothered him a little. Mostly it just throbbed. He finished out his shift and was too tired to go to the club tonight. "Why didn't they just have cold cuts like they usually do on Sunday night?"

Monday began with reveille. The sergeant told his platoon that they would begin their processing this morning with a trip to the infirmary. Now drop down for your daily dozen. They always began their calisthenics with pushups. They worked their way through the next eleven exercises and then broke for breakfast. Their last exercise was doing a dozen pull-ups on the bar before going into the mess hall. Joe just had a bowl of oatmeal and coffee. He sprinkled brown sugar on the oatmeal and doused it with milk.

He sat down with Bill, Felix and Mike. Mike asked if he checked out the dance yet but Joe said that he'd been too tired after KP and his hand throbbed like the devil.

"What did you do to your hand?" asked Bill.

"Oh, I scalded it yesterday on a pot of potatoes. I set it down too fast and the cook had overfilled it. It feels better now. I'll ask them about it when we go to the infirmary today."

"Well take care of it!"

They finished their breakfast and straightened up the barracks before falling in to march to the infirmary.

"Right face. Forward harch!"

"Why doesn't he say march?"

"Shut up Conroy!"

"I gotta girl in Kansas City,
Honey, Honey."
"I gotta girl in Kansas City,
Babe, Babe..."

It's surprising how a little song melted the miles or fraction of a mile. They were at the infirmary in no time. They filed in the building with two squads on each side. Two medics wrote down their medical history while 38 men waited. Most of their history had changed very little in the past half year. Some had experienced influenza or bronchitis. A few had pneumonia and had to repeat their training. On the whole, they were a pretty healthy bunch of men. As they finished with the clerk, they moved forward with their medical file to the chest X-ray.

They stripped down to their shorts and stuck their clothing in a locker. No lock though. The film plate was cold against the chest. Buzz! They were done. Next a nurse wrote his service number on the tag and gave him a beaker and said, "Pee in this and put it on the shelf by the door."

"Oh damn. I just went before I came over here."

"You can do it, soldier!"

He managed to get about an inch of urine in the beaker.

"An inch is as good as a mile," and he put it on the shelf.

The nurse told him to sit on the examining table and the doctor would be along. He asked if this was an appropriate time to talk about his hand. She asked to see it and said it wasn't all that bad but to mention it to the doctor. The doctor came in about that time and said, "Mention what?"

"Private Conrad burned himself yesterday and it is still red with a little swelling."

The doctor looked at his hand and told the nurse to give him a tube of that all-purpose ointment. "It has something in it to lessen the pain and should keep it from blistering. Now let's look at you."

The doctor listened to his heart and lungs. They sounded fine. He poked and prodded his abdomen. All okay there. Eyes, ears, nose and throat looked good. Now stand and drop your shorts. He checked Joe for a hernia. "Cough!" Joe pulled his shorts and dignity back up and was done. The nurse told him to go to the next cubicle for his shots. "Oh, brother!"

He stepped in and a corpsman had an array of glass syringes loaded and ready. He gave Joe three injections: one for typhoid fever, another for cholera, and the last for plague, which was feared with the amount of destroyed infrastructure following the war. He returned to get his uniform and went to a room to wait for the others. They marched back to the barracks and went to eat lunch after checking his mail. There was a letter from his mom and another from Daisy.

4/21/1945

Dear Joe,

I know we just left you an hour ago and I miss you already. I had a super day seeing you marching with all of your buddies. I imagine you and your little bunk in this sea of men. Do you ever find a place to be on your own? I'm rambling! Thanks for the movie. The music was beautiful and I appreciated holding your hand on the way home. Let's do it again. I know your time is short. Call me at Crocker 9964 please, please.

Sincerely,
Daisy

He opened the other letter from home.

4/19/1945

Dear Joseph,

News is scarce around here. Dad has been working a lot lately. Sometimes he only gets ten hours between runs and he has been pulling long ore trains from up in Michigan to Pittsburgh then he brings coal to our power plant. They are tearing up the cobblestone sidewalks on State Street and replacing them with cement. They say they will bury pipes underneath them to melt the snow in the winter. This is just in front of the department stores for a couple blocks. That's all over my head.

Frank and Marie say they are having fun calling Bingo at church. It brings in good money to pay for the new Holy Rosary Church. Your Aunt Liza got to pour tea for Bishop Gannon last week. She likes to get involved in churchy things. It would be nice if she paid as much attention to her husband as she does to the bishop. Did I say that? Forgive me.

Don and Katy are still getting their place ready to open. They have their liquor license so it shouldn't be long now. We'll need to get a ride to Sherman to see it one day. Be careful as you go overseas. I pray that the war will be over when you get there. We hear from Chuck now and then. I worry about him. They say he is going to Okenawa. Maybe you won't need to go. Patsy and Jimmy say hi.

Sincerely yours,
Mother

They finished their meal and lined up in front of the barracks. The sergeant passed out checklists to each of the troops. They were on their own now to finish checking out. They had to go to the base library and craft shop to make sure they didn't have any books or tools still checked out. That was easy because he hadn't made much use of the library. There had always been plenty of paperbacks available in the day room to satisfy his reading interests. His current book was James Hilton's

Lost Horizon about a plane crash in the Himalayas. His taste ran toward action and adventure. He and Bill went together.

They got their sheets signed off by the librarian. They proceeded to the Provost Marshall to make sure they had no outstanding fines or warrants.

"What's this about?" asked Joe. "We don't even have a car."

"This is the army, Joe. You might have got a ticket for littering. Right?"

They walked into the office of the Fort Leonard Wood Provost Marshall. It was a functional looking building. The clerk at the desk asked for their sign out sheets. "I've been dealing with these all day, guys." He looked in the alphabetical file drawer. "You guys are clean." He signed their papers and passed them back.

They wound up with the craft shop and got their sheets signed off. They lingered for a short time looking at some of the craft projects that guys had in progress. The *Terraplane* had its engine back in place and was polished bright and shiny as the day it was purchased. "I wonder what they have left to do on it." asked Joe to no one in particular.

"We've got plenty of time. Let's stop by the EM Club on the way back and have a beer. I want to check on a dance I heard about on Friday."

"Sounds good to me Joe. I've raised a bit of a thirst."

The marquee board near the door announced, "Woody Herman and The First Herd, Friday night April 27, 1945 at 2:000

hours." They walked to the bar and each ordered a 10¢ draft Budweiser. When the barman brought their drink, Joe asked him how much the dance was on Friday.

"Oh that? It's free. There's no charge for dances like that. The band is playing nearby and they just do it for the troops. Doing their bit."

"Bill, Daisy should be home from school. I'm going to call her and ask her to go. Should I get Hazel's number so you can ask her?"

"I guess I'd like to see her again. Yeah Joe! Go ahead and ask her."

Joe dialed CR 9964 and the operator said, "Deposit 10¢ for three minutes." He heard the phone ringing and a woman answered.

"Mrs. Watson? This is Joe Conrad. Is Daisy there?"

"Wait a minute and I'll call her."

"Hi Joe! Why don't you hang up and I'll call you, right back. What is your number?"

"Crocker 2275, Bye now."

A moment later, the phone rang and Joe answered it.

"There, that's better. There's no point in you putting all of those dimes in. How are you doing? Did you get my letter?"

"Woe there. One thing at time. Yes, I got your letter and yes, I want to be with you again before I leave and I'm doing fine. I got some great news today. Actually, I heard it yesterday but I just got the details. Woody Herman is coming to town and his band is playing here Friday. They call themselves the First Herd. Anyhow, there will be a dance on Friday and I want you to come with me."

"Oh Joe! I'd love to come. I'm ready to dance."

"How about if I pick you up about seven?"

"Oh no! You've got to come here for supper. Why don't you come at five?"

"Okay Honey. I'll be there by five."

"You just called me Honey."

"That's because you're so sweet."

"What are you going to be doing over there? Is it dangerous?"

"I imagine myself standing in the middle of the street directing traffic like I did in eighth grade. I've got experience. The only difference is that it will be on the corner of Eisenhower Strasse and Patton Platz."

"Oh Joe.You're funny. Do you know German?"

"Yep! Two words so far. By the way. Do you have Hazel Jones' phone number? I told Bill I'd get it for him."

"Sure Joe. It's Crocker 4692. Is Bill going also?"

"He's considering it. Now I've got to go." He wanted to say, "I love you," but knew it wasn't appropriate.

"I don't want you to leave but okay, I'll go. See you Friday."

"I'll be there with bells on."

"Goodbye Joe."

"Goodbye Daisy."

He walked back to the bar and his flat beer and gave Bill the matchbook cover with Hazel's phone number in it. The bartender said, "Here, let me freshen that up for you." He dumped the beer and refilled the glass. "You got a date for the dance?"

"Yeah and a date for dinner too."

Bill and Joe finished their beer and returned to the barracks for supper.

The next morning the sergeant asked to see their checkout lists. He noted that Joe had everything checked off but the paymaster. "Are you going there today?" asked the sergeant.

"I'd like to wait until Friday, Sarge. That's quite a bit of money to have hanging around. The poker games have already started and I'd like to stick to pinochle."

"That's a wise move, Conrad. Just remember they close at two. Go to the travel office this morning though and get your train tickets. Report back in when you're through."

The four friends, Joe, Bill, Felix and Mike, headed to the travel office with their orders. They were to be in New York City on May 4th for embarkation to Europe. They arrived at the service window at one end of the travel office and a woman asked them in her best Gravel Girty voice, "Hello boys. What can I do for you? Let me have your orders. You all going to the same place."

"Yes Ma'am."

"I can get you to Chicago on Sunday on the *Chickasaw* Number 82. We can put you up overnight at one of our contract hotels and get you out in the afternoon on a sleeper to Buffalo and then a coach to New York City. That will save us the price of a hotel one night."

She went to work and produced a flurry of tickets and papers.

Your itinerary is this.

"The bus will take you from the fort to St. Louis where you'll catch the Illinois Central *Daylight* #20 at 12:15 on Sunday, April 29 arriving in Chicago at 17:45. You've got to pick up your bags from the IC and check them again on the New York Central. They won't do it for you. Get yourselves some supper. You leave Chicago on Sunday evening at 20:00 hours on the New York Central *Niagara* #58 and travel through Canada to Buffalo by sleeper. There's not much to see until you get to Niagara Falls. There you'll move to a coach in Buffalo on #72 The *Henry Hudson* at 09:00. You've only got 25 minutes to change cars and your checked baggage will change with you. Travel to New York City arriving at 17:20 on Monday. You make your own way to the barracks at Pier 53 to await your embarkation on USAT *George Washington* on Friday noon. That gives you four nights in the Big Apple, Boys."

Joe said, "That travelling through Canada means we won't stop at Erie will we?"

"Afraid not soldier unless you want to swim."

They laughed. Joe had thought he might call his folks from the station or maybe they could stop by but now he will be on the wrong side of the lake for that.

The clerk said, "Here are your tickets boys. Guard them with your life or you'll be hitchhiking to New York."

They left to return to the barracks. Bill said, "It's still early guys. What say we stop by the PX for a cup of joe?"

They stopped by the lunch counter for a 5¢ cup of coffee and splurged on a Danish pastry. There were wild ideas flying around about what they would do in Chicago and New York. The thought of the barracks at Pier 53 sounded ominous though. Bill said, "I'm going to show those New York ladies what a real-life Texan looks like. They've had their fill of candy-ass city boys."

"You watch it Bill or they'll be packing your ass back to Goose Creek." They liked to kid him about the name of his town.

They reported to the sergeant. "I've got a job for you guys. For the next couple of days you'll work for the Provost Marshall's office."

"What will we be doing Sarge?"

"Call it on-the-job training. You'll be escorting prisoners, traffic control, wherever they need. Now go get some chow and report to the Provost Marshal and wear your spats."

An hour later, they were standing before the desk sergeant. "Reporting for duty. Sergeant Carney sent us."

"Yes, I've got some work for you. You two." He pointed to Felix and Bill. "We have a prisoner that needs to see his lawyer. Go to the armory and draw out two side arms. You there. You'll be my relief on the desk this afternoon." He pointed to Mike. It was nothing new to him. He'd worked the desk as a sheriff deputy in Jackson. "and you (pointing to Joe). I need you for traffic control at the base elementary school."

"Oh brother," said Joe. "Eighth grade all over again."

"Stop it. It's an important assignment. Here take this Sam Brown belt." He handed Joe a white web Sam Brown belt nearly identical to the one he had in school but now he had his MP helmet, white gloves and a white baton. Another PFC drove him to the school and said. "You know what to do now, If you gotta take a leak, go into the school."

"Yeah, I know what to do."

"See you at 16:00," he said as he drove away.

"What to do now? 13:30 and not a kiddo in sight."

A truck rumbled along and he walked out and waved it through. He marched around the four corners until he got sick of it. A truckload of troops roared by on their way to the rifle range. Some made obscene gestures at him from the back of the truck. "I'll see you later when you're drunk and stumbling back to base," he thought.

A bell rang deep inside the school. The first little kids marched up to the corner two by two with their pretty teacher and stopped until he waved them across the street. A jeep came along and waited patiently.

He was back at the barracks by five. The next day was a change of pace. Mike got along well with the desk sergeant so he stayed there for another day. The desk sergeant told Joe to checkout a sidearm from the armory. He was to accompany a criminal investigator to pick up a deserter. He strapped on the holster and inserted the magazine in the pistol but did not chamber a round.

Joe said, "That sounds serious."

"It is but I don't think you'll have any trouble with this guy. He lives on the other side of Richland, which is about twenty miles from here. The CID guy has a staff car so he'll be driving."

Joe had never learned to drive. His dad didn't have a car so it never came up. The detective came into the lobby and asked Joe if he was the guard. "My name is Captain Williams, private. Are you ready to go?"

"Yes sir! I'm all set."

They both went out to the 1940 Army green Chevy and began their mission. They drove to St. Robert first. He smiled as he passed the Watson's house and said, "My girl lives there."

"You're lucky. Have you known her long?"

"It's only been three weeks now. I'm taking her to the dance on Friday and then I ship out on Sunday. What is our mission today? They told me we're picking up a deserter."

"Yeah, it's a sad case. The fellow was drafted early in the war. His wife became ill and he left infantry training to go take care of her. He had four children and she eventually died. The days went by and he just never got around to coming back. Two days ago, he walked into the draft office in Richland and surrendered. He said his son was old enough to run the farm now. The old guys at the draft board didn't know what to do with him and turned him over to the constable. They held him overnight and called us. He seems peaceful enough. His conscience just got the better of him."

"That is sad. What do you think they'll do with him?"

"He could be executed but I doubt it. They could save a lot of money by just giving him a dishonorable discharge and he can go back to his farm. That is just my opinion."

They arrived at the constable's office and went inside. Joe kept quiet while Capt. Williams did the talking.

"I understand you have a prisoner here for us."

"Glad to see you. We don't run a hotel here for the US government. This guy is costing us money. Here, sign this receipt for Mr. Ritter and you can have him."

They were surprised to see Private Ritter in his class A uniform that he'd kept for three years for this occasion. It was a bit rumpled from being in jail for two nights but he was still proud of it.

"I'm sorry to put you men to this much trouble but I had a family to feed and the time just got away from me."

The prisoner got in the back seat on the left of Joe and the captain drove back. They went directly to the stockade where they fingerprinted and booked Ritter. He was just a skinny guy who needed a shave. No threat to anyone. The captain said he would take it from there and that Joe could go back to the office. Mike was at the desk when he walked in.

"That desk seems to suit you, Mike."

"It sure does, Joe. Did you get your man?"

"Yeah and a sad case it was," and he told Mike about his mission. "I got to meet the constable in Richland and he was tired of entertaining a federal prisoner. He was kind of grumpy about it." He turned in his pistol after removing the magazine and wiping it down with an oily rag. It was time for lunch and the two of them went to the consolidated mess hall after Mike got a relief for the desk.

Joe had his pocketbook with him when he returned and read in the office until someone was free to drive him back to the school to guard the intersection.

Friday morning came and went. He was asked to take a low-level offender to a dentist appointment on the shuttle bus. The prisoner was handcuffed and Joe was armed with a baton. The other passengers gave them wide berth. He escorted the prisoner into the dentist office and handcuffed him to the chair. He sat nearby and pulled out his novel. He returned the offender to the stockade and met Mike at the mess hall.

"I have to go pick up my cash after lunch. Have you gotten yours yet?"

"No, I don't have that kind of will power. I'll go with you. We need to let them know at the office."

They went and bid farewell to the Provost Marshall. The desk sergeant asked them if they needed an armed guard while they picked up their travel pay. They went to the paymaster, which was kind of like a bank with one teller where the company clerks picked up the payroll on the last day of the month. They would get paid for this month and next plus separate ration pay for their food on the road and field pay whatever that was. Joe's share was one $100 bill, one $50 bill, two twenties, a five, three ones and 27¢. The Army always pays in the biggest bills possible.

Joe asked, "Could you please change the hundred to twenties. Nobody will ever cash a hundred."

The paymaster complied and gave Joe five twenties and did the same for Mike who got about twenty dollars less since he was still a private.

Joe pulled out the money belt that he bought the previous evening at the PX. "This is what I've been waiting for. Now to hang onto it." They returned to the Provost Marshall but were told they were done with their service. They returned to the barracks and got ready for inspection in the morning and pressed their uniforms for the dance in the evening. Felix and Bill were already there, doing the same.

Joe asked Bill if he was taking Hazel.

"Nah," said Bill, "She'll be there but as a USO volunteer. That way, I don't have to buy her dinner."

"You asked her then."

"Yeah. She's not that big on me and besides we'll be gone like the wind on Sunday. You'll be leaving Margaret too. How are you going to handle that state of affairs?"

"I don't know. We're just friends. It's not like we're in love."

"You may not be in love. What about her?"

"I've gotta go now." He left the barracks and began to look for the Toonerville Trolley. None in sight.

He began walking toward the gate hoping that the bus wouldn't catch up with him between stops. He kept turning around and saw it coming so he turned and jogged back to the stop he just passed. "Hi" he said.

"Hi yourself! I would've stopped for you. No need to run."

"Thanks. I'll remember next time." (Not that there'll be a next time.)

He got to the gate just as two chemical corps guys were hailing a taxi. "Do you mind if I share a ride with you?" said Joe, always trying to save a buck. And why not?

"Sure, hop in. We're just going to St. Robert."

"That's fine with me. So where are you heading?"

"We have a couple of girls in town that we're taking to the dance tonight."

"Small world. I'm doing the same but her parents invited me for supper."

They arrived in front of Daisy's house and he asked the driver to stop. "How much do I owe you?"

"That'll be 50 cents." Joe gave him seventy-five. He walked up to the front door carrying the Whitman's Chocolate Sampler and bouquet of daisies he bought earlier at the PX. He rang the doorbell.

Daisy opened the door and wrapped her arms around his neck nearly dropping the candy box. "Oh Joe! I've missed you."

"I've missed you too, Honey. I've brought daisies for my Daisy." He looked over her gray shirtwaist dress with the sailor color and said, "You look lovely."

"Oh, this is just for supper so I don't soil my dance dress. I'm wearing something special tonight."

"I can't wait to see it."

Charles called from the kitchen, "Come on in Joe and have a Bud."

Joe and Daisy went to the kitchen. "Good evening Mr. Watson, Mrs. Watson."

"Oh. Hi Joe. We're just heating up the oil. We're having blue pike from the Great Lakes, potatoes au gratin and corn, peas and carrots from our garden. Thank you for the chocolates. Daisy please put the flowers in a vase."

"It all sounds wonderful Ma'am."

"Joe, you're such a gentleman."

"It may be all of the Southerners I've been hanging around. Maybe I just grew up a bit in the Army. I've been in eight months now. See my stripe. I forgot to mention it last week."

Charles answered, "Yes, we noticed that. You get a pay raise with that stripe?"

"Yes Sir, but it sure doesn't go very far. I got my travel pay today so it feels like I'm rich but it has to stretch quite a way."

"So this is it. Aye Joe? You're really shipping out. And I was just getting attached to you," said Charles with a grin. Joe just blushed a little. "Let's get this meal started and put the fish in the grease. You're going to love these fish, just like you get back home."

"Yes sir! I was brought up on blue pike when we could afford it. There were times when it was just tuna fish."

"You're right. The good times are here if you don't count the war. I just hope this Truman fellow can keep us out of depression when all of this spending is over and we gotta pay for it."

"I think we'll make it. You'll have millions of GI's looking for an education and homes and cars. We can melt down all of the tanks and guns and make Fords and Chevys again."

Daisy agreed with Joe. Marty came in and asked where his supper was. "Oh! Can I have a chocolate?" he asked.

Ann just frowned at him. Charles took the fish out of the fryer. "Come on folks let's eat."

They sat down and Charles said Grace, the traditional Grace and not that silly one that Fr. Richard said, "Amen"

Joe picked up the platter of fish and offered it to Ann. "No Joe. You take some and pass it on." Joe passed it to Daisy without taking any. He did the same with the vegetables. Ann dished out the hot au gratin potatoes for each one. The fish came around to Joe and he took one of the big fillets that were left. His strategy worked again.

Ann asked Joe how he had passed his last week on base. He told them about having KP last Sunday and burning his hand on the potato kettle. They laughed when he told them about guarding the intersection at the grammar school. Then he mentioned checking out of the library and such and guarding the fellow going to the dentist. He was sad when he told them about bringing in the deserter. That was a tough case.

Charles said, "They used to shoot deserters."

"I don't know if this guy even knew what he had done. He was swept up in something and then just had to go home and take care of his farm and family. When they could take care of themselves, he turned himself in."

Charles said that it was a tough situation. “But, enough of that. Who are you dancing to, tonight?”

“Daddy, I told you, Woody Herman.”

“Didn’t his band break up?”

“No Daddy. He just made it smaller and they go to smaller places now. A lot of the bands are doing that.”

Ann told Daisy that she better go and change.

“Not until I have dessert. We still have time.”

Ann brought out the pineapple upside down cake, already cut on smaller plates. “Who wants coffee?” Charles and Joe both raised a finger. Daisy said, “I’ll go get it.” She brought out the pot and filled the cups that were already on the table.

“This is good, Mom. Thank you,” said Marty.

“I’ll second that,” said Joe.

They finished their cake in short order. Joe liked to cut his way around the ring of pineapple and save the cherry for the last bite.

“Now, I gotta go,” said Daisy.

“I’ll come help you,” said her Mom.

Charles said, “You know, it’s going to be hard living with that girl for the next week? She’s been hard to live with this week knowing you are coming over.”

“That’s for sure,” said Marty.

"Why don't you get me some more coffee, Marty, and then go listen to Sky King."

"Okay, Dad," and he brought the percolator out from the kitchen and carefully refilled their cups.

"Do you love her, Joe?"

"Yes, I do sir, but I haven't told her. It's just that we've only known each other for three weeks now. If I met her earlier, I would have asked her to marry me. I don't think it's fair though, to get married and then leave for a year."

"Well, she loves you. I shouldn't be saying this but that's how it is. You kids figure it out. Just don't hurt her."

"I'd never do that sir."

"Care for a little glass of sherry, Joe."

"No thank you sir. That wonderful supper is enough for me."

Joe was blown away when Daisy walked into the kitchen, barely fitting through the doorway. She said, "It's my prom dress but I figured this will be my real prom tonight. Do you like it?"

"I don't know what to say. It's beautiful. Now, I wish I'd bought you a corsage. You are lovely, Daisy." The dress was kind of bone white with darker ovals around the skirt with flowers on them. There was a scalloped ribbon like decoration about six inches up from the hem that was just below her knees. Yards of crinoline underneath puffed it out. Her collar scooped down from her sleeveless top with the same decorative ribbon to border it. He felt like a clod in his brown uniform and brown shoes.

Ann said, "Don't worry about the corsage. We took care of that." She took a white rose corsage from the refrigerator. It had three blossoms on it. One was opened a little more than the others were. Joe pinned the flowers on to Daisy's right strap being careful not to stick her.

"I have to call for a taxi now."

"Nonsense Boy! I'll drive you. I wouldn't want that dress getting soiled in some old cab."

"Thank you, Sir. We'd appreciate that but I hate putting you out all the time."

"You know it's no trouble."

They went out to the driveway and both got into the back seat of the Dodge and pretended it was a limousine. They arrived at the EM club about 20:10 just as a bus from St. Robert Church brought the USO girls. They all looked very plain compared to Daisy. Hazel and Shirley came over and said, "Look at you, girl. You're really decked out. How did you find this princess, soldier?"

"I went to town for supper and there she was. Isn't she pretty?"

"You're damn right, soldier!"

They all pushed their way into the ballroom giving Daisy wide girth so as not to crush her petticoats. The band was playing and a young man in uniform was singing "Laura." He and a female singer were chorus troopers from the 5th Army. They were performing with the band tonight. Joe asked Daisy to dance.

"I know everyone's gonna be asking you to dance but will you save some of the slow ones for me. It is tough to see you dancing in someone else's arms."

"I'll save you the slow ones when I can and the last dance of course."

"This prom of yours. When is that?"

"It's in three weeks, a week after my birthday. I'll be eighteen when I graduate."

"Oh! What day is your birthday?"

"May 4th and I'll be eighteen."

"Then you'll be as old as me. My birthday is in August on the 14th. Do you have a date for the prom?"

"Yes I do or rather an escort. Bobby Pavlat asked me on Valentine's Day. He wasn't taking any chances. He's on the football team, tight end or some silly thing. His biggest asset is he is big but nothing like you, Joe. His idea of a hot date is drinking Bud in the back of a pickup at the drive-in movie. I haven't had to participate in that activity but I know girls who have."

They began the next dance when another MP cut in and danced away with Daisy. Joe turned around and saw two girls standing there. He asked the nearest girl to dance and she came right with him. She could really jump and she responded readily to all of Joe's moves. That song ended and Joe asked her partner to dance but he was keeping an eye on Daisy. She was dancing with two or three fellows with each song. He worked his way toward her. The girl singer got on the bandstand to sing "A Nightingale Sang in Barkly Square" and Joe hurried to Daisy. They worked their way to the center of the floor so they could dance together for a while. He held her more tightly than he should and said, "I love you Daisy."

"I love you Joe," and they kissed.

"Your dad asked me and I told him that I love you."

"I know."

"What?"

"Marty told me."

"That rat. I should've known."

"But I liked knowing it. I like you saying it even better."

They were still holding each other tightly when the male singer began belting out "GI Jive." They finished the dance and were ready for a breather. They moved to the refreshment table where the Officer's Wives Club was serving punch and desserts baked by the military wives. The female singer was also taking a break and greeted Daisy with, "Oh, I love your dress." She was in uniform with a long skirt and short jacket. She said her name was Virginia and her partner's name was Billy.

Daisy said that she and her mother bought it in St. Louis in March. It was considered out of fashion and quaint and was really marked down. Joe was relieved at that. She told the singer how much she enjoyed her song.

"It will always be very special to us."

"Why is that? I know it's special to lots of people."

"Well, Joe finally told me that he loved me."

"Finally!" said Joe.

"Why yes. You told Daddy before you told me."

"This sounds interesting but I gotta run. Good luck you two," said the singer.

The band went on to play "Woody'n You," "Swing Shift" and "Down Under." They were really jumpin' with a lot of trumpet jive. Lots of kids took the opportunity to take a break and load up on goodies. The next song was "The Golden Wedding" and an engineer asked Daisy to dance. The dance was exhausting and showed off a lot of Daisy's britches. She staggered back to Joe.

"I see your bloomers match your dress," said Joe.

"Of course they do and you shouldn't have been looking."

"But you are adorable."

They talked too long. Another soldier asked her to dance. It was a slow bluesy number sung by Billy. He said it was "Blue Prelude." Joe spotted Shirley Jones and asked her to dance. She was ready to latch onto Joe. He hadn't seen her since the spaghetti dinner. He felt like his whole life had changed since then. He tried to loosen up and give her a little room. She just pressed tighter where he could feel her firm little breasts against his chest.

"Shirley, you've got to be more careful. There're too many really horny guys around here that would love to get their hands on you," he whispered.

"I know the score buddy. Don't give me the big brother jive. I've got a brother and I don't need a big one."

A soldier cut in and Joe released her after whispering to Shirley to be careful.

At the end of the song, the band broke into "Woodchopper's Ball" and the crowd stopped dancing and just gathered around to listen. Some took the opportunity to have some more refreshment. Joe found Daisy and held her around her slender waist. At the end of the tune, both vocalists mounted the stage to sing "They Can't Take That Away From Me." The dancers came back to the floor and Joe hurried Daisy to the middle. The song began, "There are many, many crazy things that will keep me loving you...The way you wear your hat. The way you sip your tea."

Joe sang along, "No, they can't take that away from me."

Daisy sang," The way you've changed my life."

And they both sang, "No, they can't take that away from me."

"Say, that was fun."

Virginia, the female singer sang “I'll Get By” for her last number with Billy backing her up “As Long as I Have You.” That was the end of the evening especially when the band broke into a jazz version of “Good Night, Ladies.” It was a good night and then some of the ladies headed for their bus. Daisy asked Joe if they could give Hazel and Shirley a lift home in their taxi. She was assuming they would take a taxi.

“Sure, that’s alright...Love to have them.” He would have preferred to be alone with Daisy. Hazel said goodnight to Bill and “have a nice life.” They got into the third cab in line. Many of the troops were walking back to their barracks and the townies had either buses or private cars.

“Oh, that was a beautiful dance,” piped Shirley. It was her first with a live band. “I can’t wait until my prom!”

Daisy said, “I’ve got to keep this dress in good shape for three more weeks. I was careful not to get any food near it tonight. I’m starved.”

“Who you going to the prom with?” asked Hazel. “Oh! I guess I should keep my mouth shut.”

“It wouldn’t hurt. Bobby asked me to go two months ago. Joe knows about it.” Daisy wished she’d let them go on the bus.

She continued, “Virginia and Billy were good singers for soldiers. We met Virginia when she was taking a break. Must be good duty for them. I wonder how often they get to sing with big bands.”

Shirley asked Joe if he had long to stay here at the fort. Joe said, "As a matter of fact, this is my last weekend. I leave for New York City on Sunday morning."

Hazel asked, "What are you doing in New York?"

"I'm sailing to Europe on the USAT *George Washington*."

"I thought the war in Europe is nearly over," said Shirley.

"It's close to over. The Jerrys are on the run but it's going to take years to rebuild those countries after the Allies and the Germans bombed the crap out of them. That's why I'm going as an MP and not in a bomber."

"Is the *George Washington* a big ocean liner?" asked Shirley. "With swimming pools and deck chairs and shuffle board?"

"I don't think there will be much of that for us. We'll be sailing in steerage."

"What's steerage?"

"That's how our ancestors got to America. It is the lowest decks of the ships."

"Driver! Stop at that next house please, the one with the light on," said Hazel. She handed Joe a dollar and said, "For our half of the ride." Joe started to say no but she stuffed it in his blouse pocket. They stopped in front of the Jones's house and the girls' mother appeared at the door. "You girls are getting kind of fancy, arriving in a taxi."

"Oh Mom, we shared a ride with Joe and Daisy."

Joe put his arm around Daisy and kissed her. They were soon at Daisy's house. "Please let the cab go and come inside."

"I was hoping you'd say that."

Joe paid the driver and said thanks for the ride. Ann was already opening the front door. She saw the lights of the taxi.

"Hi Mom. Is Dad up?"

"You know we wouldn't sleep until you were safely home. Did you have a good time?"

"Everyone was so nice and the music was wonderful. Mr. Herman had an eight-piece band and there were two singers from somewhere in the Army."

"I didn't know the Army had singers."

"They were from the 5th Army Special Services Ma'am," said Joe.

"Virginia, the girl singer, liked my dress. We spoke to her during her break," said Daisy.

"Everyone likes your dress. I had trouble to get the few times that I danced with Daisy. She had fellas lined up to dance with her," said Joe.

Ann said, "How about something to eat? Are you hungry?"

"I am. I wouldn't dare eat anything with this dress on. Let me go change."

"I'll fix you an omelet then." Daisy returned in a few minutes back in the sailor dress she wore earlier. She laid the corsage in the middle of the table to show it a while longer.

"It feels good to have that corset off."

"Daisy!" said her mother.

"Joe knows. He could feel the stays through my dress. So could everyone else."

"Well you shouldn't be talking about those things. Get you two plates. The eggs are ready." She slid the two halves onto a couple plates.

"This is better than midnight chow at the consolidated mess"

"I should hope so."

They chatted about the dance and the music while they ate. "Joe and I sang some of the music while we danced. I promised to save the slow songs to dance with him."

"Doesn't Joe jitterbug?"

"Oh he dances great. He just didn't want to see me in anyone else's arms."

"A little jealousy here?" Joe just blushed.

Charles came in the kitchen and asked Joe where he was going from here.

"I've got an inspection tomorrow morning and then I have to buy a few things from the PX. I will pack in the afternoon and get to bed early. We have to get up at six on Sunday to get to St. Louis to board our train. We'll go to Chicago and actually go through Canada to get to Buffalo and then The Big Apple. That's where we board our ship, the *George Washington*."

"And what will you do in 'The Big Apple'?" asked Daisy.

"I'd like to see a Broadway show and go to the art museum. I don't know if I can get anyone to go with me."

"Where will you stay while you're there?"

"They're supposed to have a big barracks at the pier where the troops congregate before leaving."

The couple finished their meal and it was time for Joe to go. "Well, I'd better be leaving."

"How are you getting back?" asked Ann.

"I'll just walk across the street and put my thumb out."

"Are you sure that Charles can't drive you back?"

"No. I need the time alone. I would rather say goodbye here."

Daisy and Joe walked to the door. Charles and Ann remained in the kitchen. Joe said, "I want to thank you folks for all you've done for me. You've been my family for three weeks. I wish it had been longer."

"We've enjoyed your company, Joe. You be safe now. Take care of you," said Ann.

Daisy had tears in her eyes by the time they got to the door. “I don’t know what I’m going to do without you, Joe. You brought sunshine into my life.”

“Daisy, you have a good life. Just keep doing what you’ve been doing. Enjoy your last month in school and keep supporting the soldiers at the fort. I love you but you’ve got to live your life. I’ll miss you dearly. I will write you and let you know my address when I arrive. You’ve got my service number. That will eventually get a letter to me.”

“I’ll write but I’ll miss you so.”

“Good bye Daisy.” He held her in his arms and gave her a long soulful kiss. He could taste her tears by now and tears were in his eyes also. “Now go inside and close the door. It would be too hard on me to see you here as I cross the street.”

“Good bye Joe,” she stepped inside crying hard now and closed the door. Joe stepped out of the porch light and didn’t cross the street. He walked facing the traffic toward the base on Hwy 66. Joe looked back just once and thought he could see the silhouette of her head in the window. He wasn’t ready to encounter someone else just then. He turned down Missouri Avenue alone in his sweet memories. After about twenty minutes, a car stopped and the driver called, “You want a ride to the fort?” It was a sergeant, probably permanent party. “Yeah, I could use a lift.”

Part Two

Chapter 6 – Beginning their Journey

Reveille, reveille, reveille up and at 'em troopers. It was inspection day and there was a lot to be done. They cleaned the brick-red linoleum floor the day before and walked in their socks all evening. They got their fatigues on and went outside for roll call. They were all supposed to be here this morning. The sergeant began calling the roster, "Allen", "Albert A"..."Conrad", "Joseph F", "Conroy", "Jesse". What's your middle initial trooper? "I don't have one sir."

"Don't call me sir! I work for a living!" said the sergeant.

"Yes sir! I mean sergeant."

"...Wallace?" "William W sergeant"

"Inspection at 10:00 hours. Shape up. Dismissed."

They broke ranks and headed to the mess hall.

Joe ordered, "Two flapjacks, hot syrup and two fried eggs on top. Put a couple sausage links on the side."

"Right on Joe. You always want those eggs on top."

Joe moved to the table where Felix was already chowing down. "Are you anxious to be on our way Felix? Where's Mike?"

"He'll be here shortly. He had to stop by the barracks. Yeah Man. I am ready to be out of here. I want to go to Chicago and loop the Loop and then light up the Big Apple."

"I have mixed feelings about it. I'm ready to get on with my life but I am really torn up with leaving Margaret and her family. I've really gotten attached to them."

Bill Joined them. "What's up fellas?'

"Felix has been briefing me about what he's gonna do on the Loop and the Big Apple."

"And Joe's been moaning about leaving his girl behind."

Bill said, "You noticed I didn't get involved with Hazel. I can take them or leave them."

"Maybe she just didn't get involved with you. She was probably tired from lifting pickle jars all day."

"I knew we were moving out soon so I just didn't push it."

"You're right Bill but Daisy took the lead half the time. You know she approached us at the dance and then invited us to the picnic in her backyard. That really kick-started our relationship. And her family, her dad as much as asked me what my intentions were last night. I told him I loved her and then her brother overheard me and told her. That was embarrassing later on when I did tell her."

Bill said, "Well I'm footloose and fancy free. I got no strings on me."

Mike came along about this time looking a little peeked. "I think I had too much of that punch last night."

"What were you adding to the punch?"

"I had some of that mountain dew left from Devil's Elbow."

"You're gonna go blind drinking that stuff, Mike. Stay away from moonshine. Half of that stuff has been run through a car radiator and has lead in it," said Joe. "We better get back to the barracks and be ready when the Captain comes through."

They took their trays to the cutter window.

"How did you get back last night Joe? Daddy bring you home?"

"No. I hitched a ride with a chemical corps sergeant. I started walking. I wanted to be alone with my thoughts and this sergeant asked me if I needed a lift. I really did by then. I asked him what he did but he said it was secret so it's probably not smoke and fire. Charles didn't even ask me about a ride. He knew enough to just let me go."

"Oh, it's Charles now. What happened to the Mr. Watson?"

"Bill, you're impossible. You know darn well I respect the man and yes, I call him Mr. Watson or sir. Heck! I picked it up from you Southerners always calling everyone sir or ma'am."

"I just got time for a cigarette before the old man comes in the bay," and he headed for the porch. It wasn't much of a porch, just a platform at the top of the stairs, a fire exit.

"Careful of your mustache."

"You know I shaved it off after my 'accident'."

"Just checking."

Joe continued primping, this corner, that folded towel. He took a quarter out of his pocket and tried to bounce it on the bed. Maybe someday he would have a mattress firm enough to do that. Bill hurried in. "They're coming."

"Ten hupp!" They all snapped to attention beside their bunks. The company commander, first sergeant and platoon sergeant came up to each man. The banter was friendly. The commander wasn't looking to gig anyone. He asked if they had made their preparations for travel and to be careful when they get to New York. He told more than one trooper that it's not like anything you've ever seen. He even let Jesse Conroy go without any corrections. Jesse is a good guy. He just isn't always with the program. He'll make a good gate guard.

The platoon sergeant came back after the inspection was over. "You did okay men. You know the old man was taking it easy on you. I know you just want to get out of here but I don't want you leaving a tornado in your path. I'll be back in the morning when you board your bus. You're going to turn in your bedding <u>and</u> your mattresses before you leave and this barracks is going to be spotless."

They said yes sergeant in a collective groan.

"I didn't hear you."

"YES SERGEANT!"

"That's better. Dismissed!" They headed to the mess hall for lunch.

Joe went to the PX after lunch and bought some extra things for travel. He didn't want to have extra stuff to deal with during the inspection so he waited until now. He bought an extra half dozen pairs of socks hoping not to run out. He bought two tins of Colgate tooth powder and two tubes of Barbasol shaving cream. He added in a couple packs of Gillette Blue Blades and two bars of Palmolive soap. Showering at sea will be tough enough without running low on soap. The trick will be not to let on that he has this stuff or everyone will be mooching him out of it. He returned to the barracks with his secret hoard.

"Where you been Joe?" said Felix.

"PX, I needed some socks." He also bought a gift for Daisy's birthday that he kept to himself. It was a small sterling silver cross on a silver chain. It wasn't much but he wanted to let her know he was thinking of her. He put it in a little larger box that he wrapped and addressed to her. He would mail it when he arrived in New York City. That should get it to her by Saturday.

He packed his AWOL bag first with a week's worth of underwear, socks and his shaving kit. He reached in the toe of one of his spare boots and pulled out a small leather sack filled with a quarter pound of lead shot. It was a blackjack that his Uncle Clarence gave him when he retired from the Erie police force. Clarence called it a cosh. He sometimes carries it when he is in unfamiliar circumstances. It went into his AWOL bag. The heavy winter coat went on the bottom of his duffle bag. The extra toiletries went deep inside and the bulky garrison cap would go on top. The footlocker was now empty and he could turn that in. He put the lock on his duffle bag. The bag weighed a ton with those extra uniforms crammed in. He shoehorned the duffle bag into his locker and set the AWOL bag on top. He finished the *Magnificent Ambersons* a couple days earlier so he took it to the day room after he disposed of his footlocker. It was 15:00 hours. What to do? Should he call Daisy? She might already be busy and that could be embarrassing. Surely, he could entertain himself for an afternoon. He went to the base library and read through the current news magazines. He decided to write a letter to his mother.

April 28, 1945

Dear Mom and Dad,

The last time that I wrote you, I was talking about a girl and a dance. Well, I'm still talking about her. I took Daisy to a USO dance last night at the enlisted men's club. Woody Herman performed with his band. The band is half the size that it used to be. That seems to be the trend from what I hear. The military wives provided the refreshments and I had some really good pineapple upside down cake like the one you make. There was a guy and a girl singing with the band. They are part of the 5th Army Special Services Group. Daisy and I talked to the girl named Virginia during her break. She was real sweet.

I started off the evening by going to Daisy's house for a fish supper. It was blue pike, like we always eat. I get along well with her family but I couldn't bring myself to ask for a ride back to base. I thought it would be better to leave Daisy at her door than for them to take me to the barracks. Manly pride, I guess. That was only last night. I just have to get through today and I will be on my way. Our train from Chicago to Buffalo goes through Canada, so there is no way you can see me at the train station. I don't know why they do it that way but I guess they have to use what is available. We get a sleeping car part of the way. I will be sailing out of New York City on the USAT *George Washington* on May 4th. We should get a couple nights in New

York. I would like to see a play while I'm there. I may have to go alone. My friends don't seem like Broadway types. That's all I have going on.

Love,
Joe

He bought a 3¢ stamp from the librarian and dropped the letter in the mail slot. He walked back to the barracks in time for supper. The mess hall was nearly empty. He ate quickly and went to the barracks where he got into a pinochle game. That was a good way to while away the time. Mike and Bill were looking for a third hand to play. They could have played two handed but that's not all that much fun. Mike dealt fifteen cards to each player. Bill bid 250 and Joe bid 260. Mike passed so Joe named hearts as trumps and turned up the widow cards and then they laid down their meld. After a few hands, they decided they were getting thirsty and moved the game to the beer hall where they found Felix. The beer hall had bottled beer for a quarter where the PX only had beer on tap. The EM club had both but they also had a dress code. They were comfortable in their fatigues. With Felix in the game, the dealer didn't play but would be active again when his deal was done.

They played until 22:00 and decided to call it a day. Joe wanted to go to early Mass in the morning at 08:00. That gave him time enough to board the bus to St. Louis. Joe didn't bother tying a towel to his bunk. He knew he would wake up in plenty of time. 06:00 rolled around and he was wide-awake and ready for a shower. He shaved and brushed his teeth with his bath towel wrapped around his waist. He usually brushed after breakfast but he wouldn't be eating until after Mass. He put on his skivvies and walked back up to the second floor. A few guys were beginning to stir. He stopped back in the latrine to check out his class A uniform. All of his buttons were buttoned and his tie was right. He rubbed the toes of his low-quarter shoes on the back of his pants legs to shake off any dust. They would be dusty again after he walked the three blocks to chapel. He felt like he was doing so many things for the last time.

Father Kelly, the chaplain heard confessions a half hour before the service so he took advantage of the chance. “Bless me Father for I have sinned…” He didn’t have much to say. Had he had impure thoughts about Daisy? That was foolish. He had nothing but respect for her. There was that Esquire magazine in the day room. He missed Mass last week but he had KP. “Sorry Father. I’m coming up empty. But I’m travelling to Germany and thought I’d better come see you.”

“Bless you Son. Say an Act of Contrition and have a good trip.”

He went in and sat halfway down the middle aisle. He took a look at the Gospel for the day in the pew missal.

The priest came out from behind the altar dressed in his ornate vestments and carrying the chalice with its cover on it.

“Introibo ad altare Dei,” said the priest.

“To God, the joy of my youth,” Joe whispered.

Joe and a few others went to communion and soon the service was over. The mess hall had stopped serving by now so Joe went to the snack bar at the PX. They didn’t have much to offer so he had biscuits and gravy with a cup of coffee. Next stop is St. Lou.

He went up to the barracks. The guys had the place shaped up and the sergeant was there actually pleased with how they were leaving the place.

"Where you been Conrad?"

"Church, Sergeant!"

"They pray this early in the morning? Well get your bedding back to supply and be ready to board the bus."

"Right Sergeant!"

He rolled his pillow and bedding in the mattress as best he could and carried the overstuffed armload along with his sign-out sheet to the supply room and turned it in. It was the last item to be signed off his sheet. He returned to the barracks and turned the sheet over to the sergeant.

"Do I give this to you, Sergeant?"

"You're damned straight, Conrad. Now get your duffle to the bus."

There were 36 of them going on the 37-passenger bus. What happened to the other four soldiers from their platoon? Well, there were two troopers that were accepted for further training in CID. One fellow is going to Officer Candidate School; another forty-day wonder. The fourth trooper volunteered for the Pacific. He's Jewish and doesn't want to have anything to do with any Germans. This was mostly just rumors but it all sounded plausible.

They threw their duffle bags on the back of the deuce and a half where the two drivers added them to the pile. They boarded the bus and Joe took an aisle seat next to Mike. The bus filled fast as the air filled with the fresh body odor and the scent of Old Spice even though most of the windows were open. The sergeant made one last roll call and left the bus. He was done. They were on their own. These fellows were adults. They knew the penalty for missing shipment. He knew some would get in trouble but they would all make it to the ship in the end.

The driver eased into first gear and pulled away from the barracks. The truck with their baggage followed behind. He double clutched into second and got up to speed and shifted into third with a minimum clatter of gears. The guard waved them out the gate for the last time and onto Missouri Avenue. They turned right on Route 66 so he wouldn't be going past Daisy's house. That is probably for the best. Gosh, will he miss her! They settled back for the two-hour trip to St. Louis. Devil's Elbow was quickly behind them and then Rotta, St. James and Cuba. "Hey guys! We're going to Cuba." "Shut up Conroy!" They left Crawford County and entered Franklin County where they drove past the Wagon Wheel Café and through Sullivan, St. Clair and Pacific.

"That's the only Pacific I want to see in this war."

"You're right, Conroy."

The route flattened now as they entered the suburbs of St. Louis. Once in the city, they could see the big Budweiser Beer sign near the river and the stadium where the Cardinals play.

The time was 1140. That is cutting it too close. They had a half hour to check their bags and get to the train. They weren't all going together. The travel office was allotted seats on several trains so as not to bunch the troops together. Some guys would have to wait at the station or the brewery all afternoon for their trains. The truck drivers got on the back of their truck tossing down duffle bags. A couple troopers joined them while looking for their own. The trick was to identify your own bag without getting beaned with someone else's bag.

"Hey watch that! You threw that at me!"

"Incoming! Look out."

"Toss me that bag. It's mine.'

Joe got his duffle and headed for the baggage counter. Mike and Felix were already there and Bill was coming in the door. They checked the duffle bags and kept their AWOL bags with them. Joe swung by the newsstand and bought a *Life Magazine* and a roll of butter rum Life Savers that he had liked since he was a kid. The magazine had a war correspondent's photo on the cover as he was sketching the rubble. He gave the clerk fifteen cents for the two items. "There's no tax on less than a quarter."

They walked out onto the station platform and collided with that old familiar smell of coal smoke, steam, grease and maybe people. Railroads had their own scent. No streamliner here, just serviceable steel coaches. They saw a fellow with a hammer looking at the wheels on the train and they asked Joe what he was doing.

"That's the 'car knocker'. He's an inspector, who checks the rag scraps in the journal bearing to make sure it has sufficient lubricant. He also taps the axle with his hammer. If it rings, it is good. If it goes clunk, the axle may be cracked. It almost never happens on a passenger car. They take good care of them." They saw their duffle bags transported with the rest of the luggage to the baggage car up front on a big four-wheeled cart pulled by one man. It was a combined car with the baggage in front and coach seats in the rear. Trainmen usually rode there, deadheading up the line to catch their assigned train. The Union News man kept his store of goods there also. The baggage and mail rode on similar-sized carts but they were powered by an electric motor and the driver stood on the front of the cart and steered with a lever. The driver had to be standing on the treadles before the cart would move.

They climbed aboard and got two seats together in a smoking car. Some cars in the train were reserved for nonsmokers. They threw their AWOL bags into the overhead compartment. The windows opened in these cars so the air was a little fresher. The head napkins appeared to be clean as if they just changed them. These seats didn't recline. They just flipped forward and back to suit the direction of the train or the whim of a family or group. They were a prickly green fabric. He sat by the aisle where there was a little more room for his feet. He knew that the window passengers would be banging feet after a couple hours.

The conductor called, "All aboard," and they heard the steps and platforms slamming in the vestibule as they prepared to travel. The car jerked as the slack was pulled out when the locomotive chugged forward. Soon they were moving and headed for Chicago.

Felix said, "I just thought of something. They've been hustling us around so that we didn't get any lunch. Is there a diner on this train?"

"Relax, Felix. I don't think there's a diner on the train but there will be a Union News butcher here in a short while. I saw him getting provisioned on the platform."

"He better, Joe. I'm hungry."

"Tickets everybody. Get your tickets out," called the conductor. He and the brakeman were taking up tickets. The conductor had a unique punch that he punched the date on the seat tags after he exchanged them for the long printed tickets.

"Remember to keep that seat tag with you once he takes your ticket," said Joe. Two of them had to retrieve their tickets from their bags. Joe kept his in his shirt pocket inside his blouse. His New York Central ticket was in his money belt. They crossed the Mississippi River into Illinois and were on their way north. East St. Louis looked dingy but they never run trains through the better parts of town.

The conductor reached them and said, "Tickets please."

"Where are you boys heading after Chicago as if I didn't know?"

Bill said, "You're right sir. Were on our way to Germany. We just don't know where yet. We're farm-fresh military police."

"Well, you boys, be careful, ye hear. Take care of them Nazis."

"We will sir." They saw the Union News fellow entering the front end of the car with his big fiberboard basket filled with sandwiches, drinks, candy and magazines. Many people brought shoeboxes along with their own sandwiches. They could have thought ahead and brought box lunches but this is a lot more convenient. They had enough to carry. They each bought a sandwich and a Coca Cola. The butcher snapped the caps off the bottles for them. He also had ginger cookies in wax paper bags.

"You're a brave man, Joe, to eat that stuff," said Bill.

"Oh, this is the good stuff. He had liverwurst and onions on rye bread. "And it's not as expensive as your ham and cheese."

"Is that what you do to save a dime?" asked Mike.

"If it's good and inexpensive and I like it, this is fine."

"Well, you'd better get some Sen-Sen for your breath."

Joe said, "I've already got some."

The cornfields raced by the window. They finally closed it all the way. The wind was getting to be too much. The novelty of the trip was beginning to wear off. Joe opened his Life Savers and also his magazine. There was a short article in the front that gave French and English phrases that would be useful for a GI in France, like "You are very nice," and "What are you doing tonight?" How about something like, "Where do I go to get my hair cut?" There was a corny article about who was going to take care of Fallah, FDR's Scottie dog now that he was dead. The other three struck up a game of pinochle.

More cornfields and they stopped at the historic depot in Springfield, Illinois. It was just another city seen from its backside but the depot was an outstanding structure where Abraham Lincoln departed for his presidency. Bill and Mike said, "We're not real big on Abraham Lincoln."

"I know but the town is still rich in history and there's not much else in this part of the state. Let's put aside our differences for now. We'll be in Chicago soon."

Their wait was only fifteen minutes and they were on their way again. The Union News guy came through to sell a few more sandwiches. Felix and Mike each bought another coke. The conductor entered again checking the tickets of the new arrivals. Joe went back to his magazine. There wasn't a whole lot of reading in it. The issue was filled with war art. Some of the most striking was the area around Normandy, which took the lion's share of destruction. The city of Caen was nearly leveled. One striking painting was of a stone crucifix put to use as an ad hoc telephone pole.

He glanced at the Theater page in the rear of the mag and found a description of a Tennessee William's play called *The Glass Menagerie*. It was about a crippled girl and her mother's efforts to find her a boyfriend. The girl would rather spend her time arranging the glass animals in her menagerie. Joe wanted to see a Broadway play like that, if the tickets didn't cost an arm and a leg.

They were soon entering the south side of Chicago with its deteriorating tenements. It was a dismal scene. One thing about train travel is that you see some of the most beautiful parts of the country and the worst side of its cities. The brakemen announced the end of the line in Chicago and "please refrain from flushing the toilets while in the station." That would seem to go without saying.

Chapter 7 – Railway to New York City

The fellows got their luggage together. Joe stuck his magazine in his bag. They shuffled along with the rest of the passengers to exit the coach. Chicago and New York City have elevated platforms so that you can walk out without steps. They followed the crowd forward into the terminal past the baggage and mail car and the huge Berkshire locomotive. Joe assumed it was a big one, as fast as they were going at times. His father had taught him to recognize dozens of steam locomotives. The air compressor and boiler feed water pump continued to chug even though the engine was standing still. He felt the blast of heat as they walked past the firebox. He remembered when he was younger how frightened he was when the big engines roared into the station with flames spewing from that firebox.

They entered the main concourse of the terminal and looked for the baggage window to pick up their duffle bags. They actually just needed to reroute them using their New York Central tickets and then it was time for supper. They had to be back by eight to catch the next leg of their journey. Joe had been here before with his brothers and father to catch a White Sox game. They always ate at the YMCA hotel where they had good food and it was cheap. He suggested it to his buddies and they said, "You're the Yankee that knows this town. We'll follow you. It was a three-block walk on Wabash Avenue to the eatery. There was no line to speak of on a Sunday evening so they breezed right through. Joe had pork chops, mashed potatoes and green beans with an apple pie slice for dessert. He gave the clerk a dollar and got a nickel change.

They found a table nearby and took their trays back to the cart. The other fellows started right in about the next leg of their trip. Felix couldn't wait to see the Rocky Mountains in Canada. There were songs about the blue Canadian Rockies and all those movies about the Mounties.

"I'm afraid you're going to be disappointed boys. If you think Illinois was boring, just replace the corn with wheat and you have the Lake Erie plain. Of course, if you go north, you'll find a super wilderness but I'm afraid down here it will be flat. You'll be asleep anyhow. Our next journey is in sleeping cars," said Joe.

Mike said, "I didn't bring my jammies."

"They have curtains on the bunks but please put something on if you go to the latrine. There'll be families in those bunks also."

"We'll be sleeping next to girls?"

"Don't even think of it!"

Bill asked, "Where do you go to get a drink around here?"

"I'm not sure since it's Sunday night and all. There may not be anyplace open," said Joe. He didn't want them to get started someplace and miss the train. He felt he was the most responsible of the bunch even if he was the youngest.

They finished their supper and spoke of it approvingly even though it was Yankee food. "Where does Felix get off talking about Yankee food?" Joe thought.

They headed back to the station and wouldn't you know it. They passed a bar. Mike and Felix were the only ones that were 21 and they said, "Go ahead and we'll catch up."

"Not on your life. We'll go in and have a nickel Coke," said Joe.

His nickel Coke was a dime. Big city prices. He dropped a couple more nickels in the pinball machine while the others had their beer. Bill managed to add a year to his age and had a beer also. After about twenty minutes, they started back to Union Station. They retrieved their bags from the coin-operated lockers. They managed to squeeze four bags in two lockers. The next leg of the journey was on the east side of the station, track #11. The card above the door to the platform said it was #58, The *Niagara*. They started down the platform past the big Hudson locomotive. It was just a plain-looking engine without the streamlined fairings of the *20th Century Limited* or the *Empire State Express*. They passed the mail car with its hook on the forward door for snatching mailbags from remote towns. They were loading sacks of mail on board from a freight wagon. They passed the combine baggage car. Nothing much happening there. Either their bags were already on or they hadn't come down yet. They checked their bags all the way to New York City.

They found their car, #2564, *City of Utica*. Again, they walked onto the train without climbing steps. They passed five private compartments and the restroom and ahead there were twenty bunks, five on each side, upper and lower. Their bunks were numbers 3 and 5 upper and lower which put them on the South side of the train. If there was anything to see, this would probably be the better side. It was nearly dark. The porter directed them to their bunks and showed them where to stow their bags. It was too early to go to bed but the bunks were already made up. They asked the porter if there was a club car on the train and he directed them to the last car. They began their trek back but the car was filled when they got there. They had seen some empty coach seats on the way so they decided to squat in a couple until someone threw them out. This didn't take long as the train filled. There was still a lot of wartime traffic and there were a lot of military on the train. They didn't all have bunks either. They thanked their travel office.

They returned to their bunks and kicked off their shoes to relax and made the most of it. Joe hadn't finished *Lost Horizon* so he got it out and read. The train was jerking into motion as the engine backed out of the station. It seemed like they were going back to St. Louis but then the train stopped and began going forward, pulling the slack out of the cars. They were on their way. They went back to the club car one more time but Joe didn't see any point to it. He returned to his bunk, read a little bit and went to sleep. He felt fortunate to get the bottom bunk so he could peek out the window now and then. He thought he would finish *Lost Horizon* soon. He couldn't remember falling asleep but he knew he was thinking of Daisy as he drifted off. He would think of her again when he awoke in the morning. He remembered looking out the window as they passed Battle Creek. He saw the sign in the railroad station. He thought, "That's where the Kellogg's plant is located." He didn't see it though.

He awoke at six and asked the porter for help to turn his bunk back into coach seats. The porter said the dining car was serving breakfast if he wanted to go there and he would have his seat ready when he returned. Joe made his way forward to the dining car. A family of three offered him a seat at their table. Their eight-year-old son was happy to have a soldier sit by him. He asked Joe if he had his gun with him. Joe disappointed him when he said no. The waiter took his order, which was two eggs, scrambled, two strips of bacon, toast and coffee. That came to fifty cents. Everything was more expensive on the train but what are you going to do. The mother asked him where he was from. They were returning to Buffalo after attending a wedding outside of Chicago. The boy asked him again where he kept his gun. He told him that they don't travel with weapons but were issued one when he got to his new location. He asked him where his new location was and Joe said somewhere in Germany. "But there's a war going on there!" Joe said that he expected the war would be over soon, "...unless those Nazis retreat to the Alps where they can probably hold out for years."

"That's not a comforting thought, "the mother said. "You'll probably just get over there and have to turn around and come home."

The father said, "There are hundreds of thousands of displaced persons that will need help getting home and someone's gotta keep those Ruskies from charging all the way to the Atlantic. I reckon there will be enough for Joe to do."

"I figure I'm looking at least a year in Germany if not two." By now, Joe finished his meal and began looking for the waiter to pay him.

"Nonsense soldier! Your money is no good here. I'll take care of it," said the father.

"Well, thank you sir. I really appreciate that."

He returned to the sleeping car and his mates were up and around and shaved while he was eating. He forgot to shave before going to eat. What must that family have thought of him? He took his shaving kit to the latrine and was fourth in line at the basin. That will teach him. He told the others about the breakfast menu. He did not say that he hadn't paid for it. He lathered his face when he got to second in line. Finally, he got to shave and brush his teeth. Three more fellows were behind him by now. He returned to his seat. Lake Erie was visible nearly all the time now and across it his hometown of Erie. It would have been hard to have someone come to meet him at the station for just a few minutes. It was better this way. The few hills were covered with apple and peach blossoms. Some land was planted with nothing, but grapes. The others returned from breakfast and crowded into what had been his bed. These seats are a bit narrower than standard coach seats. The brakeman cautioned them that these cars would be exchanged for coaches and they would have to depart with the Buffalo passengers. They made one last stop in Niagara Falls, Ontario for less than five minutes to let the honeymooners off. "Isn't that who goes to Niagara Falls?"

They could not actually see the Falls but they could see the mist rising above it. They passed one chemical plant after another on the New York side of the river. There was DuPont, Hooker, General Aniline and Carborundum. A great many others were there taking advantage of the cheap and plentiful electricity generated by the Falls. It was so ugly though in comparison to Niagara, Ontario. He saw the tower of Central Station among the myriad of church steeples of Buffalo. They were nearly there.

They finally came to a stop in the station. The transfer was easier than he had imagined. They stepped off of the train walked across the platform where a fresh engine and crew were waiting with a string of coaches. A switching engine removed the back end of the first train and coupled it onto the rear of the new train. The Buffalo baggage remained in place while the through baggage moved to the new train, *The Henry Hudson, #72*. Well that was the plan anyway. The boys did not actually walk across the platform but made a beeline for the steps to the main concourse where they found a formidable statue of a bison eight feet in the air and a liquor store around the corner. Even Joe bought a half pint of his father's favorite rye whiskey, Old Overholt. Let's party. Three of them bought half pints but Felix bought a pint of his favorite brand, Four Roses. Mike didn't know what to buy since they don't have name-brand whiskey where he's from, so he bought Christian Brothers brandy. He wanted to support the good brothers. Now they were fortified for the eight hours it would take to reach Manhattan. They had to run back to their gate and show their tickets to get back on-board. There were no facing seats left in the car so they had to grab two seats of two. Bill and Joe sat together. "Bill, I didn't see what you bought."

"I kept thinking of all of those magazine ads I've seen and here it is all there on the shelf with prices. I bought a bottle of PM whiskey 'for those Pleasant Moments.' I also bought a couple Blackstone cigars, panatela deluxe."

"You've got to pace yourself. There will be things in New York City like you've never seen before."

"How did you make it so long in this sinful north without going completely off the track," said Bill.

"Who said I didn't?" said Joe.

The train pulled out and headed down Broadway past Depew and Lancaster and they began to see real hills again. The freshly planted farmland was beautiful under the Spring sky.

"I was too busy to get in trouble. My uncle and grandmother had a small farm in Union City and my brothers and I would go there in the summer and work our ass off. My younger brother and I would work on my uncle's farm. My older brother worked on the farm across the street for the Kopsas's family. They were mean and they took some kind of drugs also. They finally died in a murder suicide. My brother, Chuck, discovered the bodies and it haunted him at least until he joined the Navy. It probably still does. We set pins at the bowling alley after school and we were all in sports. I ran track and played basketball. Chuck played football and Jimmy plays basketball and swims."

"You hear from your family before you left?"

"My sister wrote me and she was all excited when she heard about Daisy. She's imagining her as a sister-in-law. Jimmy has the promise of a job at Marx Toys for the summer working on a defense contract. They make metal stampings like machine gun magazines and M-1 clips. Then he'll be off to the Navy after his birthday on August 24. That's a week after mine. Dad will sign for him to go in. He's already studying his brother's *Blue Jacket's Manual*. Chuck doesn't write much. It takes so long for his mail to get to my folks and then he can't say much. If he does, the censor blacks it out. What about you, Bill? Tell them about your dad. I really don't know much about you and your family other than your uncle's a mule skinner."

"My father's a millwright. He is employed by a contractor that does work in Baytown and up and down the Houston Ship Channel. They call him and his crew in when they are setting in a compressor or a big pump. He lines up the machine with the motor to make sure everything is concentric and true. If they get out of alignment, the bearings won't last a lick. They had one compressor installed across a fault line and they couldn't keep bearings in it until they brought in a geologist. He told them the compressor was heading east and the engine was heading west. We lived in a rented house in Goose Creek at first and then my folks had a house built in Baytown just before the war began. I have a sister named Nancy and a brother named Bob and they both go to Robert E. Lee High School. Nancy graduates this month and Bob has two more years. That makes Nancy the same age as Daisy and Hazel."

"My mother is kind of a church lady and is a member of United Methodist Women. She does a lot of volunteer work, hosting charity events for disabled veterans and such. Nancy is a cheerleader and plays oboe in the concert band. Bob is quite the athlete. He plays football and basketball on the JV teams. That's my family. Where are we now?"

"We're pulling into Rochester. We'll be here just a couple minutes to swap mail and pick up the passengers from the platform." As luck would have it, the couple sitting behind Felix and Mike got off.

Joe said, "Quick! Let's move over there and get them to flip their seat over. Don't forget your ticket!"

They moved over and Joe asked the other two to get up while he flipped the back of the seat forward. They flipped to see who would ride backwards. Joe and Felix lost and Joe took the aisle seat. Felix picked up a *Field and Stream* magazine and was reading about Sockeye Salmon fishing on the Ducktrap River in Maine. There was a picture of a big salmon lunging at a feathered lure. "You know? We usually go fly fishing for trout back home but someday I'm going to Maine after some salmon."

The Union News fellow came through and they bought some sodas to go along with their whiskey. Joe got some Canada Dry ginger ale to go along with his rye whiskey. It seemed extravagant to be drinking in the morning like this. They got a four-handed pinochle game going and rotated the dealer. The dealer did not play on his turn. That got them to Rome where three Junior Red Cross girls got on the train and rode for the fifteen minutes to Utica passing out box lunches to all of the military on the train. They were a giggly group but friendly and happy. It left the News butcher unhappy but he still sold out on his stuff. He was used to the girls. There was a ham and cheese sandwich, three homemade cookies, a banana or orange and a pack of chewing gum. Joe heard they used to put packs of cigarettes in these boxes but dropped it a while back. They kept their distance from the boys to avoid getting pinched on the bottom.

The girls were soon off the train. "I wonder how they get back home."

Joe said there would be another train heading west within an hour and they'll be back in school before the final bell.

They were soon in Albany picking up a few more coaches from New England. The locomotive had to take on more coal and water before they began their last leg down the Hudson River to New York. The seventeen cars of the *Empire*

State Express raced by on its way to Buffalo. The new stainless steel cars looked like the future of railroading. It was followed twenty minutes later by the *Mohawk*. Joe liked the names of the trains on this line.

Soon they passed Hyde Park where the Roosevelts lived and then into Break Neck Tunnel. A voice came out of the blackness, "What happens if a train is coming the other way in the tunnel?"

"You've lived a good life Mike. The end will be quick."

"I'm serious. What if the signals get screwed up or something?"

Joe said, "There are some things in life that you have to take on faith. Otherwise, you will go nuts. There are two tracks in the tunnel. Signals work. Elevator cables don't snap. Planes don't fly into buildings. Life is good." They exited the tunnel to see Storm King Mountain across the river.

They started their card game again as they stopped at Poughkeepsie and Garrison. They took another pull on their bottles. They stopped on a siding. "What's going on?" asked Mike. He was the nervous one. His question was answered when they were passed by a forty-car mail train on its way to New York City. They began moving and were soon in the Oscawana Tunnel.

There was a strange looking castle a short ways off shore in the river. Joe said it was Bannerman's Island Arsenal. He was looking forward to going to the Bannerman Gun Store. "I've heard of that," said Bill. "They have guns going back to the Civil War. I read about it in the *American Rifleman*."

"They have cannon shells going back that far, " said Joe. "No one knows how many are still filled powder. That's why they're on that island and not on Broadway. I really want to go to that store and also the Cloisters at the Museum of Art to see their armor exhibit."

"I can handle the gun shop but I'm not sure about the museum," said Bill. They were just pulling into Harmon where they would exchange their Hudson steam locomotive for an electric locomotive. They needed this to operate in the tunnels beneath Manhattan. They saw a gigantic wash rack where men were washing another Hudson. "I never imagined they would do that."

Felix said, "It stands to reason. They've got to turn around all of these engines. This is a good time to clean them up and fill them with coal and water."

They pulled away with a hum instead of a chug and were soon passing beneath Sing-Sing Prison with a short stop at Ossining to take a visiting family back to the city.

Felix said, "When you hear the phrase 'up the river', this is what they're talking about."

They went by 125th Street in Harlem before going underground for good on their way to Grand Central Station. The train slowly pulled into the platform and the boys gathered their things to head upstairs.

Chapter 8 – Taxi Dancers

Their first stop was the USO Canteen above the Grand Concourse. It was time for supper and this was the place for it, even if it was just a hamburger, fries and a milkshake. They would pick up their duffle bags after they had some food and got themselves oriented. A Marine corporal was playing the piano when they arrived. He played a lot of Boogie Woogie along with current favorites. They ate their quick dinner and ambled over to the information desk. They told the lady that they had to get to Pier 53 tonight and asked the best way to get there. She asked when they were sailing and then said, "I really don't think you want to go there. You have four nights in town and you want to make the most of it. There are five-hundred bunks on the pier and the security is not real good. I can give you a half-price voucher for a pretty good hotel and you can spend your time in comfort."

Mike asked, "How much would that be?"

"Four of you can stay in a room for eight dollars a night in the center of Manhattan."

"That sounds good to me. Two bucks a piece? How do we get there?"

"Here is your voucher for the Hotel Bristol. The best way to get there is just take a cab if you can all fit your luggage in it. You can learn to use the subway to get around after that and it only costs you a dime. This is also a good city for walking.

You might find the restaurant in the hotel a bit pricy but there are plenty of good restaurants in the area. Take advantage of the hotel safe to protect your travel money. You don't want to be walking around with all of your money on you."

Joe spoke up, "Are there any tickets available for shows or movies?"

"We just got some half-price tickets for a new show called *The Glass Menagerie*. We also have free passes for other movies."

Joe said, "I'd like a ticket for the play. I read about it and I would like the chance to see it. Any takers?" Silence. "Let me have two tickets. How does it work?"

She said, "Just take these coupons to the ticket office in the afternoon and you can buy the tickets half-price. You can take the movie tickets to the box office when you want to see the movie. I also have two free passes for Radio City Music Hall."

Joe quickly said, "I'll take them." The others didn't know about the Rockettes. They thought it was some kind of concert.

Joe said on the way out, "I can't believe I got all those tickets."

"That's okay for you Bub. We're going to see the girly shows on 42nd Street. Now let's head for the hotel, "said Felix.

They managed to squeeze three duffle bags in the trunk of the cab and the fourth by their feet in the back seat. They used both jump seats in the Yellow Cab. It was a short drive to

48th Street and the Bristol Hotel. The doorman welcomed them with a silent groan, "More soldiers. Lousy tippers."

They grabbed their own bags and schlepped them into the lobby. They noticed the Pink Elephant Room cocktail lounge on the way in. They presented their voucher at the counter and said they would like a room for four. They would be there three or four nights. The desk clerk had experience with young men before and asked for a deposit of $35 dollars to cover four nights and tax. Any long distance phone calls must be paid for at the end of their stay. That was agreeable to them and they each anted up nine dollars. They also asked about leaving some of their money in the safe. Each soldier put a hundred or so dollars in an envelope, which they signed and gave it to the clerk to put in a safe box. A bellboy started to load their bags on a cart before they stopped him. "We'll take those." They weren't letting their bags out of their sight. The bellhop guided them to their room on the tenth floor. It was actually two small rooms made into a suite with an adjoining door and a shared bathroom. Each room had two single beds. "We couldn't ask for any better than this." Mike looked out the window and said, "What the hell is this?" He was looking at the airshaft in the center of the building. "Where's Broadway? Where's Times Square?"

"This is what you get for eight bucks. The high dollar rooms are on 48th Street," said the cheeky bellhop.

"It'll do! We'll make friends with the folks across the hall to see out their window," said Bill. They all chipped in a quarter for the bellboy's tip.

Mike asked, "Where's the action around here?"

"You're in New York City and you're asking where the action is."

"Yeah! Where do we find the girls?"

"Oh! You want girls."

"Yeah! That's right."

"You go to the Stardust Ballroom, two blocks down the street at 1601 Broadway. Lots of girls there, good-looking ones too. Tell them Art sent you."

"Okay Art. That's where we'll go, right guys?"

They all agreed that it was a good plan. Even Joe. He would have rather stayed in and wrote to Daisy but they needed to get out and see the city. Art left them and they got slicked up and squirted on a little Old Spice. They were ready for the city. They walked out through the lobby. Four soldiers with a purpose. They exuded manliness and determination. They walked down 48th Street two by two, touching their caps to the ladies. Two blocks later, they were at Broadway, entertainment capital of the world, and standing in front of the Stardust Ballroom.

They walked up a flight of stairs over a restaurant and came to a booth that said "TICKETS."

"What can I do you for, fellas?" said an overly made up middle-aged woman.

"Four tickets, please," said Felix.

"Are you boys in a hurry or something?"

"I don't understand Ma'am."

"It's 10¢ a dance. No tickets! No dancing!"

"Hey what kind of place is this? Let us take a look"

"Be my guest. Make up your minds but make it fast."

They walked into the ballroom where two dozen couples were dancing. Several were military. Half a dozen girls stood to one side urging them on with a crooked finger, the universal signal for "Come on, Big Boy."

"I've heard of these," said Joe. "They're called taxi dancers and you pay them by the dance. It's like an Automat for girls." They agreed to stay and try it. They went back to the ticket booth.

"We'll each take a dollar's worth and see where that goes."

The woman completed the transaction and gave each of the soldiers ten tickets. They went back out on the floor and approached the women. They each had nametags on that said, "Hi! I'm Carmen." There was also Rosie, Suzanne, Frenchie, Betsy and Elaine. Joe chose Rosie. She turned out to be the newest of the girls, joining the group a couple weeks ago. She could really dance though. They all could. That is what they did. The fellow named Oscar put on an old record of the Andrew Sisters called "Here Comes the Navy." Everyone laughed. It's one of Oscar's old tricks when soldiers or Marines come along. Oscar was also the manager.

Rosie asked Joe when they got to town and he looked at his watch. "I guess it was two hours ago."

“You guys work fast.”

“We just put one foot in front of the other, check into the hotel and here we are. Art sent us. None of us really knew what kind of place this was.”

“What do you mean by this kind of place?” asked Rosie.

“Well none of us have ever paid to dance with a lady before. It’s kind of new.”

“None of us are ladies, Bub. What’s your name?”

“I’m just Joe.”

“Joe what? You must have a last name.”

“Let’s keep it at that. You’re Rosie and I’m Joe.” Joe had no real reason to hide his identity. He was just fooling around. She pursed her very red lips into a bit of a pout. Not for long though. She was soon smiling and the rouge on her cheeks took on a glow. Her copper-colored hair had what looked like natural curls. He thought they called it auburn. The color fought with her pink dress with black trim and skinny black straps over her freckled shoulders. He guessed she was Irish.

Oscar put on a new record, "I Wish I Had a Dime (For Every time I Missed You)." Rosie held out her hand for another ticket. “Pay up Joe. That Oscar has a sense of humor. You know how to polka, Joe? Oscar usually follows that with a polka.”

Oscar put on the “Pennsylvania Polka.”

“You bet I do! I’m from Pennsylvania and my dad works on the Pennsylvania.”

"That's rich, because I do too. I come from that coal heap they call Scranton," said Rosie. "I got out of there as soon as I graduated. I was going to make a name for myself dancing on Broadway. Well you see it. I'm dancing on Broadway. I gotta go pee. Why don't you dance with someone else? Oscar gets nervous when we dance too long with one fella. Like we're gonna marry him or something."

He saw Bill relaxing and asked, "How you doing?"

"I'm good. I'm half way through my tickets. I still can't get off on the idea of paying girls to dance. Well, here I go again," and he asked Suzanne to dance." Joe asked Frenchie to dance.

"So how come they call you Frenchie? You don't sound all that French."

"I'm from Montreal. That's in Canada. I'm what you call an illegal immigrant. I just came here one time and never went back."

"That's illegal? I've been to Canada a dozen times. I was in Canada last night, on the train. It seems like last week."

"It's illegal if you stay and go to work. This job is cash and carry. We have to pay Oscar a buck a night and whatever we make over that is ours. By the way, give me your ticket."

"What happens if you can't work, if you get sick?"

"I still have to pay Oscar."

"That's slavery. It's indentured servitude."

"It's how you make money to pay the rent without lying on your back. It's what they call a condition of employment. Shut up and dance." Oscar put on another record, "In The Mood."

They danced two more dances and then Joe asked Betsy to dance for the remainder of his tickets. The fellas regrouped to see what they wanted to do next. They agreed this place was kind of depressing but they felt sorry for the girls as if they were there to save them from their fate. They wound up putting together a two-dollar tip for the girls and gave it to Elaine to split. They said goodbye to the girls and headed for the street.

They walked toward Times Square past arcades of pinball machines and mechanical gypsies that would tell your fortune for a nickel. One made no bones about it. You drop a penny in the Wee Gee and it makes its way through a maze of pins to give you a Yes or No answer to your burning question. There was a machine to test the strength of your handgrip and the strength of your love potential. There was a row of hand-cranked peep shows called Mutoscopes. The marque and reel showed a Charlie Chaplin movie entitled *The Back Room Brawl*. Another featured Babe Ruth in *All American Hero*. A couple machines like the *Queen of Sheba* and *The Dance of the Seven Veils* promised much but delivered little. The latter one demanded another nickel when you got to the fourth veil and shut off when there was still a veil to go. Their eyes were tired from the flickering cards and they moved on.

"Wait! One more thing I gotta do," said Mike. He came to a game called a Booze Barometer. For a penny, you moved a ring on a handle along a convoluted foot of heavy gauge wire. The premise was that the further you moved the ring without touching the wire, the more sober you were. Mike put in his penny and tried it. He made it all the way. "I am much too sober. What do you say we do something about it?"

They were interrupted in their quest a few stores later. It was a shooting gallery, three shots for a quarter. They thought they heard gunshots but were doubtful of this frivolous use of ammunition. Felix said, "Not to worry. The Organization can get all of the ammo they want." The target was a letter B. If you could knock out the letter with three shots from six feet away, you won a prize. There were some very significant prizes, other rifles, custom cue sticks and silver cocktail shakers. The barker showed how to do it with an empty shell casing. He imprinted three overlapping circles over the letter. "That's how you do it."

The marksmen and expert marksmen knew they could do it and after spending a buck, they figured out the problem. The round nose bullet didn't cut the paper. It pushed its way through and left part of the letter behind. If they could cut the round head off the bullet, it would cut the paper but the barker loaded the rifles. They were had. "Let's get a drink."

The bars in the area looked seedy and a little dangerous. They thought back to the nicely furnished Pink Elephant Room at the hotel. "Let's go back to the hotel. At least we won't have far to go if we drink too much." They walked back past a number of night people, prostitutes and bums. Some men had taken up residence in doorways or on steam grates where it was warm. The Pink Room was crowded and lively. They took a booth. The Southerners ordered martinis. They heard of them but never been in a place that served the drink. Joe and Felix ordered beer. Mixed drinks were no novelty for them. "What are we going to do tomorrow?" Joe said,

"Here's my list. I want to go to the Science Museum, the art museum, Bannerman's gun store, Abercrombie and Fitch, and maybe a radio show. I want to go to the top of the Empire State Building and take in a show at Radio City Music Hall. I want to spend a morning walking in Central Park. I also want to see St. Patrick's Cathedral. That takes care of tomorrow. Just kidding!"

"Wow! That's ambitious."

"We're not coming back here real soon. I'm headed for bed. I want to see Central Park early in the morning," said Joe.

"Me too," said Bill. "This drink makes me sleepy."

Joe and Bill picked up the key at the desk and returned to the room to shower the cinders off their tired bodies. Bill looked out the window and still could not get over not having a street to look at, just dozens of windows. Now that he knew what it was, he could faintly hear the gunshots drifting up from Broadway. "What a gyp!" he thought. "If I could try it again with some wad cutters."

Joe finished his shower and wore his pajamas. He bought them at the PX for the train trip. He picked up a new pocket book from the bookrack in the lobby where travelers leave their finished books behind. It was *The Black Rose* by Costain. Walter attended a lecture by Roger Bacon in 13th century Oxford and was inspired to journey to the land of Cathay. After participating in a student riot and a raid on a castle – both led by his friend Tristram – Walter decided to leave England in order to escape justice. He drifted off to sleep, thinking of his Daisy. He needed to mail her gift in the morning.

Chapter 9 – Bannerman's Arsenal

Joe awoke to the uptick in traffic noise. It would be good to be at the park early. He shaved and brushed while the others snored. He walked out into the crisp spring air. His wool uniform was looking a little rumpled. He'll have the hotel laundry press it later on. He took along his little gift for Daisy and would find a post office on his way to the park. There was one on the way at 52nd Street. He spotted a sidewalk snack bar that was serving breakfast. He took a stool and asked what they had to eat. He started with a cup of coffee and then ordered a toasted bagel with cream cheese and a slice of smoked salmon on top that they called lox. It didn't seem much like breakfast, more like a hors d'oeuvre at a party.

He continued up 8th Avenue amid the crashing trashcans and the office workers hurrying to work. He found the post office and went in. He sent the gift first class. He wanted it to get to Daisy by Saturday and it wasn't worth enough to insure. He also mailed a letter to her that he'd been writing off and on. He bought a few more stamps while he was there. He bought partial sheets of commemorative stamps. He bought ten of the Iwo Jima stamps and ten more of the US Army marching through Paris. He bought ten Texas centennial stamps. Texas had been a state for 100 years. All the other stamps had war themes like the US Navy and Coast Guard and one for the recapture of Corrigador. He continued on his walk and reached Columbus Circle at 59th Street and dodged several yellow cabs to cross the street. He passed an open manhole with a guard fence around it and a Consolidated Edison truck parked next to it. A worker in a hard hat stuck his head up like a prairie dog. Joe realized how many levels of utilities were below the street.

Electricity and telephones, water and steam, trains and subways. It must go down sixty feet. All of these questions came to his mind like, how do they get water to these millions of people. He reached Central Park and all seemed tranquil again. He avoided the road and struck out over some trails to what they called Rat Rock. "Funny name!" He continued winding his way between half a dozen baseball fields to the Sheep Meadow. He was in awe to have this much wilderness in the heart of a gigantic city. There were not that many people around. He felt quite alone. He turned around and walked back to the baseball fields. He saw a policeman on horseback that he thought looked quaint. He hailed him and asked which direction the Museum of Art was located and if he could walk there. The policeman said, "I guess you could walk there. It's on the east side of the park around 87th Street about twenty blocks north of here. Are you up to walking twenty blocks?" Joe said that he already had and he should probably be getting back to his hotel. The policeman saluted him and rode off.

Joe kept heading southwest and circled around the carousel, which hadn't begun operating yet. He exited the park at 5th Avenue. That had of familiar ring to it. He would just walk down the Avenue until he came to 48th Street. He covered the eight blocks in a half hour allowing for stopping on corners and looking up at the buildings in wonder. His neck could get stiff doing this. Looming over him was Saint Patrick's Cathedral and he popped in for a visit. He chose a pew about ten down on the right and knelt. He said an Our Father, Hail Mary and Glory Be. The legend was that if you said those three prayers in a church the first time you entered it, your wish would be granted. He wished Daisy good health and happiness at the end of her senior year. He went over to the side where the candles were, put a dime in the slot and lit a candle in a blue glass holder. He said one more Hail Mary and scanned the immenseness of the church and left. He noted that there was a daily Mass at eight along with several other times and said he'd be back to no one in particular. He passed Saks Store and turned the corner to see Radio City Music Hall and back to the hotel.

"Joe, you should have been here."

"Yeah Joe! You missed it man."

"What did I miss? I went for a walk to Central Park."

"There was a naked lady out the window!"

"He means across the airshaft. I looked out the window when I woke up and there was a woman two floors down and she hadn't a stitch on and she was standing by her window," said Mike.

"She was naked as a jaybird," said Bill.

"Was she good looking?" asked Joe.

"I didn't notice. She had no clothes on."

"Do you suppose she was advertising?"

"Enough of this! I'm hungry! Do you want to go get some lunch?" asked Joe.

"We just ate," said Mike.

"What have you guys been doing?" asked Joe.

Bill said, "We gotta up kind of late and then there was this lady and then we went to the chow hall downstairs and had breakfast."

"That was no lady!" said Joe. "How was the breakfast?"

"Oh, it was good. It better be for that kind of money."

"First rule," said Joe. "Don't eat in hotel dining rooms. They are always overpriced."

"What did you eat?" asked Felix.

"I had a bagel and lox. I eat like a native would eat."

"What the hell is that?"

"It's a piece of bread shaped like a donut with cream cheese and a thin slice of salmon on it. That's the lox. It cost 30¢ with a cup of coffee."

"Umm, sounds appetizing."

"Well, it was and it filled a void. I'd like to go to Bannerman's Gun Store this afternoon. Anyone game?"

"Sure. I'd like to go."

"Me too."

"Me too."

"How about one o'clock? I'm going to lunch at the Automat around the corner. Anyone want to go with me?" They all shook their heads, not wanting food dished out of a machine.

Joe left the hotel and turned the corner onto 6th Avenue and it was in the first block, "Horn & Hardart"' It wasn't an Automat though but a cafeteria. He ordered roast leg of spring lamb with mint sauce, mashed potatoes and spinach for less than a dollar. He added on a glass of milk and a slice of huckleberry pie. He took a table by the window where he could see the passing pedestrians. He didn't mind that they could see him. A fellow came to the table and asked if the seat was taken. This surprised Joe and he said it wasn't. Welcome to New York. You can't afford a lot of free space. He asked Joe if he was going or coming. Joe said he was on his way to Europe. He wasn't going to say much more. They were warned about talking to strangers. "MP huh?" said the stranger. He was familiar with military insignias, the crossed pistols on Joe's collar. "Yep," said Joe. "I better be moving on."

He returned to the hotel and asked who all was going with him so they all agreed to go.

"Did you know they make the beds here? A maid came in while we were eating, made the beds and left new towels," said Mike.

"She put on new sheets!" said Felix

"Come on you guys we gotta go." They left the hotel and went down into the subway station and bought a few tokens. Once they were through the turnstile, they could ride all day. They looked at the map and determined the train number they needed to get to lower Broadway. They waited less than ten minutes and were on their way. Early afternoon, the train had few riders. They soon reached their stop at Broome Street and walked back to Bannerman's.

It was just like the legends said about the place. There were walls of firearms dating to the American Civil War. Other civil wars were represented also like the one in Spain. There was a wall full of the guns that won the West, the Springfield 1863 muskets that were converted to .45-70 cartridges in 1873. There was a rack of .30-40 Krag-Jorgenson rifles that came from Scandinavia and fought on San Juan hill. There was a barrel full of clunky Swiss Veterli rifles, one of the first repeating rifles. They looked at bayonets, sabers and trench knives, anything useful for killing other men.

They saw one small cannon on the floor that the clerk said was used for shooting a line from one ship to another. The line was used to secure a breeches buoy, to transfer a sailor between ships. They told the clerk there were many guns they would like to consider buying but they'd have to catch him on the return trip. The weapons were moderately priced considering their historical character but they couldn't take a chance with their limited traveling money. The clerk lost interest in them and they just wandered aimlessly and in awe. He went to serve another customer.

There was a museum of sorts off to the side where some of the more precious objects were kept. There was a decorative, bejeweled sword presented to Catherine the Great, a pair of pistols owned by the gangster, Mickey Cohen. His initials, "MC" were embossed on the holsters. There was a presentation case of a gold encrusted flintlock rifle with decorative inlays of ivory. It also contained two dueling-style pistols and two small pocket pistols. It included two powder flasks and a collection of tools for casting bullets. It was presented to Napoleon II by a grateful nation.

Their minds were finally full of it and they left the store. They walked around the block toward Soho and were not impressed. Felix suggested an early supper and he was yearning for seafood. He saw a place called Mike's Ship Ahoy advertised and thought that would be a good place to go. After all, they were on the coast and the fish should be fresh. They were already on Broadway so they took the subway to 66th Street. Mike's was a kitschy sort of place and smelled like the sea. There were few other customers at four in the afternoon. The waiter brought them water and they all ordered a beer. He brought the beer to them and recited the list of specials. Joe ordered the seafood platter. Bill asked what Today's Catch was and the waiter told him oysters. "We're only one day out of the 'R' months and these come from colder waters north of Long Island. "I'll take them," said Bill, thinking of the fine all-you-can-eat dinners the Masons and Knights served in Baytown during Lent. He wasn't Catholic but the Knights of Columbus cooked some fine oysters. Mike ordered Shrimp Creole. He knew what that was supposed to taste like. Felix ordered Finnan Haddie. Nobody knew what he was talking about so he sang a line of "My Heart Belongs to Daddy." "It's just haddock."

Joe spoke up and said, "I got tickets for Radio City Music Hall and I'd like to go tonight to see *Spellbound*. It's an Alfred Hitchcock flick. He's an English director. Ingrid Bergman and Gregory Peck are in it.

Bill and Mike both said they don't need no music halls. "We're going to 42nd Street to see some skin."

"Suit yourself. Those Rockettes are fine dancers."

"I'll go with you, Joe. Are the tickets free?" said Felix.

"Yeah, I got them at the USO the other night while you guys were finishing your French fries."

"Count me in."

Their meals arrived and they dug in to the seafood. “This chow is fine.” “These oysters don’t taste muddy. I thought all oysters tasted muddy.” “To dine on my fine Finnan Haddie.” They were so full afterward they didn’t order dessert and headed back to the hotel.

They called the front desk to send someone up to get their uniforms pressed. They were all looking a little frumpy. They spent the time polishing their shoes and brass. They would just as soon have the fellow in the lobby shine them but they could hardly go down in their fatigues. They checked the airshaft to see if any entertainment was to be had. The bellhop brought their uniforms back and they tipped him. “That was fast.”

Felix and Joe left the hotel at seven and walked the two blocks to Radio City at Rockafeller Center. “Wow! Would you look at that line?” It stretched nearly to 5th Avenue. They stopped by the box office to make sure their tickets were valid. The young lady in the booth said, “Even if they weren’t valid, I’d make them good for you fellas.” They walked down the sidewalk to the end of the line. A couple invited some friends to cut in line and the people behind raised such a ruckus the other couple decided to go to the end.

Soon they took their seats in the enormous auditorium with the arches looping over the stage like rainbows and a Wurlitzer organ where the pot of gold should be. They were handed programs as they entered and first up was an organ prelude by Debussy, a French guy. Felix just groaned. Next out of the chute was the NBC symphony orchestra playing a rhapsody on a theme from Paganini. Felix was ready to rebel. “I’m gonna get some popcorn. You want anything?”

"It's only twenty minutes."

"I'll see you in twenty minutes."

Vladimir Horowitz was the pianist and played wonderfully. Felix drifted back in after about ten minutes and said, "That guy's pretty good." Vladimir finished his performance and the stagehands cleared the stage. Third on the program was the Merry Minstrels, the Rockettes. They arose on an elevator platform in the rear of the stage to the tune of "Strike up the Band." A few of the dancers fell away from their ranks to return for the next number in red and white striped blazers with straw hats and canes. They performed "There'll be a Hot Time in the Old Town Tonight." The original chorus line returned and danced to "Old Dan Tucker" and "Camp Town Races."

"This is all someone's idea of a minstrel show but thank God, without the black face," thought Joe.

The ladies cleared the stage and a black announcer walked out and said in a strong voice, "Gentlemen be seated," another reference to the minstrels. Two negro men danced their way out to "Sweet Georgia Brown." Their names were Buck and Bubbles. These were old vaudeville performers and boy could they dance. They were nearly lost on the huge stage but the sound of their taps filled the theater. They danced a smooth rendition of "Shine on Harvest Moon" and wound up with Glen Miller's "Mission to Moscow" that brought the theater to its feet in applause. It was for the late popular bandleader and the skill of the two black hoofers.

Half of the chorus came out in feathery, skimpy, dark green, one-piece outfits and outlandish dark green bonnets with darker feathers on top. They danced to “Cruisin’ Down the River.” Their sisters joined them for their finale, “Waiting for the Robert E. Lee.”

“I guess they were supposed to be Southern belles in those brief outfits.” The dancers made their exit and the rear curtain opened to present the movie.

The movie was *Spellbound* where Ingrid Berman is a psychoanalyst at a mental hospital called Green Manor. The other staff thought she was a cold fish. The director, played by Leo Carroll was forced into retirement after fighting nervous exhaustion. Gregory Peck was the young doctor who replaced him. It got complicated when Leo offs the young doctor who himself was impersonating another doctor. Leo shot himself when confronted at the end by Ingrid Bergman. Alfred Hitchcock showed up getting off an elevator in the middle of the movie. He carried a violin case and smoked a cigarette.

They exited the theater and there was a flurry of excitement in a corner of the lobby. A half dozen of the women in their green-bonneted costumes were holding court with several dozen enthusiastic fans. Joe and Felix joined the fray. They worked their way to the front of the pack where they were greeted with a whole-hearted, “Hi soldier!” “Thanks for coming to see us.” “How do you like these outfits?” There was a cute girl in the front who claimed she was the youngest dancer in the corps. Her name was Corliss Fyfe. She signed their programs.

They walked outside into the cool evening air. A woman in a maroon dress asked them if they’d like a good time. “No thanks Ma’am. We just had a good time.” They headed back to the hotel with a stop at the Pink Elephant Room. Mike and Bill were already there. "How did your evening at the Music Hall go?"

Felix said, "I had a better time than I expected. The dancers were fine especially the cute one named Fyfe." He pulled out his program with her autograph on it. "She said that they don't let the older dancers come out because their makeup is too scary. Those black tap dancers really could move. I'd swear that the one guy danced up the wall. They were supposed to be performing a minstrel show. It was a real stretch. The movie was predictable but the director showed up a half hour into the film. They say he always does that. It's his signature."

"I agree with Felix. What about you guys?" said Joe.

"It was a gyp. Those theaters promise a bunch but are short on the delivery. There were baggie pants comedians, has-been dancers and the strippers wore pasties the size of salad plates. There was an old lady every twenty feet wanting to show us a good time," said Bill.

"We found a nice bar though. It seemed like everyone knew each other but they treated us like buddies. They all wanted to buy us a drink so we thought we better get out of there before we got snockered. We just walked in here. What have you got lined out for tomorrow, Joe?"

"I want to walk back to Central Park again but this time all the way to the art museum. I'll take the subway back. Any of you yard birds want to come along?"

"What time do you figure on going?" asked Bill.

"The earlier the better. The park is beautiful in the morning light. We have nothing like it in Erie. There is a city square where 5th Street crosses State Street but it is nothing but a few trees and park benches that the hoboes have reserved."

There were no takers for his offer. He arose with the sun in the morning and quietly made his way out of the room. He walked up 8th Avenue to the coffee stand that he found yesterday. "Bagel and lox with a cup of Java, black."

"That will be two bits."

"It was thirty cents yesterday!"

"The joe is free, soldier. I know you now."

"That's my name, Joe."

"Java, joe, mud, rocket fuel. It's all coffee."

"Rocket fuel?"

"What do you think of Hitler taking the big pill? Him and that girlfriend of his. It happened ten years too late if you ask me."

"I've got orders for Europe. Maybe they'll get cancelled before I go. I better be on my way. I'm walking to the park."

Off he went toward Columbus Circle. The Con Ed guys were still in their hole. He walked along 59th Street back to 6th Avenue where he entered the park and walked along a road where the carriages operate. There were none around at this hour. He had a pretty good hike ahead of him. He saw the mounted police officer that he talked to yesterday. The Mountie rode over to him. "Good morning soldier. You're back again. You like our park?"

"Nothing like it back in Erie. Yes, I like it especially in the morning like this when there are fewer people.

"I see you're in the police." Joe looked down at his uniform.

"Your collar devices give you away. Those crossed pistols mark you as an MP. Just like if you had your hardhat and spats on. Where are you heading? You're not stationed in the city."

"I'm on my way to LeHavre on the *George Washington* this Friday. We're living the life of Riley until then. I probably need to go to Pier 53 and report in or something."

"Take my advice. Don't let them know you're here a minute before they expect you."

"Advice taken. I'm heading to the art museum. I'm going to make a day of it and take the subway back after."

"Enjoy yourself and stay out of trouble," and he rode off. Joe thought that is a great job he's got. He walked past the amusement rides that were just opening up. He walked by a statue of Robert Burns, a Scottish poet, and snaked his way between Conservatory Pond and the lake. He was getting close now and he was starting to get hungry. He exited the park at 77th Street and walked the last 4 blocks on 5th Avenue past some really high-dollar apartment buildings. Black Bentleys and Rolls Royce automobiles were double-parked. The chauffeurs were outside of their cars, talking and kidding and polishing fenders. Joe was impressed at all of this wealth but amid it all, you can buy a two-bit hot dog. This fellow called them Texas Red Hots and for a nickel, you could have chili on your sandwich. He also bought a Coca Cola. The museum stretched over four blocks. He walked up the steps into the building and up to the ticket desk. The lady told him that military in uniform do not need to pay.

"Wow! Thank you. That's alright."

He went in and turned right into the Egyptian galleries, one after another, examples from ancient Egypt. He was soon overwhelmed by it and made his way to the Arms and Armor exhibit, which was his goal. The Russell B. Aitken Gallery of Firearms was full of hunting and sporting weapons. Most were ornately carved, and inlayed, both the stocks and the metalwork. They were the most ancient matchlocks and progressed to the wheel lock, which operated like a Zippo lighter. The flintlocks of revolutionary time were well represented and the most highly decorated. Finally, there were percussion cap rifles and shotguns from the Civil War era. Joe walked around and read every card on every weapon.

He moved back in time to the armor gallery where they had manikins in armor mounted on armored horses. God, they were big. The horses were broad like the big farm horses in Pennsylvania, Percherons and such. In the displays, they were described as Destrier, Paltrey and Courser. There were many bejeweled swords and sabers. The thing that really caught his eye was a crystal glass mace that belonged to a bishop. Evidently, it was just for ceremonial use. Amazing that it survived hundreds of years.

He kept crossing paths with a young lady who was taking copious notes from the descriptions she was reading. He finally asked if she was a student and she said that she went to City College. She wore a brown skirt that showed off her flat stomach and a Kelly-green sweater that hid anything appealing above her waist. She wore librarian glasses and her one frill was her brown and white saddle shoes over white sox. Her dark brown hair was pulled up in a ponytail. She asked what a soldier was doing here. He said that he had a historic interest in firearms but since he'd come in here, the medieval armor had taken his attention. "I thought of all that as the stuff of legend and here it was bigger than life."

She said, "I am doing research on 14th Century warfare in Saxony."

Joe said he was going to Saxony or Bavaria to study warfare himself. "Mine is more of a hands-on study."

She said she liked his sense of humor. She said, "I'm starved. Let's go downstairs and get something to eat. There is a cafeteria near the lobby."

"I could go for that. My name is Joe. What's yours?"

"Vivian, Vivian Palermo. That's Italian."

"I'm just Joe. I'm a mutt."

The cafeteria was a nice, non-committal way of enjoying lunch. They each paid for their own tray without any discussion. It was a nice atmosphere. Joe caught her up on yesterday's activities. He thought he'd leave out the part about the taxi dancers. He said how he enjoyed Central Park and had struck up an acquaintance with a police officer on horseback. "He's a midget compared to those knights we saw in the hall. It must be a chore keeping that metalwork shiny."

She was sure it would keep a crew busy. "How long are you here and what are you doing?"

"We ship out on Friday on the *George Washington* if the war don't end before then. No, I'll be going no matter what. I'm an MP and they're going to need thousands of police in Europe to get everyone back to their homes and keep the peace until the countries can establish themselves again. Hitler destroyed nearly everything, government, infrastructure, farming. What he didn't screw up, we bombed. That was going to be my first job. I studied radio operation for the big bombers but we ran out of targets so I went into the military police."

"I've been studying all my life. I really haven't done anything. Oh, I waitress at resorts in the Catskills in the summer. Now I am going for a MA in European Art History so I can come back and work at this place. They know me. I hang out here a lot."

"Meet many guys here?"

"Are you kidding? The guys that come here don't pay that much attention to girls. You are one, rare dude."

"Well my buddies are back at the hotel, hanging out the window to see how many naked ladies they can spot. I guess I'm kind of rare. I'm going to take a chance. Are you doing anything tonight? I mean, would you like to go to a play with me?"

"I think I'd like that. Yes!"

"I'm not sure of the logistics but I have to go by the ticket office and trade my vouchers for tickets."

"We can do it simpler than that. We can call them from a pay phone here. What is the play?"

"It's a Tennessee Williams play, *The Glass Menagerie*. I read about it in *Life Magazine* and I got half price vouchers from the USO. I know my buddies don't want to go."

"I'm finished up here. There are a couple of galleries across the street that I think you might like. Then we can go to my place so I can change into something for the evening. We can get supper in my neighborhood without paying tourist prices and go to our play. What do you think of that?"

Red flags began to wave. Go to her apartment. She is older than he is. Well maybe just yellow flags. "Yeah! Swell! Let's do it." They went to a payphone in the lobby and found the theater in the phone book. He dropped a dime in and called the number. They agreed to hold his tickets at will call but he had to pick them up a half-hour before the performance. He said he'd be there. "I got that taken care of and fortunately I have the vouchers in my wallet. I better call the guys and let them know."

He dialed the Hotel Bristol. "Room 1042 please." He let it ring about eight times. The operator returned and said, "there was no answer," He perceived that also. "Can I leave them a message?" She said he could. "Tell them that that Joe went to a play with a friend and he'll be back around midnight." The operator said that she had it and would leave a note in their box. "That's it! Now we can go. I hate to run out of here but I have seen more than I expected to see. I really feel good about it. I know an awful lot more than when I came in."

"Me, too," said Vivian.

Chapter 10 – Vivian Palermo

They got off at the Bowery subway stop. Vivian pointed to Sara Roosevelt Park a block away and said, "There's the Bower. See all those trees down there. We're going the other way. It's about four blocks." They arrived a short time later at Benito's Restaurant at 163 Mulberry Street. Vivian opened the door and yelled in, "Hey Tony! Save me a table by the window for 5:30."

"That's lunchtime for you Viv. Why so early?"

"Don't bust my chops, Tony! I'm going out tonight. I got a fella."

"Lucky him. I'll have your table ready."

They turned around and walked back two blocks to Mott Street. "Here we are. This is where I live." Joe noted the number 128. It was a big building with a grocery and hardware store on the ground floor. "Are you ready to climb, Big Boy?"

"How far?

"Just five floors."

"I'll wait here while you change. Just kidding."

They walked up the five floors to apartment 509.

"I thought they had elevators in these buildings."

"I bet you think the moon is made of green cheese. This is what keeps New Yorkers healthy. We walk everywhere and we're always climbing stairs."

"Give me a moment to catch my breath. I just passed a PT test but it's nothing like this."

"You're using a different set of muscles. I'll leave the door open for you."

"Nothing doing," and Joe sprinted up the stairs. They both touched her door at the same time. Joe was still panting though. Vivian wouldn't admit that she was too.

The apartment was tiny. There was a closet size kitchen with a gas stove as wide as the four burners. She said the icebox doesn't work because she can't afford the ice. The fella has to carry the ice blocks up the stairs. It keeps the food away from the vermin. She buys most of her food fresh downstairs. "You have to tolerate warm drinks. In the winter, I just set it out the window. You don't have to chill wine so I use a lot of that." There were several original paintings on the walls along with a couple of woodprints. They darkened the place though. The iron steam radiator was odd. He suspected Vivian painted it alternating blue and maroon.

Vivian pulled two dresses off a peg near the bathroom. She held them up. One was rose colored and the other dark green with a darker velvet trim. He pointed to the green dress. "I would have picked that one also. The rose is a daytime dress." She tossed it over a screen at the foot of her bed and got a fresh slip out of her dresser. She went behind the screen and tossed the sweater on the bed followed by the skirt and two socks. A mirror on a sidewall briefly showed bits of her. She brushed out her hair.

"Don't look in here!"

She slithered into the slip and then put the dress over her head. It was open enough on the top to show off a carved cameo broach hung on a black ribbon. She selected a pair of low-heeled black shoes, what would be called sensible. "Make yourself useful and zip up the back of my dress." He more than willingly complied. She screwed on a small pair of earrings that complimented her broach.

"Should I wear a hat or a band?"

"Your hair is too beautiful to cover with a hat. Go with a band."

"Why thank you. Now it's time to show you my hood."

"Your hood? I don't get it. You don't need a hood."

"No silly. My neighborhood. My neighbors."

Joe suspected that he was the one being shown off, but he eagerly went along with her plan. They walked down to the street level chatting with a couple residents on the way down. They went into the hardware and she introduced Joe to Harry the hardware guy. The wall of the store was filled with little six by six drawers of every imaginable type of screw, nail and hinge. More bins held pipefittings. Harry asked Joe where he was stationed and Joe replied that he was in transit to Germany.

"The war should be over by the time you get there."

"Yeah, but Hitler's henchmen could retreat into the Alps in Austria and hold up there for years in their underground lairs."

"We would just bomb and starve them out."

"I won't know until I get there."

"Are you two going out?"

"Yeah. Joe's taking me to a play on Broadway, *The Glass Menagerie.*"

"Well, have fun you two," and they left.

"He's a nice fella," said Joe.

"Yeah. I see him when I gotta fix or paint something or just to talk."

They walked by the green grocer, Mr. Nussbaum, who was inspecting his fruit and they exchanged greetings. She said, "You see I have everything I need on the street to prepare a meal. I really don't need a fridge. They arrived at Benito's precisely at 5:30. Tony joked about the military precision. He had two glasses of dark red wine waiting for them and a lit candle in the chianti bottle. Moments later, he brought a small flat piece of bread with tomato sauce and cheese on it. Bits of sausage were sprinkled on top. He called it pizza. Joe asked, "Is that like the leaning tower?" Tony had to say, "Mama mia, it's pizza like p-i-z-z-a. And the sausage is pepperoni that we age by hanging it from the ceiling."

The restaurant had a pleasing garlic and spice odor to it. It smelled old and well used. Next was an antipasto salad with three kinds of lettuce, beans, cheese and anchovies. The anchovies were overly salty. That called for more wine. Joe admired the mural of the Bay of Naples on the long wall. Mount Vesuvius was near the center and Isola di Capri was on the far end. The rolled and pleated velvet in the booths was elegant at one time but was starting to show signs of wear. The entree was a heaping platter of Bucatini all'Amatriciana with three large meatballs. "Are we expecting someone else?" He thought, "It looks like spaghetti to me."

"No, this is how they serve it. You don't have to eat it all. They'll package what we don't eat and I will pick it up tomorrow. The pasta is like spaghetti but it is bucatini."

"That sounds like a good plan. Are you related to Tony?"

"Only as a neighbor. We do things for each other. Do you see the art on the walls? I helped him with that."

Joe wondered how but kept his questions mute. She must eat here an awful lot but she looks so trim.

Joe asked for the check and it came in less than four dollars. He said to Tony, "There must be some mistake. You didn't include the wine or appetizers."

"I don't make mistakes! You are my guests. You honor me by coming into my establishment. You serve my country and I serve you."

"Oh! Thank you very much." Joe left a five-dollar bill on the table.

They walked back to the Bowery on Grand Street and caught the subway to go to the theater district. They had to make one transfer on the way. There was a photo booth in the underground and Vivian suggested that they mark the event with some pictures. They got four images, two were silly and two looked blissful.

They arrived at the Excelsior Theater with minutes to spare and Joe paid for their tickets. They were even more reasonable with his military discount. They took their seats in the center of the orchestra section after Vivian went to the powder room. They looked over their programs. Julie Haydon played Laura Wingfield, a physically disabled young lady who spent her days playing with her glass figures of animals, her menagerie. Eddie Dowling played her brother, Tom, who was charged to find a clean-living suitor by his mother, Amanda. Amanda lived in the past when she was a pretty southern belle dancing at cotillions with handsome men.

They went to the lobby and drank a coke during intermission. They stepped outside into the cool spring air and admired the endless lights marching down Broadway. The lights in the lobby dimmed briefly and they returned to their seats. Well, Tom didn't do so well in his choice of a man for his sister. She knew of the gentleman in high school and admired him from afar but was thoroughly shaken when he arrived at their apartment with Tom. She withdrew into the company of her animals. It turned out that the gentleman was engaged to be married. Tom hadn't done his research well.

Maybe it was the cool air but Vivian snuggled closer to Joe with his arm around her neck. She pulled his hand a little closer to her ample, firm breast. Joe's mind was bouncing off the walls and not on the play. He had to be careful. The play ended in darkness when Tom neglected to pay the electricity so he could renew his Merchant Seaman's Union card and get out of town. The applause was enthusiastic with two curtain calls. The writer, Tennessee Williams, won an award from the New York City Drama Critics when they voted this play the best of the season. Joe got to see the award-winning play with a lovely young woman.

If they were going to stop somewhere for a drink, they'd better get back to her neighborhood where she felt safe. They went down the stairs to the subway, which was quiet this time of night. They had to wait ten minutes for the next train going south. Vivian's gaze was enough to keep the panhandlers at bay. The train thundered into the station and then hurtled through the tunnels at seemingly impossible speed. Time to get off to transfer to the last leg.

They were standing there talking, when this fool in a zoot suit walked up and asked for the time. His suit was silvery and shiny, maybe sharkskin. His hand-painted tie was wide as a bib with a dancing girl on it. His trousers were pegged at the cuff, barely larger than his ankles. Joe said it was about 11:30.

"I don't want to know about what time. I want your watch and your wallet."

He flicked a switchblade knife out with his right hand and held it menacingly. Vivian gasped. Joe reached into his back pocket as if to pull out his wallet. Instead, out flew a leather sack full of lead that knocked the knife out of the thug's hand and nearly broke his wrist. Next, Joe hit him full in the face with a left jab and a right hand to his stomach with an oversized fist full of lead shot. Vivian kicked the evil looking blade off the platform as the train arrived. She made a fist with her right hand and slugged the guy in the ear. "Take that you jerk!" She took Joe's hand and ran into the train car as the doors were closing. "Come on Conrad!" The train jerked to a start and they stood there in the near empty car holding onto each other. They were both panting. She looked up at Joe and he kissed her full on the lips. A laboring man sitting nearby said, "Way to go!" They sat down for the remainder of the short ride.

"Where did you get that cosh? It was like an angel dropped it into your hand."

"It belonged to my Uncle Clarence when he was an Erie police officer. I carry it when I am in unfamiliar circumstances like zoot-suited muggers."

"I am glad you had it. It's probably illegal in the City."

"We won't tell anyone."

They got off at the Spring Station. She said, "It is a little farther but it keeps us away from the Bowery. We're going to Benito's first and then to my place."

They walked in Benito's. The chairs were on the tables. Tony said they were closed.

Vivian said, "Tony, give us a shot of bourbon, a big one."

"Viv, you know we don't serve liquor here, just vino."

"I don't want to buy it. Joe needs a drink. He just clobbered a mook in a zoot-suit. Let me use your phone. I need to call his buddies and tell em he ain't coming home."

Tony brought a bottle of rye whiskey and three glasses. He asked where Joe was staying and said he would call the hotel. Vivian poured three fingers of whiskey in Joe's glass and the same in her own. Tony could pour his own. "He's at the Bristol."

"What room?" Tony asked.

"1042"

The phone rang twice and a voice answered, "Hello?"

"To whom am I speaking?"

"Bill Wallace and who is this? It's almost midnight."

"This is Tony. Your boy, Joe, won't be coming home tonight. He'll be there in the morning."

"Is he okay?"

"Oh, he's fine, really fine," and he hung up.

Vivian said, "That was rude. You probably scared his friends half to death."

"So what am I gonna say, he's too loaded to come home."

They sat with Tony for twenty minutes and told their story. Tony said, "Let's see the cosh." Joe took it out to show him. "It's a good one." It was made of tan leather worn darker from contact with a sweaty pocket. At four ounces, it felt substantial. "This will do it!" said Tony. "You should have hit him in the head."

"I think I did enough damage. He may look into another line of work."

"Nah! He'll be out there tomorrow preying on some other tourists."

"Are you calling me a tourist?"

"We got native New Yorkers and tourists. You're not a native. I don't mean to diminish you. You are my guest."

"Drink up, warhorse! We gotta get some sleep."

"I can't sleep in your apartment."

"What is your choice? You can't go back on the subway this time of night. You don't have to ask your mother. It's my mother that would have a conniption. Come on General Patton."

Joe and Vivian left the restaurant to walk to Mott Street. Joe looked over his shoulder every fifty feet. Up the stairs. Up more stairs. "How does she do it?" Apartment 509 looked wonderful.

"You take the sofa. I don't love you enough to give you my bed and you damn sure better not try to get in it. Here's a quilt."

"Calm down! I have no intention of ravishing you. I have had a wonderful evening, better than I could have imagined, 'zoot-suit' not withstanding and I don't want to mess it up."

Joe went to the bathroom while she spread out the bedding. He returned and kissed her on the cheek and said, "Goodnight Dear."

"Goodnight Dear," and she kissed him back.

He was gone almost immediately. She still had some prep to do in the bathroom before she hit the sack. It was ending too fast. The past day was like a storybook. "Yeah, he is young but what a guy."

Joe awoke in this strange place to the pleasant odor of hot wool as Vivian pressed his pants. "Good morning, sergeant. You got promoted overnight. You're a sergeant to me now. Here's your trousers. You look funny in those baggy shorts."

Joe quickly hopped around pulling up his trousers. Vivian touched up his shirt with her iron and put it on a hanger. She said, "I put a fresh blade in my safety razor, so you don't look like a bum when you go out on the street." Joe shaved and finished dressing. She cut the photo strip from last night and gave him his half, "so you'll remember."

They left the apartment for the street. Ladies in front of the grocery said, "Good morning Vivian. Good morning Joe." Mr. Nussbaum called, "Good morning Joe." Knots of people on the sidewalk parted as they walked along on their way to breakfast.

"They knew," thought Joe.

They entered a little lunchroom on the block. The waitress greeted them with, "Good morning Vivian. Good morning Joe."

Joe said, "Good morning."

"You know this is kind of unnerving with everyone knowing my name."

She said, “The jungle telegraph worked overtime last night. They all know how you saved me from the ravages of the zoot-suit. They’d award you a bronze star if it were up to them.”

“I’d rather forget it. I’m just glad I didn’t rate a purple heart.”

“You acquitted yourself nobly with that slapper of yours.”

Joe ordered a short stack of pancakes with two fried eggs on top and sausage on the side. Vivian had scrambled eggs and dry toast. “You ought to get a haircut before you go on that boat. I mean you look good but in a few days, you might be a bit shaggy. Let’s go see Nick after breakfast. That’s who cuts my hair.”

They walked around the corner and Joe saw the red and blue barber pole. The sign in front proclaimed “Nick Fattah Barber.”

“Good morning, Vivian. This must be Joe. What can I do for you two?”

Joe said he could use a trim before he sails tomorrow.

Joe sat down and Nick began to cut. A snip here and snip there and soon he was done. He handed Nick a dollar and they were out of there. Vivian said, “I’ve held onto you long enough, and it’s time to go face your compatriots. It’s been a marvelous 24 hours and I wish it could last longer but I know you’ve got to go. I’ve got a class at eleven so I have to get my books. Goodbye Joe. You’ll always be in my heart and prayers.”

Joe held her close and kissed her. "Goodbye Vivian. I will always remember you and this day," and they parted. He walked away on Grand Street. He crossed the street and looked back and Vivian waved. She was holding her handkerchief to her eye. Joe felt this dull ache in his chest. He thought, "Is this what love is? Is it this bitter sweet physical feeling deep inside you?" He walked into the subway station and looked at the photo that he took from his breast pocket.

Chapter 11 – The Palace

"Where have you been, Joe?"

"Who was that goon that called last night? He scared the crap out of me!" said Bill.

"Did you score?" asked Mike.

"Where did you stay?" asked Felix.

Joe went on to relate the past 24 hours to them. He showed them his slapper and the photo from last night.

"Va voom! We been wasting our time when we should have been checking out the museums."

"Madone! What a woman. And she didn't invite her hero to her bed."

"Ya know, it's almost lunchtime and I haven't been in an Automat since we came to this city. What do you say we go get some lunch? Then, I think it is about time to check out Pier 53, do a little reconnaissance," said Joe.

The automat was located around the corner on 7th Avenue, just a short ways. It wasn't noon yet so the place was half-full but all of the windows were full so they had plenty of selection. Joe selected a veal and ricotta meatball sandwich with fresh parsley sprinkled on the sauce. He had a coke with it and said, "That was fine." He went back and drew a piece of lemon meringue pie from another window and ate it with a cup of coffee.

He asked the guys what the lady in the airshaft was doing. "You wouldn't believe it! She waved at us yesterday but she wasn't there today," said Felix.

"The cops probably nabbed her. Indecent exposure."

"She was not indecent. She was a lady. Probably one of those nature-loving nudists."

Joe said, "I think you normally find them out in the woods, not in Manhattan airshafts. Who's going to the dock with me? I got a plan for this evening that you might enjoy. Have you ever heard of Sally Rand? She is appearing at the Palace this evening."

They all begged off from going to the dock but they were eager to go to the Palace. "I'm going to check out Pier 53 and I'll be back for supper at six. The show at the Palace starts at eight with some vaudeville acts and Sally Rand winds up the evening. At least that's what I read in the paper."

"Where have you guys been hanging out?" asked Joe.

"We found some bars and pool halls in Hell's Kitchen just west of here and we've been kicking around there."

"You could do that in St. Louis!"

"Nobody's tried to knife us yet. Can you say that?"

"You got me there, "said Joe.

Joe had to walk about six blocks through the meatpacking district to get to Pier 53. It was next to the pier where the ill-fated Lusitania sailed before WWI. He decided that they better take a cab tomorrow. They would be hauling duffle bags. Two MP's were guarding the entrance. He showed them his ID and a copy of his orders. They told him to go in and see that master sergeant at the standup desk.

"What can I do for you trooper?"

"Me and three buddies are supposed to ship out tomorrow and I wanted to be sure of when we should be here."

"What's your name?"

"Joseph Conrad."

"You were supposed to be here three days ago. You're AWOL. It's a good thing you haven't been here. We've got guys stacked to the rafters and it's killing us to feed them all. They've been cooking aboard ship and hauling it out to us. Where have you been bunking?"

"The USO recommended the Hotel Bristol and that's where we've been staying."

"At least they didn't put you up in a brothel."

"Do they do that?"

"Just kidding!"

"What time do we need to be here tomorrow?"

"The ship shoves off at 14:00 hours. You need to be here at 10:00 hours."

"Why?"

"To get in line."

"Are the berths assigned? Do you know where we sleep?"

"Yeah. You're in a room with three other MP's, Wallace, Jackson and Schneider."

"That's great. We're all friends."

"On your way with you and be back at 10:00 hours."

"What's for lunch?"

"They'll have box lunches for you at the pier."

"Supposed we use part of that 'standing in line' time to eat nearby?"

"Do you know what the penalty is for missing a shipment?"

"I ain't said anything about missing a shipment. I just want a decent meal before we embark."

"You better not be late," and Joe hit the road looking for a likely restaurant. He found one nearly across the street. It was the Brass Monkey and a look at the menu said that it was a working man's lunchroom. He took one last look back at that awesome ship that would be their home for a week, the USAT *George Washington*.

He had to do one tourist-like thing while he was here so he took the bus to the Empire State Building. He got a military discount here also and took an elevator to the 60th floor. It was the local. Then he took a second elevator directly to the observation deck on the 86th floor. That was a fast ride and his ears popped on the way up. The wind was blowing up a storm when he arrived. He folded his cap over his belt to keep it from blowing overboard. Central Park looked like a green jewel from up here. He could see the lake in the distance. New Jersey was to the West and looked like a giant waste dump in the haze.

He could see Pier 53 and the *George Washington* to the southwest with Hoboken across the river. They had the best view of Manhattan at night. The open sea was to his south but there was a lot of land between here and there. He went back inside and took the elevator to the 102nd floor, Top Deck. He didn't think it was worth the extra price of the ticket. You can see further but it was hazier and you were stuck inside. He would have rather been outside like *King Kong*. Now that was a picture.

He left the building and began walking north on 6th Avenue to Bryant Park on 41st Street. He bought a roll of caramel popcorn from a vendor with one of those glass popcorn wagons with the whistle on top. The fresh popcorn is good but this caramel roll is the best. He chose a spot on the green near the stage and lay back looking at the tall buildings and eating his popcorn. "It doesn't get any better than this. Unless? Unless Vivian or Daisy were here. What if they were both here? That's uncomfortable. I won't think of that." He covered the last seven blocks in a half hour. There was just so much to see along the route.

The shoeshine man was reading a paper when he entered the lobby of the hotel. He asked him if he was on break or ready to make some money. The man told him to get up in the seat. His brown shoes had gotten a bit scuffed in the past day.

"What do you read in the news? I've been out of touch for a day."

"Italy and Yugoslavia have been liberated. The Ruskies have taken Berlin. It's just a couple days before Germany throws in the towel."

"That day can't come soon enough for me." He paid the man and gave him a tip. If he is careful tonight, that should be his last shoeshine. He picked up his key. Nobody else in the room yet. He hung his uniform on the corner of the bed and took a shower. The other three came bounding in while he was in the bathroom.

"Hey Joe! You in there?"

"Pick up any girls today?"

"I'll be right out."

"No hurry!"

Joe came out with a towel around his waist, "Are you still game to go to the Palace with me tonight? It's the last vaudeville show in town."

There was a staggered reply of "Yeah."

"We don't seem to be doing much good on our own. You've been seeing the town and the women. You didn't pick up any this afternoon, did you?"

"No I came up short. I visited the dock and talked to a master sergeant there who told me to be there in line by ten and that they have boxed lunches for us."

"What did you say?"

"I agreed with him but I think a better plan would be to leave here in a cab at ten and go to the Brass Monkey for lunch. It's a saloon in the meatpacking district. Then it is just a walk across the street to our ship. Whatever happens, the absolute limit is one o'clock. If we miss shipment, we spend the rest of the war in the stockade."

"That might not be so bad."

"It's not for me. Not with a dishonorable discharge."

"Enough of that! We're not missing shipment! Now suit up and let's eat."

Joe put on his uniform and the rest freshened up a bit. They had been passing a restaurant on 8th Avenue called The California and decided to try it for supper. It looked to be a moderate family-type place. They had seen others in the city with state's names. They wondered if the menu reflected the namesake. They left their keys at the counter, gave the shoeshine man a nod and were out on the street. The noise of 48th Street reminded them of their quiet airshaft with its early morning scenery. They heard recordings of Carmen Miranda belting out "Brazil," "Frenesi" and "Green Eyes" as they passed by dives and cocktail lounges.

They reached their destination and were seated with their menus. It was good plain American food just like in the mess hall. They ordered drinks, Manhattans and Old Fashions and then their dinner, nothing fancy. They asked Joe what he thought of the ship.

"It's bigger than anything I've seen on the Great Lakes. It's more than two football fields long and tall with two big smokestacks. The sergeant said we'd be bunking together in a compartment."

"That's okay with me. I'm used to you guys and Joe finds himself other places to sleep."

"That was once and it was for safety," said Joe.

"Yeah, the safety of a young lady's apartment."

They finished their meal with coffee and let the dessert go. They had to walk about three blocks to the Palace. The marquee proclaimed Sally Rand as the headline act. They paid their admission and took their seats as the organist played a medley of songs about women, Mary, Jeannie with the light brown hair, Cherry and Daisy. The first act was for the dogs. A man and woman performed with a dozen trained dogs jumping through hoops, poodles walking on hind legs and little yappers bouncing off the walls. Every time the man bent down a large dog would push him over. The poodles danced in between the woman's legs. And it was over.

A young lady came out and changed the card for the next act, a baritone who sang "Vesti la Giubba" from *Pagliacci.* He was dressed as a pointy-hatted Italian clown applying makeup before a lighted mirror and he sang his soul-wrenching aria. The young lady returned and turned over the card for Paul Winchell and Jerry Mahoney, a ventriloquist and his dummy. It was a funny act. Jerry played the funny dummy and Paul was his straight man. Winchell began as a ventriloquist on the radio with Jerry Mahoney. The program was short-lived, as he was overshadowed by Edgar Bergan and Charlie McCarthy. The radio wasn't big enough for two illusions that have to be seen.

An old comedian in a baggy suit took the stage and told some fast-paced jokes.

"The weather was very hot, and a man wanted to swim in a nearby lake. He didn't bring his swimming suit. He was all alone. Who cared? So he undressed and dove into the water. After some delightful minutes of cool swimming, a pair of old ladies walked along the shore in his direction. He panicked, got out of the water and grabbed a bucket lying in the sand nearby. He held the bucket in front of himself. The ladies got closer and looked at him. He felt awkward and wanted to move.

Then one of the ladies said, "You know? I have a special gift. I can read minds."

"Impossible," said the nervous man, "You really know what I am thinking?"

"Yes," the lady replied, "Right now, you think that bucket you're holding has a bottom.""

There was a titter of laughter and he told another.

"My wife says I drink too much. I keep a picture of her in my billfold and I keep tossing back the shots until she starts to look beautiful to me and then I go home. Anyway, I got loaded last night and went to the cemetery. I found Robert's gravestone and I knelt there and cried my eyes out. I never met him. He was my wife's first husband. I cried, 'Why did you have to die? Why? Why?'

I suppose you're wondering why I'm wearing these pearl earrings. I've been wearing them ever since my wife found them in the front seat of my car."

The following act was a soprano who sang "The Barcarolle" from *The Tales of Hoffman*. That was enough classical music for this audience. Three girls came out billed as the Andrew Cousins and sang several songs by their more famous cousins like, "One Meat Ball", "Shoo-Shoo Baby, "Six Jerks in a Jeep" and "Lullaby of Broadway."

The card changer returned with the Will Mastin Trio minus one. It was Will Mastin and Sammy Davis Sr. The minus one was Sammy Davis Jr. who was still serving in the Navy. They were tap dancing fools. Joe and Felix kept comparing them to Buck and Bubbles that they saw on Tuesday. They were all really good but they were a lot closer to these two fellows and the tapping really got going in your head. You couldn't keep your feet still on the floor.

Finally, the act they came to see arrived. It was Sally Rand. She appeared at the Chicago World's Fair. She walked on stage behind a giant balloon with the organ playing a lighthearted "I'm Forever Blowing Bubbles." Sally stepped back stage for a moment and returned in a gossamer gown with two large ostrich feather fans. A pianist played "Clair de Lune" to accompany her dance. There was a translucent screen on each side of the stage and when she danced behind them, her figure stood out in sharp detail. The gown seemed to hide a bit more. She danced behind the right screen and the gown seemed to melt away. She alternated the fans front and back but never revealing much. She used the screens to display her figure. Toward the end, she turned to the back of the stage and arched her back toward to the audience displaying her lovely breasts. She finally faced the audience and displayed her beauty with her arms upraised holding her fans like wings. The crowd exploded with applause.

"That is one fine woman," exclaimed Mike.

Joe said, "I thought you'd like it. One more thing I'd like to do before we leave. Let's go to Schraft's for dessert. It is just around the corner from the Bristol on 6th. Who wants to go?"

"That's about all of the money I've got left. I could have an ice cream cone," said Bill so off they went, enjoying their last view of the city's lights.

They arrived at Schraft's and each chose his favorite confection. They called it a night and returned to the hotel for their last night.

In the morning, they went to the automat for breakfast. Joe told them he'd be along later. He wanted to give Daisy a call. He stopped by the desk and got five dollars in quarters. He dialed the operator and asked for Crocker 9964 in St. Robert Missouri. The operator said to deposit $3.50 for three minutes. Joe put in 14 quarters. The phone rang and Ann answered it.

"Hello?"

"Mrs. Watson, this is Joe Conrad. Is Daisy nearby?"

"She has a mouthful of cereal but I'll get her. It's Joe."

"Hello Joe. Where are you?"

"Happy Birthday Daisy. This is my last day in New York and I wanted to call you before I sail this afternoon. That's why I'm calling before you go to school."

"I received your present yesterday. Thank you so much. I'm wearing it now."

"I bought it before I left the fort. I mailed it as soon as I got to New York." He went on to tell her some of the things he has done. He left out the part about the art student and the mugger. "I went to most of the places I wanted to see."

"It's been boring here since you've been gone. I really miss you. School keeps me busy but not busy enough."

"I'll keep writing you when I get to Europe but your letters won't catch up to me until after I reach my unit. You have my APO."

The operator broke in, "Please deposit $1.25 for an additional minute."

"Goodbye Daisy. I love you!"

"I love you Joe."

Joe walked down the street and joined his companions at the automat. He had a cup of coffee and a bagel with cream cheese and lox. "What the hell is that?" asked Mike.

"Lox and bagel. Never heard of it?"

"No I haven't! It looks like one of those fancy things they serve at cocktail parties in the movies."

"That's what I thought the first day I had one. It seems like a week ago."

"Well not all of us got a silver star for taking down a mugger," said Bill.

"I didn't get no reward for preserving my own life and property. I just wasn't going to turn my wallet over to some thug."

"Joe, you could have named your reward and she would have been glad to give it to you."

Chapter 12 – USAT George Washington

They paid off their account with the hotel desk. Their deposit covered most of it except for their cleaning and laundry. Joe was the only one who got his money back from the hotel safe. The others had withdrawn their money and gone through most of it. They went out and piled into a Checker Cab. The doorman helped them squeeze their duffle bags into the trunk. It was a few minutes before ten. Joe asked the driver if he knew where the Brass Monkey is near the docks. The driver told him, "I know where every monkey is. Just sit back and leave it to me." It didn't take all that long to get to the restaurant. They could see their ship from the door. It looked huge.

They entered the restaurant, which was crowded even at this early hour. They spotted a few other GI's like themselves avoiding the dreaded box lunch. This would be their last meal on shore. The barman told them to stow their bags in a secure spot behind the bar. "Don't worry about em! Eat your dinner!" They began with a beer and looked over the luncheon specials. It was a working stiff's bar. Seventy-five cents would get you a darn good meal. A couple butchers in white coats came by the table on the way out and said, "You guys run those Krauts back to Berlin and watch out for them Ruskies also."

Bill said, "It looks like those Ruskies already got Berlin."

"They've gotta go home and rebuild their country too."

The waiter brought their orders and they dug into their food with more impromptu conversations with the locals. There were more butchers, stevedores, truck drivers and ship's crewman. Each had a different slant on the war and advice to give the soldiers. Only a couple recognized them as MP's. They had to have dessert. No telling where their next dessert would come from. They left the restaurant along with the few other GI's with a rousing cheer from the bulk of the patrons. This was probably their habit whenever a troopship was sailing.

Their little troop crossed 12th Street and then had to make their way across the highway carrying their sixty-pound bags on one shoulder and their AWOL bags in the other. They got across with no mishaps and made their way into the cavernous Pier 53. It looked different to Joe than it did yesterday. The endless rows of cots were stacked against the wall and mountains of mattresses were stacked on tarpaulins to keep them somewhat clean and dry.

Mike said, "That money we paid the hotel this morning was worth every penny of it. This place must have been a snake pit."

"You're right! It looked awful when I was here yesterday. It was mostly deserted except a few guys reading magazines or comic books."

Joe saw the same sergeant that he spoke to yesterday. "You're late soldier. I said to be here by ten."

"We ran into trouble. The cab driver took us to the wrong dock and we had to walk from there." Joe crossed his fingers behind his back.

"Well don't expect anything to eat. The box lunches are all gone."

"Awe Sarge, not even some K rations"

"Shut up you guys and get in line."

For the next hour, they slowly made their way forward in a serpentine fashion toward a hole in the black wall that was the USAT *George Washington*. The sergeant gave them a pamphlet to tell them about the ship. It was an old liner that was built in Germany before the Great War. It was taken by the United States after the war as part of reparations and sailed under the flag of United States Lines until 1931 when it was mothballed. It was returned to service at the start of WWII and given to the United Kingdom under the lend lease arrangement. It was called the USS *Catlin* for six months and then returned to the US due to its slow speed. The name, *George Washington*, was returned after the coal-fired boilers were replace with oil burners. This gave her the speed needed to outrun German subs. These were no longer much of a threat.

They reached the gaping maw at the end of the gangway. It was flanked by black painted steel plates, riveted together decades ago. Overhead a plume of grey smoke wafted from the funnel. A sergeant and a corporal stood there with clipboards to identify the soldiers seeking access. Here they were given their room number, 347. "That's on deck #3."

Felix looked at the main deck and counted up from there. "That's right on top!'

"No soldier. You count from the waterline."

They made their way into the new iron universe that would be their home for the next ten days. They shuffled along until they came to a companionway and went down and went down again. Two times and they were on deck 3. Their cabin was on the starboard inside. The even cabins were on the port side. Bill opened the door and looked in at the two double bunks. "No window. It's got no window. Not even an airshaft like the hotel." They soon found out that corporals and above got the outside cabins with portholes and they were two to a room.

"This sucks, man!"

A voice from behind said, "Consider yourself lucky private. We're sailing with 2900 on this cruise. A year ago, there were 7000 troops on this ship. That was half of the 100th Infantry Division. They slept in hammocks three high in every corner of the ship." This was from a Merchant Marine crewmember. "We're your guides today. The showers are at each end of the hall. There's no smoking while we're in port so don't light them up." He told us that we were free to explore the ship as long as we wear our life jackets. He also said to keep clear of the troops that were still coming on. The bulky life jackets made passing in the halls a bit hazardous. "Once we cast off there will be a life boat drill on the boat deck. You must attend. No exceptions."

The four of them began with a swing around the current deck. It was all cabins on the sides and center. There was a large enclosed space in the center that they took to be the smokestack. Aft was a day room and library. There were game tables and writing tables and even Ping-Pong but no pool tables. That probably wouldn't work. The game could play itself at sea.

Joe picked up a copy of *The Razor's Edge* by Somerset Maugham from the library while Bill chose *Great Tales of Terror and Supernatural* by Herbert Wise. They went down a deck but it was all pipes and valves and what looked like the tops of the fuel tanks. What's more, it smelled like fuel too. They didn't waste any more time down there.

They climbed to deck #4 and noticed the cabin doors were further apart. "This must be the second class deck." Mike said to no one in particular. There had been a nice saloon forward on this deck but they just served soda pop. They also could make cold sandwiches. They noticed that the deck was called the Saloon Deck. There was a handball court aft. Deck #5 seemed about the same as far as the size of the cabins. The ship sounded its horn and they all jumped. "How often are they going to do that?"

"I think they may be getting ready to cast off." They ran up the stairs to the promenade deck and lined the rails with a thousand other GI's.

The ship was loose from the pier. Two little red and black tugboats squeezed the ship away from the pier. They then pushed the massive ship into the Hudson River where it gave another toot. They had to cover their ears for that one. The ship moved majestically down the river between Governor's Island on the left (ok port side) and Ellis Island on the starboard side. Soon the Statue of Liberty was to their starboard. A thousand cheers went up as they passed the Lady. Upper Bay was behind them and the Lower Bay ahead where the pilot boat comes out to retrieve the pilot. The loudspeaker called out for all enlisted men to return to their cabins by 16:00. That gave them a half hour to view the last of their country. They knew it was too good to last. They were also told they could remove their life jackets below deck but they must still be worn on deck.

"How am I gonna get my tan?"

They slowly made their way back down to deck three. They went to their cabin and drew cards for their choice of bunks. Joe got an upper bunk. He was close to the overhead where he could lie on his back and read the graffiti left by their predecessors. "Kilroy was here." He was everywhere.

"On the chest of a barmaid named Gail
Were tattooed the prices of ale
And on her behind
For the sake of the blind
Was the same information in Braille."

"A Salvation lassie named Claire
Was having her first love affair.
As she climbed into bed,
She reverently said:
'O please let us open with prayer.'"

"Hey guys! There was a poet here ahead of us. Maybe it was Kilroy?"

There was a knock on the door and a voice hollered, "Fall out!" They went out in the passageway. A sergeant said that the dayroom aft will be our muster station. "Follow me." There were about thirty of them plus a few NCO's. The sergeant began by calling roll. It didn't seem like it but somebody had organized them. It turned out there were 36 of them in nine rooms. "Every three rooms was a squad, led by a corporal. The three squads is a company even though you are only one platoon. Until we reach the shore of Europe, you are the 203rd

Military Police company charged with keeping the peace on this ship."

"My name is Staff Sergeant Fredrickson. Your Company Commander is Lieutenant Michael Keane. The US Marines are charged with guarding key points of this ship like the bridge and the brig. We will supplement them where their numbers are too small. You won't have to think about KP. This will be your primary duty. You will rotate your duties so that you stand guard for a few hours and form roving patrols in between."

"I never even considered KP on a ship," thought Joe.

"Any questions?" asked the sergeant.

"When do we start?"

"Tonight at 20:00 hours. That is the third shift. Khaki uniforms, armbands and spats. We will issue helmet liners and Billie clubs. The first shift begins at 04:00 and the second shift begins at noon along with the afternoon watch. One more thing. The ship is on Greenwich Mean Time. We will change to GMT at midnight so set your watches ahead four hours. That means the third shift will only serve for four hours tonight."

"Right!"

"Supper hour is 18:00."

"Sarge. What happens when we're on duty at suppertime?"

"Half of you go to chow for a half hour and then you switch. You even get to buck the line. Breakfast is at 07:00 and lunch is at 1230. Any other questions? The duty roster is posted here in the day room." All eyes turned to the bulletin board. "Now I'd like to introduce Lt. Michael Keane."

"Thank you Sergeant Fredrickson. Men, we're charged with the safety and order of this ship and its 2900 passengers and crew. We're not going to impose our will but we will defer to the Marines and crew wherever there is a disagreement. We're just here to help."

"And keep busy."

"Did someone have a comment?"

"We need to get busy, Sir!"

"Third squad report here at 1950 hours. There will be an inspection in the morning at 10:00 hours. This will reoccur each day we are at sea. Dismissed!"

They all crowded around the bulletin board that would decide their fate. It all seemed somewhat logical. Cabins 341, 343 and 345 are the First squad. Cabins 347, 349 and 351 are the Second squad. "Hot damn! We get to sleep in 'til noon tomorrow," said Felix. 353, 355 and 357 are the Third squad. They were blessed with the first duty.

They went back to their cabin and dug out a fresh pair of khakis to wear for supper. Shoes and buckles need a good polishing. The cabin took on the odor of Kiwi polish and Brasso. It was a familiar smell. They left for the chow hall at 1745 and were taken back by the line they encountered. It wound halfway around the ship. They dutifully lined up like the lemmings they felt like. "I thought we could buck the line."

"That's when you have your hard hat on."

They ate off the same tin trays that they used shore-side. The food was shoveled onto the trays by other soldiers who had just got on the ship and discovered they had KP. They were none too neat about it. The stew ran into the bread and cake. They drank cold milk from hot cups. There were few tables and they were full so they stood up to chest high metal shelves and ate there. The ocean was pleasantly calm so it was no trick to stand straight. They took their trays to the cutter window. There was no joy in hanging around this place.

They went to the day room and the four card tables were in use with six to eight players at each. They were locked into five-card stud with that many players. They tried to watch the games to judge the strength of the players. The players let it be known they didn't like guys looking over their shoulder so they moved off to their cabin. Someone had posted nametags on their cabin doors while they were gone. They looked at the two doors by theirs to see who else was in their squad. The names on the door next door, 349, were Dick Santomeno, Ronald Steffee, James Stevens and Walter Vanderhoof. William Wyatt, Charles Boll, Gary Haag and John Polzin were in 351. They were all from Fort Wood. The guys went up and down the passageway. They remembered all of the names from their company. Joe thought they were lucky to have traveled on their own.

Cabin 359 had no names on the door and was vacant. No mattresses on the bunks. They had found their game room. Joe probably had the most money but he kept it in his belt and didn't talk about it. The boys searched around and found a piece of plywood and a tea box that was the right height and Felix came back with a fire blanket. He wouldn't say where he found it. Bill rounded up some butt cans from the mess hall.

They could smoke below decks now after leaving port. He and Mike found some soda-pop crates to sit on. Joe was surprised to see that the other three had been hoarding change after living out of the Automat. They left the door open to attract a few more players. Joe bought five bucks in coins from Mike and Bill. It was time to play. They decided on nickel ante with a limit of a quarter to keep the game friendly.

Felix produced a well-worn card deck and they drew cards for the deal. Bill won the deal. He called the game five-card stud and they each anted a nickel. High card opens. Felix opened for a nickel with a 6 of spades. Bill dealt another card and Joe bet a nickel with a Jack of diamonds. Mike had a 7 of diamonds and threw in another nickel. "Did anyone shuffle this deck?" They were coming out in order. Felix bet a nickel with a Queen showing. Joe raised him a nickel. No one could beat Joe if he had a pair of Jacks so they folded. Joe didn't need to show them his King high.

Felix dealt and Mike opened for a nickel with an Ace. Felix dealt again and now had a pair of Kings showing and bet a dime. Bill had a pair of aces showing. Joe had a pair of Queens. Bill bet a dime and Joe and Mike folded. Did Felix think he could deal another King? He didn't but gave himself another deuce to go with his hole card. Two pair beats a pair of bullets. This was a nice pot for Felix.

Charlie Boll and Bill Wyatt poked their heads in the door and asked, "Is this game private or can anybody join in?"

"You can play if you like. You're family, second squad - right?"

Charlie said, “We ought to set our watches ahead so we don’t play too long.”

“Good idea.”

“Hey! It’s almost midnight and all we got in was two hands.”

“We’ll take care of that. Deal!”

So they played until 02:00 and decided they had enough. Joe dropped out earlier after he lost $5 and just dealt for the rest of the evening. Charlie and Mike were the big winners with about ten apiece. They never woke up until 09:00 GMT.

“Holy crap! We missed breakfast and we got inspection in an hour.” Well, what could they really do for inspection except make their beds and sweep the floor? Hang a fresh towel on the end of the bunk that they wouldn’t use and save for inspection. Polish their shoes. Their brass was beginning to look a little green from the salt air. “Pass me your Brasso. Please?”

Lt. Keane and Sgt. Fredrickson arrived at 10:05 and looked around. The lieutenant told them that the overhead could use some work. “There is dust on that pipe.”

“Yes, Sir!”

They departed. “Joe, your pipe is dusty.”

“Hand me a sock and I’ll dust it.”

They put on their spats and armbands and went to the chow hall to see if they could sweet-talk them out of an early lunch. The KP’s were eating when they got there and they served themselves a sandwich and soup. They even got to sit down for this meal. Charlie Boll joined them.

"That time change screwed over my mind. Between that and not seeing the sun, I don't know which end is up."

He brought a mimeographed sheet with him that was titled "The Hatchet." It was the ship's daily newspaper named after GW's cherry tree hatchet. This initial issue spoke of the many units represented by the passengers. It also had the latest war news.

German forces in Holland and Denmark surrender to British.
Tribute to the Iwo Jima flag raising. Heard over MBS/WGN.
Adolf Hitler confirmed dead in Berlin bunker.
Many American units prepare for redeployment to Pacific.

"That last one is what worries me. I'll take springtime in Germany. I don't need no tropical Pacific islands."

"That Iwo Jima scared the hell out of me. I've got a brother out there somewhere," said Joe.

The Hatchet also listed the movies for the week. They appeared in the Officer's Mess at 20:00, the EM mess at 14:00 and 20:00 and on the poop deck at 21:00 weather permitting. Some of the movies were *Arizona Whirlwind, Bathing Beauty, Bowery to Broadway, Canterville Ghost, Dancing in Manhattan, The Fighting Sullivans, Going My Way, The Yellow Rose of Texas* and *National Velvet*. They saw many of them at the base theater in Missouri but some of them would be fun to see again. Not much else to do but play cards.

They took their trays to the cutter room to be washed and headed to the Day Room where they met Corporal Badger, the corporal of the guard for their shift. Charles Badger had washed out of Officer Candidate School with a temporary rank of corporal. All it did was make him mean, pissed off at the Army and everybody in it. "You guys are late!" he growled. It was 1145. That's the time they were told to be there. "We've got a lot to cover. We're here to guard the officers and keep enlisted men out of their facilities."

"That's what I thought," mused Joe.

"You'll stand guard for two hours and then patrol in pairs for two hours. You eat lunch before you come on duty and eat your supper when you are on patrol, one at a time. You are to challenge any EM's that wander into your area. You are to act as fireguard and make sure that drunken officers do not fall overboard. You'll keep an eye out for any unauthorized gambling and report it. There are sound powered telephones at each guard post and others at critical points on the ship to report back to me and I can contact the duty officer."

"Corporal, what is authorized gambling?"

"There should be no money visible. Chips are available in the game room."

Mike and Joe were assigned to guard the entrance to the Shelter Deck with its Officer's Bar and Lounge. Bill and Felix started on roving patrol on decks 2 and 3. They wore their distinctive helmet liners. They did not carry any weapons. Joe secreted his cosh in his pocket just in case. It was boring duty. The only activity was saluting every officer who passed and receiving a half-hearted nod in return.

The roving patrols walked their post in a military manner keeping always on the alert just like the General Orders demand. The only thing was, no one else walked in a military manner. They wanted to stop and shoot the bull. What is the gossip? Since they stood out, they were questioned as experts about everything that was happening. They could have started all kinds of rumors if they were creative and devious. They were neither.

At 14:00, Cpl. Badger arrived with Privates Wyatt and Bolls to relieve Joe and Mike. They were then assigned to patrol decks 5 and 6. This was their first time above deck since the boat drill on Friday. It was a pleasant day, a sunny afternoon with enough of a westerly to dampen the wind of the ships movement. There was little to disturb their walk except an officer to salute now and then or a hastily discarded cigarette pack to be picked up. An officer could walk past a piece of litter a dozen times in a day but Lord help a private, if he doesn't stop and pick it up. A corner of a piece of canvas had lifted on a lifeboat but it was out of reach. He would note it and report it to the corporal. They found a craft shop on deck 5 that was nearly deserted but open to all ranks. They had a few machine tools like a grinder and drill press and a little jeweler's lathe. The most popular products of this shop were cribbage boards. They had lumber salvaged from freight pallets and when GI's ran low on cash, they reverted to pinochle or learned cribbage. The board has 120 holes in it arranged in groups of ten for keeping score.

There is a handball court aft near the poop deck. The sign on the door said, "Officers Only." The poop deck had tackle for mooring the ship in port. "So this is where they have the movies. You got to get here early to find a chock or bit to sit on." They continued around the deck enjoying the fresh air and the mesmerizing effect of the ocean.

It was time now to relieve Felix and Bill. That made it two more hours before they can eat. The time went fast though with all the comings and goings. There were a lot of officers on this ship. At least you didn't have to worry about breaking up card games when you are standing at a post. They tossed a quarter to see who would eat at six. Joe lost. Mike would eat at six and Joe would walk through decks 2 and 3. This was safe territory since it was home and nobody belonged on deck 2. Supper at 1830 wasn't all that bad. You didn't have to be polite and you could serve yourself. Few people were at the tables so you could sit down. At the end of their shift, Corporal Badger told Joe that the lieutenant wanted to see him.

"I wonder what that's about?" said Joe.

Joe checked himself over and went to Lt. Keane's cabin.

"Private Conrad reporting, sir."

"How's it going, Joe? Are you getting used to shipboard life?"

"Yes sir. This is a lot better than the horror stories we've heard about troop ships."

"What is this about?" he thought.

"Conrad, we've had a complaint from the New York City Police Department that someone with your name and description assaulted and robbed a citizen."

"That is preposterous sir. What is this about?"

"A well-dressed gentleman was discovered bleeding and injured in a subway station in Manhattan by a transit officer. He said that he was assaulted by a soldier and a prostitute who then stole his wallet and escaped on a train. He heard the woman say Conrad and noticed you were an MP."

"That was very observant of him. Did he also say that he drew a switchblade on me after asking for my wallet and watch? I knocked the blade from his hand and punched him in the face and stomach before escaping on the train. The woman was not a prostitute. She was an art student."

"What was her name?"

"I don't see where that is relevant."

"She was a witness. It could be relevant."

"I'd rather not say, sir. It could get back to that mook and he would go after her. I think he's just fishing for her name and address."

"Is this your statement then?"

"Yes sir. Would you like me to write it for you?"

"No. That won't be necessary. The police also said that this fellow had a number of convictions for petty theft and robbery. Your story seems to hold up. What happened to the knife?"

"My date kicked it off the platform as the train entered the station."

"That checks out. The policeman said there was a knife between the tracks. It would probably have the victim's prints on it if they dusted it. I believe that's all private. You may go."

Joe saluted and said, "Goodnight Sir."

Joe buried his blackjack in the bottom of his duffle bag. He didn't need to get caught with something like that after the night's questioning.

Chapter 13 – Life Aboard Ship

Sunday at sea. "This should be a new experience."

There was a Catholic Mass service in the EM mess hall after breakfast. The Protestant service would be after that. The lieutenant said they could skip inspection on Sunday. Joe would have to forgo breakfast and fast.

Joe asked his freshly awake partners if they remembered that girl's name that he met in New York.

"Beats me!"

"I don't even remember Daisy's name. Oops!"

"I forget. Don't you know?"

"Of course I remember her name. It's just better that you forget it if anyone asks."

"What's up?"

"That mugger that tried to shake us down, had the nerve to bring charges against me for assault and battery. A policeman probably arrived and found him messed up. To save himself, he made up the story that he was the victim. I don't think the cop bought it but he reported it anyhow. The zoot heard my name and knew I was an MP. The police followed up on it. As far as I know, he didn't mention the cosh. I'm going to forget I have that for a while and I don't want that lady's name dragged into it."

"Our lips are sealed."

"That's good! I'm off to Mass." He passed Bob Cole and John McInnis walking their beat on his way back up to the mess hall. He took a seat with couple hundred like-minded troops and a few dozen officers.

"Introibo ad altare Dei," said the chaplain.

"To God, the joy of my youth," Joe whispered.

The priest read the familiar Latin words of the Mass. Everyone usually did his or her own thing while the priest did his. There were women here, the first Joe had seen on the voyage. There were some nurses and Red Cross women along with a few WACS. A few field-grade officers' families were aboard also. Most of the faithful made a pretense of following it in the English - Latin missal. They would synchronize when the bells rang or some familiar phrase was spoken. Nearly everyone went to communion. No telling when they would get another chance. He couldn't believe it had been a week, half a continent and half an ocean ago since he last received.

He had an hour before he could eat so he dressed for duty and caught up with some writing. He wrote to his parents and told them about his four nights in New York, Radio City, the Palace and the play. He mentioned Vivian but called her an older woman and left out his adventure in the subway. Some things could wait to be told. What would he say? I got to use Uncle Clarence's blackjack.

He went to the day room and reported to Corporal Badger. It was a quiet shift. The whiskey that the troops had brought on board in their duffle was about run out. Even the officers did not imbibe as much on the Lord's day. The mess hall served roast beef and mashed potatoes at lunchtime and had the traditional cold cut sandwich supper.

Joe went to the card room after his shift but it had been taken over by the 1st squad. Money was running low among the losers so there was a seat for Joe. Cole, Monk and Reilly were playing. There were a couple of others that Joe hadn't met. They were Kensington and Price. Bill Wallace stepped in to deal. He was broke but could make some money dealing. They wanted to play seven-card stud or "down the river," with a dime ante. Two queens were showing on the first deal so Price bet a dime as the first queen. Price bet a dime again on his queen ace. Reilly raised another dime Cole and Kensington folded. They called him Ken. Bill dealt another hand and Joe and Price folded. Reilly bet a quarter with a queen high. Monk saw his quarter and raised him a quarter. Reilly had two pair so he saw Monk's quarter. Bill dealt the last two cards face down. Reilly bet a quarter on his queen. He still only had two pair. Monk saw him and raised a quarter. Reilly saw his quarter and called it. They flipped over their hole cards and Monk showed his full boat with no pairs showing. What a hand! They anteed a dime for the second hand.

Bill dealt again with three kings showing. Monk bet a dime on the first king. Everyone matched him and Bill dealt another hand. Monk bet a quarter on his king ace. Everyone stayed in. Joe bet a quarter on a pair of nines. Bill dealt the last up card. Joe bet a quarter on three 9's. Cole folded with a pair of 6's. Monk folded with his 7's. The next three also folded. Joe didn't have to show his two queens in the hole. Bill never dealt the 7th card. "Great hand but not much of a pot."

They all anteed and Bill dealt the first three cards. Ken bet a dime with an ace. "Ace still bets," and Ken put in a dime. "Ace bets again." Ken kicked in a dime and the others followed. Bill dealt the last card showing. Ken now had a pair of aces. He bet a quarter. Cole and Price folded. Bill dealt the last down card. Ken bet a quarter and the rest folded.

Joe began to win after that and the pots were larger. He had $23 on the table after putting a twenty in his shirt pocket. They called the last hand so the 1st squad could get some sleep. Monk opened for a quarter with the first ace. He opened again for a quarter with a second ace. "Bullets open again for a quarter." Joe had a pair of nines showing. Monk bet a quarter. Cole, Reilly and Ken folded. Joe raised Monks quarter. Price had two pair so he stayed in. Monk called Joe who had to show another full boat, nine high. "That beats my bullets," said Monk. Joe had an ace in the hole. He wasn't drinking. The others were finishing off the pints they brought on-board. Joe got his life vest and went up to the poop deck to catch the end of *The Yellow Rose of Texas* with Roy Rogers and Dale Evans. He wasn't worried about missing most of the movie. He had seen it on base at Fort Wood.

This was the one where the singing cowboy is an insurance investigator sent to find a stash of money lifted from a company payroll. Portraying a performer on a showboat, Roy meets Dale, the daughter of the alleged robber who has recently escaped from prison. Together, Roy and Dale set out to prove her father was wrongly accused and track down the real criminal. So they began the movie on opposite sides of the law and ended with the two of them fighting for truth, justice and the American way. Joe looked off the stern where America was receding rapidly. He went back to deck 3 and hit the sack.

At about 0230 they were all awakened by a combination of horns and sirens. They grabbed their trousers, life vests and helmet liners and tumbled out in the hall. The noise stopped and the loudspeakers shouted, "Man overboard!" They lined up by squad. Lt. Keane came running. Corporal Prosser announced, "Squad 1 present and accounted for." Corporal Badger called out, "Squad 2 present and accounted for." Sergeant Fredrickson went to the dayroom to check on the duty squad. Corporal Bechtel told him ten men were accounted for and he was waiting for Privates Luce and Morgan. The phone rang and Luce and Morgan reported in. Sergeant returned to the cabins and announced, "Squad 3 present and accounted for!" This drill was repeated throughout the ship. A pair of lifeboats was made ready with their crew standing by. It took twenty minutes before the all clear was sounded.

The ship's captain came on the intercom and said this was a serious and dangerous breach of discipline. "If anyone has seen someone throw something overboard, report it to your commanding officer. If anyone is caught throwing anything overboard, you will spend the remainder of your trip in the brig and will be court marshalled when we arrive at our destination. Stand down on boats 1 and 21. That is all."

"Fall out men. First squad prepare for duty."

"Who the hell would pull a stunt like that?" asked Bill.

"I never really thought throwing something overboard would be taken that seriously," said Felix.

"Well now you know!" said Sergeant Fredrickson.

They went back to their cabins and surprisingly got back to sleep after the excitement. Joe woke up early enough to snatch some breakfast before they shut down the chow hall. He went back and prepared for inspection after their day off. Another routine day at sea. They used up their excitement last night. The card players in the day room began to dwindle as the money concentrated among the winners. Joe was able to buy a seat at the table and even leave with a few extra bucks but their kind of card playing wasn't for him. There were too many wild cards and they changed every hand. The cards felt like baloney slices with smudges on the back. He'd rather play penny ante with his buddies.

Tuesday morning began with the headlines in the Hatchet, "IT'S OVER, OVER THERE." Today is VE Day, Victory in Europe. There would be no inspection and duty would be relaxed as much as practical. There was additional information about the peace agreement that was signed yesterday in Rheims, France and today in Berlin. Winston Churchill and the King and Queen greeted the crowds at Buckingham Palace from the balcony. Princess Margaret and Princess Elizabeth celebrated incognito among the crowds. "I wonder if anyone calls Princess Margaret Daisy?" wondered Joe. Two cans of beer were issued to all of the troops on board. These sold for as much as two bucks among fellows who really liked their beer. Joe drank one and sold the other to Felix for a buck.

A special dinner would be served from 14:00 to 18:00 with the menu in the newsletter.

Menu

Appetizers

Shrimp Cocktail ----- Scotch Beef Broth

Salad

Hearts of Lettuce with Russian Dressing

Entrees

Broiled Filet Mignon a La Montgomery

Roast Spring Chicken a La Eisenhower

Sides

Asparagus Polonaise Carrots & Peas

Parisienne Potatoes

Desserts

Baked Alaska

Cookies Fresh Fruit

Beverages

Coffee Tea Cocoa Fresh Milk

Their patrols went without incident. They ignored most of the tipsy troopers, unless they endangered themselves or others and those weren't many. They got an hour off to enjoy the sumptuous dinner. The Special Services troop broke out a cache of records and played music in the chow hall all afternoon. Some of the soldiers lounged on the 3" and 5" gun mounts on deck and bragged about how they would like to bag a German U boat. These guns had remained unused since their installation. The ship relied on her speed to keep out of harm's way. Joe asked for a deck of cards from one of the Special Services troopers, a cute brunette named Kathy.

An impromptu talent show developed in the chow hall after dinner. Many acts were three or four soldiers lip-syncing Andrew Sister's songs. There were some really good dance acts, primarily tap dancers. "Who carries tap shoes with them?" Joe mused. There were jugglers and an amateur magician or two. Several soldiers could really belt out a tune. One fellow sang "I'll Walk With God" from the *Student Prince* that brought tears to your eyes. Joe and his partner went by the chow hall as much as they could on their patrols.

He went to the day room after his shift and filled a vacant seat at the poker table. He said that he picked up a new deck from Special Services and since their deck was so worn, they might want to use a new deck. One guy said, "but this is our lucky deck" but he reluctantly agreed to the new deck. Joe was careful not to contribute to the large pots and win a steady stream of smaller pots. They ended the game after midnight and Joe walked away with $45. He returned a couple nights later and there was an empty chair. He asked if it was okay if he sat in. "That's Fred's chair. He's coming right back."

"Well, let me just play until Fred comes back."

"Fred don't like a hot chair. Why don't you find another game?"

Joe saw he wasn't wanted and walked over to one of the writing desks. He wasn't going to let them run him off. He picked up some writing paper and began a letter to his family. Fred never did come back to finish the poker game.

May 10, 1945

Dear Mom and Dad,

It doesn't matter when I write to you on this trip. The letter isn't going in the mail until we get to England. We've been at sea on this "luxury" liner for nearly a week now. You get used to being out of sight of land after a couple of days. The MP's have been on duty every day we've been at sea. It's not bad though. It gives us better hours in the chow hall and it keeps us in touch with the whole ship. If we didn't patrol, we'd probably spend every day in a card game. I have been doing well at cards, too good in fact. I was just froze out of a game for winning too much the other night. I'll go back to playing penny ante with my friends. I am bunking with the same three guys I hung out with at Fort Wood.

This ship we're on, USAT *George Washington*, goes back to 1908 and it was built in Germany. Funny thing is it was named after our president from the beginning. The US took possession of it in WWI and turned it around as a troop transport. We gave it to England for a while and they couldn't make it work so we took it back and changed the boilers to oil fired. They added big guns but I don't think they were ever fired in anger.

VE Day was a big deal here on the ship. They had a festive menu in the chow hall and we had more time to spend eating it. There was a talent show after the meals ended. It was a lot of fun. I don't know when we'll get to England, maybe four more days and then a day or two to get to France. It just doesn't seem like it should take this long. I hope Chuck is doing well. I feel certain that he is somewhere off Okinawa. We see it frequently in the newsreels but we have no updates since we left New York City. They have a broadsheet called the "Hatchet" that gives us some news and the movie schedules. They printed the VE Day menu in it. I got a couple copies. I will send you one later on from Europe. I just realized that today is Ascension Thursday and I completely forgot about going to Mass. I think I'll call it a day. Give my regards to Jim and Patsy.

Love,
Joe

He couldn't figure out why he was feeling so blue on Saturday. He chalked it up to being at sea for eight days then he realized that it was the day of Daisy's prom. She would be with Bobby Pavlat tonight, a bird in the hand...He ought to write her so he'd have a letter on the way when they dock. They kept doing the same thing every day. It let up a little bit on Sunday when they had church service instead of inspection. They got through today's inspection with no sweat. It must be boring for Lt. Keane also. It's the only time we get to see him though unless something goes wrong like that man overboard the other night. Joe and his buddies went to the chow hall before their shift began. Their first posting after noon was roving patrol on the upper decks. The weather had turned sour and they had to wear rain gear and life vests. Now and then, a wave would wash over the forecastle. They really shouldn't be up here. They hung onto a cable and stayed far away from the rail. Occasionally, they would help somebody up who had lost his footing. They called Cpl. Badger and told him that conditions were too dangerous to be on deck. They requested permission to stand guard inside the passage. The corporal came up and looked at the situation and agreed with his sentries. They had to keep their life vests on in case a situation developed that required them to go on deck.

"Joe, what kind of a situation would cause you to go out on deck?"

"That has me stumped too, Felix. I can't think of a thing out there that I want or need. I'm really happy in here." They took off their life vests and ponchos and set them nearby. Occasionally an officer would come to take a look outside and they would say, "You don't want to go out there sir," and that would be it. They got no disagreement. They were glad when they got back down to patrolling their own deck. Guys were getting sick left and right. The ship's crew set buckets of coarse sawdust around to throw on top of vomit to clean up later. Most everyone found things to do in their cabin so they could sit or lie quietly. Supper was an exercise in balance and agility. If you were lucky enough to sit, your drink wanted to meander around your tray. If you had to stand, you had to keep yourself and your drink upright while trying to hit your mouth with your fork. Any rougher than this and the cooks would fall back on serving sandwiches.

He went to the day room after his shift ended and wrote Daisy a letter. He told her about leaving New York and the joy of VE Day and a little about life aboard ship. He said that he hoped that she was having a wonderful time at her prom and he imagined how beautiful she looked in her prom dress. "Thank you so much for wearing it to the Woody Herman dance." He didn't want to say anything about Bobby. That was best unsaid. He hoped that his mail would be catching up with him soon because he missed her letters.

He went to Mass early enough the next morning to catch the chaplain hearing confession. "Bless me Father for I have sinned. My last confession was about five weeks ago. I missed Mass on Thursday."

"Did you miss Mass deliberately?"

"No. I just forgot about it."

"Well, then it's not a sin. Is it?"

"No."

"Is there anything else going on in your life?"

"I've met a couple of real fine girls. I punched a thief and ran away from him. I've been doing well playing poker."

"Sounds pretty normal to me. Say an Our Father and Hail Mary just for drill. Go and sin no more. Now say an Act of Contrition."

That was it. He read his book, *The Razor's Edge,* while he waited for Mass to begin. The priest talked about the joy of VE Day in his sermon and the need to help rebuild Europe when they arrive there. He asked the congregation to do their part in the restoration. Southern fried chicken was on the menu today but it was baked because they couldn't take a chance with a kettle of boiling grease in rough seas. There was also boiled okra and he didn't know what to make of that. He ate it even if it was a bit slimy. The sea was still rough and it would have been uncomfortable to eat standing up. They went on watch at noon and were told ahead of time to stay inside unless there's an emergency. The passengers must be getting used to the situation or they're hiding out because there wasn't so much sawdust on the deck. The news was that this was their last full day at sea. They would be seeing land soon.

He got together in their card room for a friendly game of penny ante poker. Everyone could still afford that. They mused over what it would be like seeing a port the next day. They knew they must remain on board unless they could figure some ruse to get off board. They'd be on duty most of the day anyhow.

Monday dawned and they found themselves in the Irish Sea. Most of them had never heard of the Irish Sea. Ireland was off the port bow and England was on the starboard. It was tantalizing but they weren't scheduled to enter the River Mersey until 22:00. The ship would anchor in the roads overnight and move into port on Tuesday morning. It was almost mystical that they could continue sailing all day and still not reach their destination. The rest of the activity was normal. Lieutenant Keane had his inspection. They stood their watch from noon until 20:00 but they spent as much time as they could seeing the hills come in and out of the mist. Occasionally their vision would clear and that vision would persist long after the clouds closed it up again. Supper consisted of ham and beans. They hoped for fresh food tomorrow but Joe wondered if they could really expect that much with the shortages that were experienced in Great Britain.

Joe wound up the day going to the movie on the poop deck. They had nicknamed it the Poopadrome. The movie was "The Canterville Ghost" with Margaret O'Brien (his favorite) and Charles Laughton. It was about a cowardly ghost destined to haunt the castle forever. Miss O'Brien lived in the castle, which was taken over by Yankee GI's as their headquarters. The misty weather and movements of the ship added to the charm of the movie. The ship dropped its anchor midway through the film. The long blacked out lights of the harbor twinkled again on the horizon. The movie wound up with the ghost bravely riding a blockbuster bomb to his death and his soul was freed for eternity. The guys tried to make out what they could of the shore and gave up to hit the sack. They were awakened by a strange vibration in the morning as the ship weighed anchor. A pilot joined them from the pilot boat as two little tugboats snuggled alongside the transport for its journey into the harbor. Joe was in time to have breakfast this morning. It was easy to find a seat at a table since so many guys avoided breakfast. He went back on deck to check things out.

This was at a time when every berth had a ship alongside, vessels were waiting off the Port to enter, and they were inching toward the locks on the Liverpool side of the river. There were endless queues of lories on the Dock Road, stretching as far as the eye could see bringing the lifeblood of Great Britain in from the sea. This idea of locks was new to Joe. The tugboats helped to thread the great ship into a lock for its passage into the lagoon that held their dock. The waterfront was built like a fort with solid granite walls. The locks isolated the dock area from the vagaries of Mersey River tide. The tugboats pushed the ship around a tight turn and up to the Hornby Dock. The tugboats left through the lock to wherever tugboats go until they are needed again.

The damage to the port was extensive but was mainly limited to the support buildings like the customs house. It was the first time Joe had seen a bombed city. Saint Luke's Church was destroyed with incendiary bombs but this was all before January 1942 when the attacks ended and Hitler turned his attention to Russia. Enough of this! Joe had to get back below for inspection. The lieutenant remarked that their brass was getting a bit green so they got out the Brasso to shine their buckles and collar devices. It was time for lunch and then they were on duty. They looked forward to their patrols today especially the time they could spend on deck. The smoking lamp was out today so they would have to pay attention to that.

There were designated areas where the smokers could pursue their habit. They received a popular music radio station over the radio and it was broadcast throughout the ship. It lent a festive air to the day.

Five hundred passengers would disembark during the day and the rest would sail to LeHavre on the high tide tomorrow. Many thought it would just be an overnight to LeHavre but it was a fifty-hour trip. Today was time to view the complexity of the port. The gathering of war ships preparing to sail back home was fantastic. The returning troopships would mainly evacuate liberated POWs, the sick and injured. The armies left in Europe were trying to reorganize and restore law and order to a wild west scene of disorder. Joe's first patrol was on the smelly fuel deck where no one ever went. It smelt worse in port without the ventilation gained from the ships movement. Duty on deck got to be disagreeable in a short time knowing there were all those British pubs out there just out of reach. Only the Merchant Marine crew could go ashore in two alternate watches. No one would ever trust a thousand soldiers loose on the town.

They made do with a couple movies. Joe was getting tired of poker all the time. He went to see *Bathing Beauty* with Esther Williams. "They say her language would make a sailor blush," thought Joe. The galley provided popcorn for the viewers and a can of beer each was passed out to the troops. You had to think twice about drinking it because it was still worth a couple bucks if you chose to sell it. Joe decided it would taste pretty good with the popcorn. The fog set in around 22:00 and by 23:00, it was uncomfortably damp.

The great ship cast off at 09:00 and they went topside to view the port activity. The tugboats were on hand to guide the ship back out through the locks. Joe and his buddies had to go back to the dayroom to receive their assignments. Joe got to go back on deck again as the ship left the harbor of the River Mersey. He said to Felix, "We can say we've been to England now and France is straight ahead." He worked his shift as the land fell off behind the ship. He went to the library and wrote Daisy a letter. He should have written more to her a couple days ago before they entered English waters.

May 16, 1945

Dear Daisy,

The letter is not going in the mail until we get to France in a couple of days. We just spent a day in the Port of Liverpool. We had to remain on board and just look at the dock activity all day. The docks look absolutely Medieval like they had been here forever, solid granite. I wonder how old they are. We got a can of beer out of it to celebrate. Somebody threw something off the ship a few nights ago and it upset the whole ship. Everyone had to fall out at two in the morning while they counted noses. They take it serious. I'm anxious to get to France with solid ground under my feet.

It was hard thinking of you on your prom night but I don't begrudge you having fun. I just hope Bobby treated you like a lady. You are a lady to me. Time to go now.

Love,
Joe

He went topside to see what was happening at the Poopadrome. The *Fighting Sullivans* was playing. What a movie to be shown onboard a ship. It was about the five Sullivan brothers who grew up in Iowa and insisted on serving in the Navy together wherever they wound up. They served on the

USS *Juneau* that was sunk at Guadalcanal in 1942. What were they thinking to ask for an assignment like that? They were survived by their sisters. There was a short movie before it with the Kay Kaiser band and Ish Kabibble played the coronet and clowned around. It was difficult watching the *Sullivan* movie and he was so glad the war was over for him. His heart went out for his brother, Chuck , who was still in the middle of it. The movie wound up and the fog had chased them down. All of the metalwork on deck was wet with dew. He was off to bed.

They were going north in the English Channel in the morning. They were still out of sight of land but there was a lot of ship traffic, both military and civilian. The lieutenant advised them to take a shower and get cleaned up before going ashore because the facilities in the camps on land are going to be primitive and crowded. This was at inspection in the morning. They had an hour off before mealtime. He was tempted to write to Vivian but decided against it. No sense getting into another long distance relationship. Felix challenged him to a game of Cribbage and he took him up on it. That made the time go quickly until lunch. They served beef stew but it didn't exactly taste like beef. He thought it may be canned beef but a server told him it was mutton. That's what they get for stopping in Britain. It was time to go on shift and he and Bill wound up guarding the officer's mess at noon. Not much going to happen at that time of day. The fog from last night was just beginning to clear. They could see the ships coming at them at a distance now instead of appearing alongside them.

Joe began to get a cold. His coughing was disturbing the other three guys at night so he went by sickbay after his shift. The Navy corpsman on duty gave him a party-size bottle of GI cough syrup and a jar of Vicks Vapo-rub. He rubbed the Vicks on his chest and took a swig of the red syrup. It had codeine in it. The corpsman also gave him a bottle of APC's, Army jargon for all-purpose capsules. Back home we called them aspirin. He was told to take them if he had a fever and he didn't think he did. He woke up too late for breakfast and got in line to take a shower. He heard that they were in sight of land. He shampooed, showered and shaved. He put fresh Wildroot Cream Oil in his hair and combed his Pompadour just so. He was ready for inspection. The sergeant told them to report to the day room instead of inspecting their quarters. He and the lieutenant inspected the troops and only a couple guys got gigs, which were soon corrected.

The lieutenant told them that they would be disembarking from the ship later this afternoon. "You'll be transported to Camp Lucky Strike about fifty miles up the river by truck or rail. It's only a two-hour trip. There are thousands of troops there already who have faced the Battle of the Bulge or been liberated from POW camps. All their effort will be directed toward these men. Don't expect anyone to be concerned about your welfare. You're just a bump in the road on their way home. They see you getting off a cushy ocean liner and they have trucked and marched across France to get here. You'll just be there a day or two and then you will travel to your permanent assignment. Any questions?"

"Do they know we're coming for supper?" Everyone laughed.

"They know that another two thousand troops are coming for a visit. Yes. They're expecting you. Anything else? Dismissed!"

Joe was hungry so he wore his helmet liner and went to the chow hall to see if he could eat with the KP's. They said, "Sure, come on in." He served himself some rice and chili con carne with corn bread. He sat with the KP's and conjectured about what they were getting into when they docked in France. These fellows were combat engineers and would be joining the 488th Engineer Company that was already in country. They had no illusions. They would be clearing landmines, rubble and debris. There was lots of unexploded ordinance to find and destroy. The British had dropped 12,000 tons of bombs on the area. When they finally saw the harbor, they had trouble identifying anything. It looked like a gigantic bulldozer had pushed through the city.

Joe's first two-hour tour was on deck. The pilot boat brought the pilot to the ship and then remained in front of the ship to guide it through the sunken ship hazards in the outer harbor. A pair of little tugs joined the ship to lend a hand. The pilot boat pulled away and the tugs pushed the ship into a dock. It turned out not to be a dock but a canal and a huge gate pushed across the opening. The ship came to a stop with the tugs trying to keep it still. By now, it was 14:00 and Joe was relieved to take a post below deck. He could feel the ship beginning to move again and he tried to plot it's movements in his mind. The ship moved forward carefully playing dodgem with partially sunken ships. Workboats and men with cutting torches were working to clear wreckage. Joe was back on deck again at 16:00 when there was an announcement for everyone to come by the mess halls for a sandwich. They didn't know where their next meal was coming from and even a baloney and cheese sandwich was welcome. The dockhands secured the bow and stern lines to the bollards on the dock. A gangway was rolled up to the ship. The corporal of the guard came along and told them to secure their station and grab a sandwich. “We’ll leave the ship as a unit and form up on the dock. Then we’ll march to our transportation. You got it?”

“Right corporal!”

Part Three

Chapter 14 – Uncle Bill Conrad

They got rid of their AWOL bags and slung their newly issued musette bags over their shoulders. It contained the same stuff, shaving gear, a toothbrush and a change of underwear. They now had to carry GI mess kits and tableware. Joe had a new book after reading *Lost Horizons*. He picked up *Animal Farm,* a short one and *Cannery Row* by John Steinbeck. They wore their helmets, spats and armbands proving to everyone they were newly-minted Military Police. Full canteens were added to their pistol belts. They formed up on the pier in three squads of thirteen and marched to the railhead across the street from the dock. "They're freight trains!" They exclaimed nearly as one. They couldn't believe their eyes. The sergeant said, "Relax men. We only have an hour ride. It's 56 kilometers to Camp Lucky Strike."

"That don't sound so lucky to me."

"Quit your griping. We have two cars. First squad goes in the forward car with all of the bags. Second and third squads go in the second car."

"That's 26 men! Where are you riding?"

"These are made for forty men. It says so on the side. The lieutenant and I will travel in the forward car with First squad."

Sure enough, a board on the side of the car read, "HOMME 40, CHEVAUX 8." "What's a chevaux?"

"That's a French horse, Champ."

"Oh great! We're travelling in horse cars. Those must be tiny Frenchmen to fit in there with their eight horses. Are we really riding in those things?" The grey painted cars were about twenty-feet long and eight feet wide. They only have four wheels instead of the eight that Americans were used to seeing. The wheels were fixed by leaf springs to the bottom of the car. They don't need to swivel with that short of a wheelbase. They seem to have airbrakes because there was a heavy duty hose connected between cars. The couplers were a hook and loop arrangements with fat mushroom bumpers separating the cars. The inside of the cars were recently painted white as if that would erase the smell of death of the thousands of Jews transported east in these cars. It was also a blank canvas for a graffiti artist like the one who wrote, "Kilroy was here" on the end of the car.

"First squad, pile in the forward car and stack the duffle in the front of the car." The second and third squads tossed there duffle bags in the front car while Cole, McInnes and Munk piled them up. Charley Boll and Gary Haag opened the panels on the topside to let some air into the car. The last two squads jumped into the second car. There were twenty boxcars on their little train and a flat car with two Red Cross Clubmobiles. Around 300 more soldiers climbed on the train for the short trip to Camp Lucky Strike. The locomotive whistle tooted and their car jerked into motion. They were in the sixth car back and the black smoke swirled around them as the train chugged up the grade from the waterfront. Joe began to cough and couldn't stop. He took a swig of his cough syrup that he carried in his new bag. That seemed to take care of it.

The train followed a canal from the harbor past acres of bombed out rubble. "These tracks must have been torn up too." Joe was amazed that they were working again. There was a couple inches of straw on the floor of the car. "Careful of your smokes, guys." They took turns looking out the openings of the car. Once they got away from the city, it was kind of pretty with only a bomb crater now and then. The canal joined the River Seine where the train turned north and soon Felix announced they were passing though Bolbec. It had seen better days but he saw signs of new construction. The same went for Fauville-en-Caux, which appeared on the next railroad station they passed. Valmont was the next station. Joe looked out the opening and saw an industrial area like chemical plants that seemed to be operating with steam venting from various stacks. He hoped they made fertilizer. France would be needing it. They soon pulled into Cany-Barville where they could see Camp Lucky Strike. It seemed to stretch to the horizon, a sea of green tents. There were several transfer camps in France and all named after cigarette brands.

A truck took their duffle bags into the camp and two of the fellows rode along to guard them. Lt. Keane insisted on that. The rest of the company formed up into marching order along with the rest of the occupants and paraded into the camp. Joe thought his unit looked the best. The camp was huge, tents as far as you could see. The camp was centered about a German airstrip that had the bomb craters repaired. The traffic was as bad as in New York City. It was very dangerous to those pedestrians that would risk crossing the street without paying attention to traffic directions. They would be flattened like a pancake. The permanent party MPs had their hands full. Occasionally the airstrip would clear of traffic and a plane would land. They passed a cobblestone pad where duffle bags were being stacked. Jack Sadler and Paul Munk were guarding them. They entered a hospital-sized tent with a dozen desks in it with signs designating units. The 203rd MP Co. was represented. A sergeant and a captain sat at the desk.

The sergeant stood up and gave them a brief orientation about the camp.

"This tent city is divided into four sections: A, B, C, and D. Each section has around 3000 tents under which are housed about 15,000 men. The Red Cross has offices in the neighborhoods: nurses and girls who serve hot coffee, cake, and newspapers day and night. There are also saloons: one for officers, another for NCOs and a beer garden for soldiers. They serve the best liqueurs, as well as Coca-Cola, whiskey, gin, and American beer. The bars are open from 19:00 to 22:00. Each sector has its own auditorium, which serves as a theater, cinema, and chapel. Catholic service is at 08:00 Sunday. Protestant services are at 9:30 and Jewish service is at 11:00. Any questions?"

"When can we eat?"

"You get a meal card for three meals a day. You eat when you can. When you leave here, a guide will take you to your tent. You will have three squad tents. Don't get attached to them. You will only be here for a day. We're moving 10,000 men a day in and out of here. Six thousand will leave on that ship you just brought in. Now file past the desk with your orders in your hand. We need to check them. Then go grab your duffle and follow your guide to your tent area. Oh! One more thing.

You weenies have just got here after a luxury ocean voyage. The majority of the men here have fought their way from Normandy to Berlin and back. They're not going to take any crap off you so give them wide berth."

They left the tent and a grizzled old soldier walked up to Joe and said, "You're Charlie Conrad's kid. Is it Joe or Jim?" His dark worn face could use a shave. A cigarette hung from his lips. His fatigue uniform was freshly washed but tattered.

"How do you know me? Oh my God! Uncle Billy! Yeah! I'm Joe."

"I saw you in that parade coming in and I recognized your face. You put on a swell parade for a bunch of green soldiers. Are you bound for Germany?"

"Isn't everybody?"

"Not me. I'm out of here. Back to the US of A on that boat you came in on."

"How do you know what I came in on?"

"We keep tabs on the comings and goings. I've got my orders for the USAT *George Washington*. Is she a good ship? Anything is better than a liberty ship. They're going to pack us in like sardines."

"Uncle Billy! I gotta go find my tent. Where can I meet you?"

"Le Manureva Bar! Just think of manure. This place is full of it. I'll be there 'till ten – drunk as a skunk I hope."

"I'll be there, " and Joe joined his platoon to march to the tent area. There was a tent for each squad. The sergeant bunked with the 1st squad rather than try to fit in the NCO tent. The lieutenant got a bunk in an officer's tent. There was a blanket on each bunk. The weather was mild and they would be here for a night. The sergeant told them they were on their own until inspection at 11:00 in the morning."

"We can't do without that inspection. Can we fellas?"

"If they don't inspect you, you'll just go to seed like a dandelion. What are you up to Joe?"

"I'm going to have that sandwich I brought along from the ship and then go to Le Manureva Bar to meet my Uncle Billy."

"You've got an uncle here?"

"I do now! He landed on Omaha Beach with the 29th Division but he's taking our boat back home."

"If that don't beat all! You travel halfway around the world and run into a relative. You can't get away with nothing"

Joe padlocked his duffle bag to his cot. "Like that's going to do a lot of good." He went to the latrine to wash some of the cinders out of his hair and neck. His face actually looked a little blackened. The wash rack was outdoors, just a long shallow trough with a spigot every two feet and a little bit of a mirror over every other one. Bare light bulbs were hung above but it was still light out. Is this the same day they left the ship? What a world of change. He made his way back to his bunk. It was easy to get turned around here with row after row of identical tents. They seemed to be all fresh troops in his quadrant so he was unlikely to encounter anxious veterans. He ate his sandwich and the peanut butter cookie the ship provided. He decided to find his way to the mess tent so he could find it when he was hungry in the morning. It was as big as the reception tent with a chow line at each end and rows of standup tables in between. They didn't want you lounging around here. The tables were half occupied. He took them to be French men and women that were serving the food and cleaning up the eating areas.

He moved to the airstrip to find La Manureva. A signpost pointed the way to the mess hall he just left. It pointed to the PX, the Red Cross tent, the cinema, several bars including Le Manureva, La Moulin Rouge, Café Laffite and Le Bombay Bar. Joe followed the signs to Uncle Billy's hangout. The tent was packed with humanity jostling for drinks at the plywood bar. Most of them wore khaki uniforms. Little tea box tables were set on the side of the tent opposite the bar. Blue, red and green light bulbs were hung with the clear bulbs to create some sort of "atmosphere." It just made people's faces look peculiar. French women made the rounds picking up glasses and orders and taking the teasing of the troops. They didn't mind the jibes. Anything was better than occupation by le Boche. That's where he found Uncle Billy and three other sergeants from his battalion. They were all in fatigues. Nobody hassled them. When he looked around, he saw nothing, but three stripers. He asked if it was okay for him to be here in the NCO bar.

"You're my guest. Anyone give you any guff, their ass is mine. Grab a stool. Mademoiselle? Drinks for my nephew, s'il vous plait. Whatcha having Joe?"

"Rye whiskey, water side. Old Overholt if they have it."

"You drink like a man. Who taught you that? Your old man? What's Charlie doing these days?"

"Dad is back to driving a locomotive on the Pennsy after that layoff in the thirties. We have a house on 26th Street now."

"That's good to hear. The last time I saw Martha and Charlie was at the reunion on Presque Isle in '41. I was working in Cleveland then and then I joined the Army in '42. We trained and bothered the British for a couple years before D-day."

"How did that go for you? It must have been hell."

"It was hell alright. That's where I picked up my Purple Heart and a Bronze Star. After that, I learned to keep my ass down and we made it through. Right guys? The other sergeants affirmed his story. All the survivors gathered against the bluff and ran up a ravine together. A lot of men didn't make it but when we got to the top, we were behind the Krauts and just picked them off. There was still plenty more ahead of us. We never ran out of Jerry's until we got to Berlin. Then they began rushing us back here as if our pants were on fire but I'm glad to be here. Right guys?"

Mademoiselle brought their drinks and Joe downed one shot and put the glass back on her tray. The other drink he took to sip. Bill put a dollar on her tray and said, "Keep the change, Darling, and bring us another round, s'il vous plait."

"Did they tell you that MPs came ashore on D-Day?"

"They mentioned it." said Joe.

"Yeah! Some even came in with the airborne units. They had backpacks full of 'Off Limit' signs to put on all of the bars and brothels before the infantry got there. I'm just kidding. They did a lot of good, directing traffic and clearing up jams. They would stand out there with their whistle and white gloves keeping the trucks going. It was as if their MP armbands protected them from rifle bullets. They had balls. As we moved forward and took Jerry prisoners, the MPs would come in behind us and herd them up. Right guys?"

"Right Bill!"

"You know, Joe? You're the last of a long line of Conrad soldiers going back to Captain William Conrad in the American Revolution. He had a fort named after him in Pennsylvania. It wasn't much more than a blockhouse but it was his blockhouse. That was in the Indian War before the revolution."

"I didn't know that. Is he related?"

"He certainly is. The government gave him land near Easton after the war as a bonus."

"Are Conrads living there now? I never heard of that."

"No. Two spinster sisters owned it after the Civil War and they never married because there were no men of their class in the area to marry and they didn't care for what was left. I guess the county or the state got the farm. Enough about history. What have you been up to Joe?"

"I began training to fly. I studied to be a radio operator in a B-24. Mom, Dad, Pat and Jim came out to Scott Field when I finished school. Then, the Air Corps didn't need me. They had enough weenies to bomb Germany. They offered me MP school or transfer to the Pacific. That was a no-brainer. One Conrad in the Pacific is enough. So, I got an eight-week course in keeping the infantry out of trouble and they sent me here. I met a girl named Daisy when I was at Leonard Wood and we had a torrid courtship for three weeks before I had to leave. It seemed like her family was courting me. Daisy and I went to a dance a couple days before I left. Woody Herman's band played that night. I took the train to New York City with my buddies and we had a great time. We stayed at a hotel for four nights and took in the sights. I met another girl but that was only for a night. We got into trouble and I had to use Uncle Clarence's blackjack to get out of it."

"How did that go? Why the blackjack?"

"Some mook tried to stick up me and the girl at a subway stop. He had a switchblade and I had the cosh and I broke his wrist. My partner kicked his knife onto the tracks. The guy had the nerve to try to bring charges against me for assault. My commander put it down as mistaken identity. The mook said I was with a prostitute and she was really an art student." They all got a kick out of that story. Joe started coughing because he was talking too loud. It was tough being heard in that tent. A bit of rye took care of it.

"How is Clarence doing?" asked Billy.

"He keeps himself busy. Did you ever hear any more about who had it in for Uncle Clem? It was six years ago but it was on Joe's mind much of the time he was in New York."

"No. That is still a mystery. I'm not sure that all Clem did there was on the up and up. Just sayin'! How about another?"

"Keep them coming but let me pay the next round."

"Your money's no good here soldier. They only take NCO gelt."

The waitress said it was last call so Billy asked for another one for the road. "Merci beaucoup. I parlez-vous the hell out of this language." Joe just groaned.

"What do you hear from your brother Chuck? Did he fight at Iwo Jima?" asked Bill.

"I don't think he did. I don't hear much but what my folks tell me. I think he went right from the Philippines to Okinawa. That scares the hell out of me with all those kamikazes crashing into ships. He only writes home because his letters would never find me."

They parted outside the tent. Billy and his buddies were nearly home. "Au revoir neveu."

"Bonsoir oncle," said Joe as he walked to the runway and made his way to the tent. His muscle memory knew the way. Most of the squad was already there since their walk from the saloon was shorter.

"What's it like to talk with a war hero?" asked Mike.

"Mike, there are a million war heroes passing through this camp on their way home. Uncle Bill was pretty low key about it. He just said he kept a minimum profile after he got out of Normandy with a bullet in his backside. We talked about historic Conrad soldiers. He said there was a Captain William Conrad in the Revolution who had a fort named after him in Pennsylvania. That and we drank a lot. They seemed to be familiar with the waitress. It was a NCO club and I felt odd for being there but there was no one going to challenge me with those four guys."

Bill said, "We tried a bit of everything, didn't we guys? I never saw so many brands of liquor before and good stuff too. I liked the Benedictine and Brandy. It was smooth."

The lights went out. "I guess that's a hint to go to sleep."

Chapter 15 – Donut Dollies

Joe awoke to a glorious day, bright and sunny. Mike and Bill were already awake. Bill gave Felix a shake and said, "Come on lazy bones. It's time to get up." They did a minimum cleanup. They had plenty of time to shave later. They walked to the mess tent, which was close to the runway for logistical reasons. The runway was the highway from which, all good things flow. The serving line was short. It was still early and there was little incentive to get up early unless your ship was leaving. The food was labeled in French to give them a sense of place. A duty sergeant punched their meal tickets. The servers were mature French women, maybe in their late twenties or early thirties. First, a cup of café noir. He held out his mess kit and chose œuf et bacon. It was pronounced like *erf*. Then he chose some dry pain m grille. They had no toaster so they browned the bread on the grill. It was the famous crusty bread of the French. That was all his mess kit would hold. He walked to one of the long standup tables made of bare pine boards stained from too much jam, jelly and ketchup. It was clean, just funny colored, somewhat expressionistic and abstract at that. This is France after all.

The guys ate with little ceremony. They went to the cleanup station afterwards. There was a garbage can to scrape your pan. Nothing to scrape. Then there was another garbage can filled with soapy water and an oil-fired immersion heater to keep it hot. Joe scrubbed his kit out with a GI brush, the same kind they used for toilets. The mess kit had a folding handle on which, to hang the cover and silverware. Joe dipped it in a heated clear water rinse and it was done. The kit was so hot it dried in seconds and you could put it back into your musette bag. They went back to the tent and then the latrine to shower and shave. The water was cold so the shower was brief. They didn't know when they'd see another one. It took Joe's breath away and he began to cough. "You got something for that cold, Joe?"

"I'll have a swig of cough syrup back at the tent."

They took a walk around their area, avoiding the veteran's turf. The veterans would laugh if they knew the new guys were wary of them. They found the movie tent although they wouldn't be seeing any movies today. The Red Cross tent was nearby so they stopped in to see the Donut Dollies. They outnumbered the men at this early hour. They were gathering here before journeying into France and Germany. The guys picked up a cup of coffee in a real china cup that didn't burn your lips when you drank from it. They helped themselves to the doughnuts and sat down to talk to the ladies. There was a group of five who came up by truck yesterday. Their Red Cross Clubmobiles were on the boy's train from LeHavre. They were from all over the States. One was from Miami, Florida. "I didn't think anybody was from Miami," said Felix. Her name was Carolle Frieze. She told them about their introduction to France.

"We had to learn how to drive an ambulance before leaving England. Then, they put us in the hold of a Liberty Ship. We didn't travel first class as you fellows. We ran into a storm and the captain had us evacuated into a landing craft but we had to hitchhike to the port to find our Clubmobiles. They were taken to LeHavre. They are filled with cigarettes and toiletries that we are trying to protect from pilferage. They are worth a king's ransom. We will ride on the train with them to the field hospital at Metz. That's as close as we could get to the German border. They're not ready for us in Germany yet. We're just waiting for the next train east. It shouldn't be long with so many guys coming here and they're filling the trains with food and medicine to send to Luxemburg, Belgium and Germany."

Carolle was a prophetess as well as good looking. Her pretty face was framed by short, curly blond hair. She had an upturned nose and a few freckles to accent it. They were told they would be shipping to Germany when they got back to the tent. The second squad was going to Company C of the 713th MP Battalion in Munich with Corporal Chuck Badger. The first and third squads were going to Frankfurt. Lieutenant Keane was going to Frankfurt along with Sergeant Fredrickson. "The train leaves at 12:00 so get some chow before we leave," said Badger. "Oh yeah. You can forget about inspection. Just look sharp when we move out."

"Does the train have a dining car, Boss?"

"Sure it does along with a club car and each of you get a Pullman roomette. Any other questions?" asked Badger.

We had a couple hours to kill before going to the chow hall again. I repacked my duffle bag and floated the overcoat up near the top even though it was May. It would be colder as we travel away from the Gulf Stream. We made a stop at the PX tent to fill our musette bags with candy bars and snacks. I bought a couple boxes of Cracker Jacks even though they were bulky. I just liked them. We went to the chow tent and had this beef stew they called *veal ragout*. There was a basket full of baguettes and we each took a whole loaf so we would have some for the train. There was some hard cheese that looked like it would travel well so we took a bit of that also. Corporal

Badger told us to fall out on the runway with all of our gear at 1130.

When the time came, we dutifully lined up on the edge of the runway with traffic zooming by us and around us. Thirteen of us in our MP helmet liners and unwieldy bags on our shoulders moved out amid the derisive comments of the passing veterans. "You go, guys!" "Go get you some Nazis, fellas."

They marched to the end of the runway and into the rail yard. There was their train, the locomotive puffing and wheezing. A railroad engine is like a living being. Even while stopped, the boiler feed water pump continued to supply high-pressure feed water to the boiler, bump – bump...bump – bump. It had a distinctive odor of hot metal, lubricant, steam and the sulfurous soft coal, maybe even the sweat of the crew. A little 4-4-0 engine pulled twenty boxcars and one flat car with two Clubmobiles. "You know what that means, Joe?"

"Yeah, I hear you."

They had a whole boxcar to themselves. They threw their bags on board and clambered up inside. They piled their bags at the head end of the car. They brought their blankets along. They were getting settled when Sergeant Fredrickson came to the door and said, "I need three volunteers." Nobody spoke. "One more time and then I'll pick three."

Joe had pretty good luck with volunteering so he said, "I'm in." Bill and Felix reluctantly volunteered.

"I need you to ride in the third car with the Red Cross women to guard their cargo."

Mike said, “Wait a minute, Sarge. We’re a matched set, a fire team. I gotta go also.”

“Okay, Schneider! You go too and bring a case of rations with you. Leave your duffle in here. There’s not that much room in the other car.” There were three cases of mountain rations in the car for them to eat along the way. There was a whole boxcar loaded with them on the train. They were supposed to provide three meals for four men. They were bulkier than the normal K rations. They proved to be more than the average man could eat. They included powdered soup and milk, canned meat and butter, cereal, chocolate, biscuits, compressed fruits, sugar, tea and coffee and powdered lemon. They walked back toward the engine to the third boxcar with the open door. “Not much room. Sounds cozy.”

Sergeant Fredrickson knocked on the boards and said, “Ladies, I brought these men to ride along with you.” It was Carolle who answered, “What, do you think we can’t take care of ourselves? Now we have to fight off four of your soldiers too. Why didn’t you bring the whole squad. We can entertain them also.”

“Come on boys and climb in. This shouldn’t be a long trip. You’re Joe and that’s Felix. Who are these other dudes?”

“This is Bill Wallace and that is Mike Schneider. Bill is an oilman from Texas and Mike is a sheriff out of Mississippi. We’re all destined for Munich.”

“Well boys, I’m Carolle and these are my sidekicks, donut dollies in training. We climbed down a cargo net into a landing craft in a storm and made a landing in Normandy. A photographer from *Life Magazine* took our picture. We had to hitchhike to LeHavre to find our clubmobiles. They were loaded with cigarettes so it was like searching for Hitler's gold. Any who, this is Sandra Stalter from Buffalo and that's Mary Ruth Manchester from New Hampshire. The other two are Kathleen Donahue and Betty Ann Crocket." They were dressed in dark green uniforms, a tunic and skirt. Kathleen and Betty Ann wore sensible jodhpur riding slacks. They did nothing to flatter their hips but they were good for climbing up the two-foot step into the car. A cap not unlike the German soft cap perched on their heads with a ribbon in the front supporting their Red Cross pin. Kathy was nailing a poncho to make an enclosure for the pail in the corner with the heel of a shoe. "Could one of you guys tack this sheet to the roof?"

Mike came over and said, "Let me get that for you, Darlin."

"I'm not your Darlin, Bub! Get that straight!"

"Yes ma'am!"

They got into chit chatting about their origins and how they got into their line of business. Enlistment in the WAC's was being cut back and they wanted to contribute to the war effort when they got out of high school last year. They needed to experience the world before getting tied down in college. They had been working with the USO and Travelers Aid helping service men as they travel around the country. Now they made their amphibious landing at Normandy and were on their way to the German Border. They hoped to travel into Germany soon. Time seemed to be dragging. It was nearly 14:00 hours. Sandra said she was going to go find out what was going on.

She returned and said, “You’re not going to believe this. They need to top off the coal hopper and the loader bucket they use is out towing a truck out of the mud. Relax, we’ll be here for some time.” She went back and told the rest of the squad. “They’re cute guys too. They were just playing poker. I don’t think they even noticed that we aren’t moving.”

“What about you ladies? Do you have your board games with you?”

“They’re packed in the Clubmobiles. We got some cards though. We could play strip poker.”

“I don’t think that’s a good option on this straw. Besides, we hardly know you, “ said Mike with a blush.

A trainman came along and closed the door on the car. The train jerked to a start after a few more minutes. The boys opened the upper doors on the rear of the car. They couldn’t get to the others because of all the cargo in the way. The dust and straw began to blow around and Joe began a coughing fit. He reached for his bag and took a pull on his cough syrup.

Sandra was concerned. She asked Joe how long that has been going on. Bill said he thought it was as long as they’ve been on the road. Joe said, “No. It started on the ship when they were entering LeHavre.”

Mike said, “That’s when you went to sick bay. You were coughing before that and keeping us awake.”

Sandra held his forehead and said he wasn’t feverish. “You need to take care of that when you get to where you’re going. Where are you going?”

A couple of them said, "Munich. It's München on the map. I think they drink a lot of beer there."

Bill was looking out the trap door. He saw a kilometer post. He checked his watch. The next one appeared in about four minutes. "Hey somebody! What's 15 kilos per hour."

"Not much, " replied Sandra. She did some quick math and said, "a little less than 10 miles an hour." They continued at this pace until they got to Rouen where they stopped to take on water. "Holy cow! We're never going to get there."

No, they wouldn't. It was 16:00 and the engine crew reached the end of their shift. They banked the fire in the engine and left for the day. A new crew was not prepared to take over, so the kids would need to entertain themselves. Their baguettes were calling to them. Mary Ruth had a bottle of burgundy that she bought at the officer's club. They passed it around and poured the contents into their canteen cups until it was gone. Everyone got a little bit. They broke bread and shared it. Joe thought of it as communion. Holy it was not but it was communion never the less. The fellows who grabbed the cheese laid it out on a mess kit tray and cut it in small pieces. Betty Ann and Kathy surrendered their apples and cut them in segments.

"That was a nice snack. How about the main course?" Felix broke open a box of rations and read the contents. I don't believe this. He opened a daily box and pulled out a package labeled soup and shook it. It sounded like noodles or rice rattling in the bag. "We gotta cook this stuff. How we going to do that? We need a pan."

"And a fire!" said Sandra.

They looked out the car door at the moonscape around them. It didn't look like a brick was still fastened to a brick.

"There were houses out there. Houses have cook pots. Why don't a few of us go check out the area. We seem to have the time and we may not later," added Carolle.

Two guys and two girls went off to the edge of the train yard about a half a click from the partially rebuilt train station. As they got closer, they saw some rag-a-muffin kids running barefoot over the piles of rubble. They had sticks they were using to shoot at each other. One boy had a cook pot on his head that he was using as a helmet, right out of an "Our Gang comedy."

"Bon jour amis. Parlez vous Anglais?" The kids shook their heads no.

Mary Ruth said, "Je voudrais acheter le pot. (I'd like to buy your pot.) C'est combine? (How much is it?)"

"Un million francs!"

"Vous pouvez baisser le prix? (Can you lower the price?)" asked Mary.

"Mille francs!"

"C'est trop cher! (Too expensive)"

Joe took a dollar out of his pocket and handed it to the boy. The boy shook his head. Joe added a Hershey bar. The boy smiled and shook his head. Finally, Joe got out his gold, a pack of Old Gold cigarettes and handed it over. The boy jerked the pot off his head and handed it to Joe.

"I' ai plus le pots," said the kid.

"Joe, he has more pots."

They followed the children into the bombed street to a cul de sac where they found a rubbish heap. There were a few sad looking dented pots in the pile and Bill picked out one that would hold about three liters. The leader of the boys held out his hand and said, "Un Old Gold." Bill took out an unopened pack of Lucky Strike and gave it to the boy. "O Luckies!" exclaimed the boy. They couldn't believe it but there was a green grocer shop open behind a boarded up window. He had a bushel of turnips, three pear-shaped tomatoes, some sad looking apples and several cases of Evian water in 1.5-liter bottles.

Joe asked, "C'est combine?" "25 francs."

"Per boite?" (box)

"Non, per bouteille!" (bottle)

"C'est trop cher!"

Joe took out a ten-dollar bill and said "per boite!"

"Merci!" and the fellow picked up the case of water and handed it to Joe.

Joe said, "I think I paid too much."

Mary Ruth picked up three turnips and an onion and handed the grocer a dollar. She was older than the other women were and looked like she had managed a house in the past.

"Merci, Mademoiselle."

They made their way out of the rubble-strewn neighborhood. It was all these people had left of their lives."

Back at the boxcar, Joe set down the dozen bottles of water and began coughing after the exertion of carrying 40 pounds of water across the rubble-strewn train-yard. He took another pull on his diminishing bottle of cough syrup. He said, "I'm selling this water for a buck a bottle." Bill took the extra pot back to the squad boxcar and offered it to them for two bucks.

"What do we want that for? It's a battered old pot."

"You'll need it to cook your food." They took up a collection and handed him eight quarters. He made $1.80 on the deal. "I'm an entrepreneur," he thought.

Sandra began breaking up a kitchen chair that she found. She lifted it overhead and smashed it on the railroad track. Then she broke the spindles individually on the track. She built a little teepee over a piece of waxed paper wrapping from the box of rations. Meanwhile, Mary Ruth cut up the onion and a turnip and sautéed them in the pot until the onion browned a little. She added the contents of her canteen and asked for another canteen and poured it in. Bill added two packets of the soup mix and let it come to a boil. It simmered about twenty minutes and it was soup. They used a battered tin cup to scoop it into their canteen cups. Two eastbound trains went by while they were stopped. They were closed boxcars, probably filled with commodities. The westbound trains were filled with British and American soldiers. Some looked like POWs.

Their fire burned out by 20:00 hours and a trainman came along and told them to get back into their cars. They were moving out. They used their time to gather more firewood like broken chairs and table legs, hardwood when they could find it. They hardly had any place to put it. There was barely enough room to lie down but spooning with Red Cross girls was not such a bad deal. The girls didn't think it was all that bad either. The train jerked to a start and they tried to go to sleep, as it was just getting dark. They could tell they were still moving slow but they were moving in the right direction. It took three hours to cover the 35 km to Les Andelys. They didn't stop except for every train that passed them. They must have had the lowest priority on the French rail line. It was almost midnight.

Around two, they stopped in Vernon, probably for water. They heard the latch rattle on the outside of the door but they had prudently wedged a table leg behind the door. One of the girls said that there were half a dozen young men with flashlights. They moved back on the train for easier pickings and pulled the door open on the squad boxcar. They could have just put a stick in a hornets nest and got the same results. Nine mad MPs with sticks and pipe came boiling out of the car. "Merde! Je suis vraiment navre! C'est horrible. Pas de probléme. Au revoir." A few of them looked out the port to see them running out of sight with their flashlights waving in the night. "Nice going guys," yelled Sandra. Charlie Boll walked down and yelled, "How about it guys? Do you want some relief?" Sandra yelled back, "No thank you. We're doing all right. Be sure to block your door." They tried to go back to sleep.

They woke up as they were passing Pontoise. Mike got up and looked out the upper door. "Hey guys and gals! Look at this! I can see the Eiffel Tower." Sure enough, Sandra looked out and there it was with the sun rising behind it. “He’s right. We’re not far from Paris, fellows.”

“Wake me up when you see Notre Dame,” said Felix.

“How are you feeling, Joe? We can see Paris from here. You seem kind of quiet,“ Sandra was concerned.

“I’m not going to Paris. I want to get to Munich and it is still a long way from here.”

“Let me feel your forehead. I think you have a fever.” She took a thermometer out of her kit and stuck it in Joe’s mouth for a minute. “Mm mph frumps.” “Quiet and leave it alone soldier!” said Sandra. She removed it and said, “99.5°. You better stay quiet today. We’re taking you off KP.” She uncapped a bottle of his Evian water for him and said, “We need to buy some more of this.”

The train pulled onto a siding near Paris a couple hours later. The train crew disappeared with the engine. It just continued down the tracks like it was going to Metz without them. A switchman approached them and said the “Moteur est finis.” Betty Ann could speak his lingo and said that the locomotive is worn out and they are replacing it with a rebuilt unit. He had no idea how long it would be. Betty Ann said, “The good news is we’re getting a new engine. The bad news is we don’t know when. We had better use our time wisely and buy some food. There are some shops nearby with bread, cheese and wine.” That was the plan. Four from their car and four from the other fanned out in the village looking for food. They took their empty bottles along to save money on the Evian deposit. It was Sunday so they found many stores closed. They managed to bring back two cases of Evian along with plenty of bread, cheese, more wine and a few vegetables. They even brought a sack of charcoal along so they wouldn't have to smell the varnish on the furniture they were burning. Felix got a fire going and had some hot water to make coffee. The shoppers had already purchased some really strong coffee from a café in the village. Nothing was seen yet from the engine crew so they switched to allow Felix and three of the women to go see the village. They told Joe to stay put and he offered no argument. He gave them a couple bucks to bring back some brandy or cognac since his cough syrup was running low. He allowed that he could try some French cold medicine if they saw any.

The shoppers went straight to the café Les Deux Magots. "No Felix, they don't serve maggots," said Betty Ann. It has something to do with a nest egg like money or savings. It's a famous Paris bistro. They paid too much for café au lait and an assortment of pastries. It was still a bargain to them. They found a half-liter bottle of cognac for Joe and some licorice-flavored cough syrup, **Arzt Lapeer's Lakritz Husten elixir**. It had higher alcohol content than the cognac. They saw a one burner Primus stove that would really serve their needs but they had a day to go and they could rough it with charcoal. Maybe later on a Primus stove would be a good addition. They returned to the train enlivened by the good coffee and food. They gave Joe the liquor and medicine and let him make the choice. They even provided a small glass so he wouldn't have to use his canteen cup. He tried the licorice and decided to save it until later. Betty Ann poured him 50 ml of cognac and he said that was much better. He sipped it and enjoyed it. It made him feel better than he actually was.

The new locomotive showed up and they got back on the road again just before noon. So much for their Paris outing.

They were passing through an industrial area. They left the side door open so they could see any nice scenery if it should appear. They tried playing cards again but the cards were at odds with the wind from the door. They had to close the door as the train picked up speed to keep the straw out of their cheese. They continued their wine and cheese party as they highballed it at 20 km/hr. They had to stop a couple times as an express barreled past them. They really got to know each other, their families, and their background. They could not get enough of Bill talking about Texas and Bill was happy to oblige. He told them about the cowboy who died and went to Heaven. There was considerable excitement in heaven when he reached the pearly gates. The arrival of a real Texas cowboy was considered something of an event in Heaven. Saint Peter himself came right over and insisted on giving the cowpoke a tour. Things were right friendly until the Texan spotted half-a-dozen cowpokes staked out like broncos. "Why are all those men tied up like that?" he asked Saint Peter. Peter replied, " Every time we let them loose, they try to go back to Texas!"

He had another story about Brit Baily down on the Brazos. Brit got to Texas a little ahead of Stephen Austin and grabbed up as much land as he could in the fertile Brazos Valley. It was good land and he fought to protect it from the Indians and the impresarios who had legal standing with the Mexicans. He had a good life and passed away as all people do. He left instructions with his slaves to bury him standing up with his rifle and his jug of whiskey so no man would say, “Here lies Brit Baily.” They thought wasting a good rifle and jug of whiskey was a sin. To this day, you can see a ghostly light roaming the Brazos River Valley as Brit searches for his rifle and whiskey.

Joe said that he always liked that story, all the dozens of times he had heard it. He also asked for another dose of cognac. They passed the bottle around for everyone to try a little. Most thought it was quite pleasing and would buy some more the first chance they got. They were approaching Rheims and the train crew let it be known that they were taking a break for supper. Joe just shook his head. His dad would be fit to be tied. Felix and Sandra started a fire next to the adjoining tracks and put some charcoal on it. They gathered an onion and a couple of turnips and chopped them up for soup. They sautéed the onion in olive oil, added the turnip pieces and a can of cooked sausage to brown a little before adding water. They boiled the turnips for about twenty minutes and added the contents of a couple of soup packets. Carolle said, "Have any of you thought, that we're living like hoboes?"

"Yeah! We're a band of hoboes all right and fighting for our life at night. This isn't the way it's supposed to be. Somewhere at the end of the line is the Army we signed up to serve. I'm going to lodge a complaint with Herr Himmler and Dr. Goebbels for putting us through all of this, " said Joe. There was a titter of laughter. At least Joe still had his sense of humor. They dished out the soup into their canteen cups and ate it with bread and wine. They had canned ginger bread and dried fruit with a bit of cognac after their meal. "Okay train crew. It's time to go." They had mingled with the rest of their squad during their meal. The crew showed up again. Everyone wondered how much vino they had with their meal. Chug. Chug. They were on their way again for their final run to Metz, 160 km. They should be there in eight hours or at least by morning.

Chapter 16 – Pneumonia

Joe awoke in a strange room with a dim light in the hallway. Now and then, a woman's voice in German drifted into him. His rear end hurt like the devil. "Was I shot? Am I captured?" Hell no! The war is over. He touched his tush and found a Band-Aid there. I must have had a shot. He felt the prick in his arm where the IV drip was attached. He swung his other arm out in the air and found he was enclosed. An oxygen tent? This is getting serious. What was the last thing he remembered? "Fire! Fire? Our railcar was burning." "Where is everybody?" he asked. "Nurse! Nurse!"

A female shape entered the room carrying a flashlight. "Guten Morgen!" greeted the nurse. Joe asked, "Was ist los?" That was the sum of his German. "Du haben die Lungenentzündung." The nurse coughed and pointed to her chest.

"Pneumonia?" asked Joe.

"Yah!"

"Wo bin ich?" His high school German was coming back to him.

"Nuremburg! Standort Lazerett Kaserne," she answered. The nurse left the room and returned a short time later with a syringe. "Dreh dich um!" She made a rolling motion with her hands flashing the light around the room. "Penicillin," she said.

"That answers that. I didn't get shot in the ass," thought Joe. "Was ist tag?" asked Joe.

"Mittwoch," she said.

"Midweek? Wednesday? I've really been sleeping. Ich hunger haben," another phrase that Joe remembered. He was always hungry but this was a gnawing ache.

"Selbstverständlich," Joe hoped that meant yes.

She left the room and the sunlight broke through the curtained windows. His room faced east so he got the full impact of the rising sun. The tent he was in was made of light canvas with some sort of plastic window in the front. He could hear the slight hiss of oxygen entering the enclosure. His bed was white painted metal, chipped and old-fashioned in appearance. He couldn't see to the side but there was a narrow chest of drawers with a mirror, basin and pitcher at the foot of the bed. Soon he had to pee. "Nurse! Nurse!"

She hurried back and said, "Was ist los?"

"I gotta pee!" He never learned the German for that.

"Ach! Urin." She handed him a funny shaped bottle and he emptied his bladder. "Sehr gut," she said.

"I guess that's the drill whenever I have to go. I can't drink less," he thought. "This drip in my arm is relentless."

She was back again with a blood pressure cuff and stuck a thermometer in his mouth. She checked his blood pressure and said, "Sehr gut." She looked at thermometer and said, "39°."

"Sehr gut?" asked Joe.

"Nein. Nicht gut." She gave him zwei Aspirin.

Another lady came in a short time later with a tray of breakfast.

"Joe frühstücken?" she asked.

"Yah! Ich frühstücken," Joe answered. There was a cup and a little carafe of coffee, a bowl of oatmeal, two sausage links and some kind of streusel pastry. "Milk, bitte?" he asked.

"Nein. Nein Milch," she answered.

"Oh well! I'm lucky to have food and penicillin." He had oatmeal without milk during the depression and this place was about as depressed as one could get. The food was hot and well prepared. The coffee tasted a bit off but the oatmeal wasn't lumpy. Maybe it wasn't coffee. Considering our shortages in the States, these people must be living on nothing. Actually, the Reich had been robbing the surrounding countries to keep their larders full. A nurse or aid came in with a cart full of towels and washcloths and a basin of warm water. He just followed her lead. She shut off the gas valve and lifted the hood from him. "This would have helped when I was eating." She opened his gown and began scrubbing him.

"You look better. You very dirty on Monday and you smelled. Today you smell better." She handed him the washcloth to scrub his private parts. Then she rubbed him with alcohol. "Bring down fever. You very hot."

"You speak English. That is great. Where am I besides Nuremburg?" asked Joe.

"This German field hospital. Some Yankees. Some Deutsch. Others, Polski, Russian, Brits."

"Why am I here?"

"You very sick. I must go now." She took her things and hurried out the door. The nurse came back in and repositioned his tent and turned on the oxygen again.

Joe laid there trying to make sense of his situation. "What happens to a guy halfway to his assignment who gets stuck in a strange hospital and alone at that?" The light on his side table suddenly came on as well as a fan that was hung on the wall. "What is that all about? No lights at night but you get lights in the day?"

A doctor and a nurse came in his room. "Joe Conrad?" the doctor asked. "Good morning. I am Doctor Watkins and this is our nurse, Natalya Baganov." She shut off the oxygen valve and lifted the tent from Joe. "You look much better today. Can you tell me where you're from?"

"Erie, PA."

"Do you know where you are?"

"Nuremburg."

"Who is the president?"

"That's a trick question. I almost said Roosevelt but it's Harry Truman."

"Congratulations. What day is today?"

"Wednesday but I haven't a clue as to what today's date is. Do I pass?"

"May 23rd. You pass. You're still a sick man. You've got pneumonia. How long has it been going on?"

"It really got bad on Sunday. I sacked out most of the day while my friends were enjoying Paris. I remember the second attack and a fire."

The doctor didn't say anything but checked Joe's pulse and then listened to his heart with his stethoscope. He got behind Joe and listened to his chest. He told Joe to cough but when he did, he couldn't stop. "Take a swig of this." It was Arzt Lapeer's Lakritz Husten elixir, the stuff that Bill bought for him in France. There was still a little left. The doctor waited for Joe to get hold of himself and just listened without coughing. There was plenty of fluid in his lungs.

The Doctor continued, "There were two attacks as I understand it. The second was at Verdun and the nurses were still with you. Your buddies repulsed the attack after the thugs opened your car door. A train came by and drove the gang back. After the train passed, they threw a petrol bomb at your car hatch. A quick thinking nurse threw a pail of urine on the flames and put it out. That's why you smelled so bad. You also got a lungful of smoke. It could have killed you. They gave you artificial respiration after the smoke cleared. That saved your life."

"They tried to put you off the train at Crailsheim and Ansbach but there was no hospital that could take you. The station agent at Ansbach telegraphed Nuremburg and we agreed to pick you up at the rail station with the ambulance. You were a sorry piece of work."

Joe asked, "Who are you and what are you doing here?"

"I'm a conscientious objector. I worked at the Friend's Mission in Holland when I was captured, sent to Germany and put to work here. Nurse Natalya is Russian and a prisoner of war, but she speaks German and English so she is very valuable. She is deathly afraid of being deported to the Motherland because Stalin is killing returned POWs. He believes they've all been turned. Many of the hospital staff fled when Germany folded but a good many stayed on to take care of whomever we can. Our resources are skimpy. We have a week's supply of penicillin. Oh, you should be well by then."

"And if I'm not?"

"We may have to get some on the black market but be assured that you'll be provided with what you need to regain your health."

"I can't figure it out. I was fit as a fiddle when I left the States and now I'm an invalid. What happened to me?"

"You sailed with 3000 people, you traveled in railcars unfit for horses. People died in those cars. Your body is run down from stress and uncertainty. You were an open vessel to infection. Now we have to get you fit as a fiddle again."

"How many patients are here?"

"We have around forty patients in residence and we see another hundred billeted nearby. Portions of the building have bomb damage so we're limited as to what we can do."

"I'm glad we have the lights back on again. How often does that happen?"

"They'll be off at 19:00 when the supper dishes are washed. That's when the engineer goes home. He operates the dynamo among other things."

Natalya said, "Let me remove your IV. You must drink lots of water and other fluids. I'll have the aid bring you some pajamas so you don't have to wear a gown."

The doctor said, "You won't be needing this tent anymore and we'll move you in with some other men so you'll have some company. You must remain in bed and use the urinal bottle. If you must get up for der Stuhlgang, call an aid or orderly to take you to the toilet. Do you have any questions?"

"A million of them but they can wait. Did my buddies go on to Munich?"

"They never even got off the train. The ambulance received you from the boxcar door so to speak."

"I can't wait to get to my unit. Do you know where my gear is?"

"That's all locked up and your money is in the hospital safe. You have a receipt for it on this clipboard."

"That's a relief! Could I have my shoulder bag? It has my books and writing paper."

The aid and an orderly came in Joe's room with a pair of pajamas and new bedding. He got up and tottered around a bit before slipping on the PJ bottoms and then he got rid of the hospital gown and put on the PJ top. In the meantime, the orderly dismantled the oxygen tent and wheeled the gas bottle back to storage. The aide took him in a wheelchair to his new room with two other men and two empty beds.

"G'day Mate. You the Yank? I'm Rodney Patterson and this is Darrel Woods, the great fighter pilot. He augured in his Hawker Hurricane trying to take out a Jerry milk truck."

Joe coughed, "You got to cut me some slack here and not make me laugh. I'm coughing my lungs up. I'm Joe Conrad from Erie, Pennsylvania. I'm supposed to be an MP. Before that I was supposed to be a flyer."

"Pennsylvania? That's where they make the steel like in Birmingham?" recalled Darrel. "You a steelmaker, Chum?"

"Naw, we don't make steel in Erie. General Electric makes locomotives, big motors and dynamos. I never did anything but set pins in a bowling alley."

"Set pins like in Ten Pins? They pay you to do that?"

"We had to work for tips."

"That's what Yanks and canoes have in common. They both tip better than Brits. Right Rodney." replied Darrel.

"Please, don't try to make me laugh guys." Joe thought, "They stuck me in a ward with Laurel and Hardy."

Rodney had wild curly black hair, puffy cheeks and a broad nose. His eyes seemed to bulge out of his lids. Darrel was thin with a narrow nose and close-set eyes. His complexion was darker than Rodney's ruddy skin. His left leg was in a plaster cast and his arms were bandaged. His chest and neck appeared to be burned. "I was burned trying to get out of the cockpit, rather difficult with a broken leg. Lucky I came down near Allied troops and they beat the fire out. Rodney has some strange unnamed disease that they haven't figured out yet. They treat it with plenty of beer and schnapps."

The aid came in carrying Joe's shoulder bag. It looked like she was struggling with it. "I know it weighs a ton. Danke Shön!"

"Gern gschenhen," (Glad to do it.) she replied. She spun around and left.

"She just seems to speak English when she feels like it."

Darrel said, "She doesn't speak English. Watkins and Baganov are the only ones that speak English."

"Okay?" answered Joe.

He rifled through his bag and pulled out his two books, writing paper and the last box of Cracker Jacks. He peeled back the waxed paper covering and found a popcorn brick. The covering hadn't held up to the humidity. It was still tasty and he munched away. The Cracker Jack brick reminded him of the popcorn man in Bryant Park and the round wafers of fresh caramel popcorn. He rummaged around and found his Gillette razor and a package of blades. He called for the aid. He pointed to his razor and asked her for Wasser. She said, "Ja, rasieren." She returned with a basin of water, a mug and a brush. "Ich rasieren du!" She soaped her brush and applied it to Joe's stubble. She put a new blade in his razor and began shaving his face. Joe never expected that. She did it skillfully and painlessly even though his long whiskers pulled once in a while. She wiped his face with a damp washcloth and took out a comb. She straightened out his hair and gave the front a little flip. She stepped back, put her hands on her hips and said, "Sehr gut?" "Sehr gut!" answered Rodney and Darrel. She gathered up her things and left the room. "Danke!" called Joe.

He picked up his writing pad and fountain pen. He checked the ink in the pen by holding it with the tip up and raised the lever until a little drop of ink formed and decided he had enough. He would have the aid fill it later. Ink was something you didn't want to carry in your gear. He began to write:

May 23, 1945

Dear Mom and Dad,

I had hoped to be in my unit in Munich by now but it hasn't worked out that way. I am in a hospital but don't panic. I only have pneumonia and they have it under control with penicillin. I have an American doctor and a Russian nurse. The rest of the staff seem to be German. The US Medical Corps will take over this facility next month. I just beat them to it. I am in a ward with two British soldiers who are determined to make me laugh. The other bed is empty. I had a cold on the ship and they put us in these rickety boxcars in LeHavre. They weren't much better than cattle cars. It only took a few hours to get to Camp Lucky Strike. I ran into Uncle Billy there. He's a staff sergeant after fighting his way across Europe and now he's headed back home on the *George Washington*. He seemed very well, even though he said he has a couple of bullet holes in him. He received a Bronze Star for valor. He was with three other sergeants who had been through it all together. I travelled across France and Germany in the same sort of car but we had the company of five Red Cross women. They were protecting their cigarettes and stuff and we were protecting them.

A couple of bands of thieves tried to break into our train but we resisted them. The last group set our car on fire and one of the women put it out with the contents of a slop pail. I inhaled some smoke and they got me into an ambulance and to a hospital as fast as they could. I woke up in an oxygen tent not knowing where I was. This doesn't look like such a good introduction to Europe but I'm safe and no one is shooting at me. I had a young woman wash me and shave me this morning. They don't want me to move a whole lot. I got my books to read and I'll try not to laugh too much at my British buddies. Say hello to Jimmy and Patsy.

Love,
Joe

He addressed an envelope and put the letter inside. He didn't put a stamp on because he had no idea how to post it. He would talk to Nurse Natalya about it. He began another letter but just addressed the envelope when lunch arrived.

Miss Vivian Palermo
Apartment 509
128 Mott Street
New York City, New York

Lunch was sausage and fried potatoes, apple and a half-liter bottle of Helles beer. That took Joe back a little. Rodney said that they had a little Lowenbrau at first but the damn Yanks bombed the brewery and they ran out. The meal was tasty and was served with spicy mustard. He got a bit sleepy after the meal but Nurse Natalya appeared with a penicillin syringe. "Roll over, Soldier! I've got to stick you." She was so fast and accurate that he felt just a little sting. He finished reading *Animal Farm*. It was a short book and left him with something to think about Uncle Joe and his band of thugs in Russia. Eastern Europe would be falling to communism. Then we'll have to bail them out when their economies crater. He asked Natalya if she had read the book. "Ya, some animals are more equal than the others. I know all about that. I will not go back!" He asked if there were more books in the hospital. She said, "Ya, but they are mostly written in German. A woman from the American Red Cross comes once a week on Monday with a cartful of books and stuff." Now he was tired and closed his eyes.

Joe woke up and began a letter to Daisy that was a carbon copy of what he had written to his family. She seemed so far off now. Toward the end of the afternoon, he began the letter to Vivian. He thanked her for her hospitality and sharing her neighborhood with him. He told her how the mugger had the nerve to accuse him by name of robbing him but his CO understood what was happening and let it slide. He told her of the train trip in the 40 and 8 boxcars with the Toonerville Trolley engine and its casual French crew who worked when they felt like it. On the positive side, there was the comradeship with the ARC women, their hobo meals and foraging trips for groceries. There were the nightly attacks by hungry youth gangs that they had to fight off. Finally, he spoke of his own situation with pneumonia exacerbated by inhaling smoke from the firebomb. He said he was taken care of well and would write more if his situation changed. He signed the letter and put it in the envelope to go out with the other two letters. Natalya came in the room and said he needed to go downstairs for a chest x-ray.

The x-ray machine survived the bombing and they needed a baseline image of his lungs. The orderly came in with a wheel chair, an old-fashioned wooden structure. He got a ride as far as the stairs and had to walk down since the elevator didn't work. He saw the sky through the roof in the center part of the building. "Good work, Yanks! You bagged a hospital." They picked up another wheelchair on the lower floor. He went in the room and the technician motioned to him to remove his pajama top and stand with his chest against the cold film carrier. He heard the buzz of the x-ray tube. The warning sign on the tube housing said, "Nicht berühen!" He'd learn what that meant later. The technician took the film into the darkroom to develop it. The nurse's aide joined them for the trek back up the stairs. One-step at a time they climbed to the first landing. Joe leaned against the wall with his two companions supporting him. Another flight and they rested again. He was alternately panting and coughing. One more flight and Joe had to sit down. "Kommen sie, bitte," said the orderly. "Nein! Nein!" said the aid. They helped Joe rock up to his feet for the last flight. He collapsed into the wheelchair coughing and wheezing. The aid went to fetch his cough medicine. It was nearly gone. "Good riddance!" he was tired of the licorice tasting stuff. He preferred the Cognac. They both did about the same thing. He also trusted the contents of the Cognac more than the French concoction. He would talk it over with the doctor.

At supper, Joe had his choice of beer or wine to go with his pork, red cabbage and warm potato salad. He chose Moselle wine that came from a jug instead of the tall skinny bottle. The aid filled a quarter liter carafe with the light wine. The Brits each had beer. He picked up his John Steinbeck novel, *Cannery Row*. As far as he could tell, it was about a marine biologist who lived on the docks amid the prostitutes and fishermen in Monterey, California. He looked forward to visiting Monterey someday. He only had a half hour of light left before the lights went out and then he could only chat with Rodney and Darrel.

Ten days had gone by each punctuated with three sticks in his rump and as many ways to serve sausage. It was Saturday June 2nd. Everything they cooked was so sour but he lost his sense of taste after six days. He could still taste the beer and sometimes wine. They alternated between Beck's and Helles beer and one day, someone found a cache of Lowenbrau. That tasted special. "Anybody here ever heard of Budweiser?" he thought. Natalya procured a bottle of cognac for him but limited the doses to 15 ml. That's about a tablespoon. He had to treat it like cough syrup but boy it was good. The ARC lady came by on Monday as they said and he traded his two books for five more. He felt like he could read a novel each day. His choices were not much to speak of, just crime novels, Ellery Queen, Dashiell Hammett and Agatha Christie. She had the latest *Life Magazine* and also *Yank,* the military mag. The *Life Magazine* was the VE Day edition, a catalog of advertising the wonders awaiting GI's on their return to the States. It had a Robert Capa photo of an American soldier standing in front of a wreath-framed swastika. There was also an article about the millions of displaced persons finding their way home in Europe. He'd read it cover to cover including the letters to the editor.

Joe received his last dose of penicillin on Monday. His x-ray showed his lungs were clear and he was no longer coughing blood. He was just about free to go. Natalya came to him and told him that he had a visitor, a sergeant.

"Who could that be?" he wondered.

In walks Captain Williams that he met over a month ago, only he'd been demoted to tech sergeant.

"What gives and what are you doing here?" asked Joe.

"I flew over two weeks ago and my first assignment is to pick up some high value prisoners and return them to Nuremburg. I need a guard and I thought of you after our experience together. I knew you were going to the 713th MP Battalion but they don't know where you are. You are AWOL as far as they're concerned. I knew you were no deserter and I talked to some fellows that knew you and they said you went to a hospital in Nuremburg. I thought I'd find you and try to clear it up."

"How can I be AWOL when I'm in an Army hospital?"

"Well that's the thing, Champ. This isn't an Army hospital. It's not on the map or anyone's radar. They knew of a German hospital but it had been bombed."

"Oh! This place has been bombed all right. Part of the roof is gone and there's no electricity at night. I had to help the surgeon remove a guy's appendix one night. I got to hold the flashlight. Why the sergeant stripes."

"It's easier for me to move around that way and ask questions. Nobody bothers with a sergeant. I spoke to Bill and Mike and Felix and they told me about the wild ride you had through France. They said that you were sick and the Red Cross girls were mothering you. They said that in the second attack by a communist gang, you stood your ground, wailing away with a blackjack until you got knocked to the floor. Someone tossed a Molotov cocktail at the car and caught the straw on fire. That's when you got a lungful of smoke and an ARC girl threw a pail of piss on the fire to put it out. An ambulance picked you up in Nuremburg and that was the last anyone saw of you."

"They said I smelt awful when I arrived here."

"Bye the way, my name is Dennis, Dennis Williams and I really am a captain. I can wear whatever uniform suits the job. Are you game to pick up another prisoner? This one is an SS Sturmbannfuhrer, a major who commanded a slave labor camp. He got his jollies shooting prisoners with a sniper rifle. We picked him up trying to make his way to Austria. They have him under guard in Passau. It's a straight shot southeast of here."

"You two Yanks plotting to break out of here. Ye can't do it," said Darrel.

"No Darrel! I'm cured. It's time for me to go to my unit. First, we got a job to do. We're going to arrest some German mook."

"What's a mook?" asked Rodney.

"It's a Kraut that gets a kick out of shooting innocent people with a sniper rifle. That's what a mook is!"

"I need to remember that one," said Rodney.

Joe went to the door and hollered, "Nurse...Doc?"

Natalya came to him and asked what is wrong.

Joe said, "Nothing's wrong! I feel fine! I want to get out. I hope you have my medical records." Soldiers traveled with their med records sealed in a manila envelope.

"I will have to get Dr. Watkins to examine you. Wait."

"They treat you all right here?" asked Williams.

"Yeah, this is good. They seemed to make do with nothing and take care of patients. I had no problems with the care. I think they have a conduit to Wehrmacht stockpiles. One orderly made me stretch and exercise. I dare not call him a Nazi but he is firm. The nurse's aide seemed to temper him though. I never figured her out. She would speak English to me when nobody was around but would speak only German otherwise."

"Maybe she's a secret agent," said Dennis.

"Well, she's one cute secret agent," answered Joe.

Doctor Watkins entered and said, "I hear you want to leave us. Let me take a look at you. Sergeant, would you mind stepping out for a couple minutes?"

Dennis went out to talk with Rodney and Darrel. Darrel's cast was off now but the scars on his arms were nasty looking. His face had healed nicely though with a minimum of scarring. He told Dennis about crashing his Hurricane. Rodney kept any smart remarks to himself. He was feeling fine now and just wanted to get back to England. Doctor Watkins opened the curtain again and told Dennis, "Joe is fit for duty but I recommend that he takes it easy for a couple days. His muscles are weak from his many days in bed."

"We don't plan any hard duty, just a drive in the country. Who do you work for and what will you do now that the war is over?" asked Dennis.

"I guess I worked for the Germans after I was captured in Holland. I suspect that I'm persona non grata in the States so I may just find a position here in Europe, maybe with the UN or some missionary group. The American Army takes over this place next week and they won't want me around."

"Here's my card. If you ever need a reference, look me up." Dennis offered him a business card that said Capt. Dennis Williams.

"What gives? This says you're captain."

"I'm a chameleon. I use whatever uniform gets the job done. It's easier to move around as a sergeant. Joe! I took the liberty of checking your mail and I have a half-dozen letters for you and a *Life* magazine." He removed them from his musette bag.

Joe was thrilled. He had felt so cut off from his family. There were three letters from Daisy, two from home and one from Miss Vivian Palermo. He was shocked to see a letter from Vivian. Yes, he had written to her but she was more enterprising than he suspected. She wrote:

PFC Joseph Conrad
RA 12241332
APO MP unit somewhere in Germany

"Yeah! That puzzled me too," said Dennis. "Some mail clerk took a liking to you to track you down to where you should have been. She must really like you or do you owe her money? Let's get going. Do you have your gear here? What about money? Are you broke? We can get you an advance."

"Whoa sir! One thing at a time. My money is in the safe or at least they tell me it is. I won enough on the ship to last me a few weeks. They have my duffle bag locked up but I have my shoulder bag."

The orderly arrived with Joe's duffle bag and his cleaned suit on a hanger. Joe sniffed it and pronounced it clean. The duffle bag was locked but he had the key in his bag. Dennis was wearing a short wool jacket made popular by General Eisenhower but only authorized for use in Europe. Joe put on a dress shirt with wool trousers and his long tunic and black tie. "Where did you get that shorty jacket? Are they issuing it or do you have to buy it?"

Dennis said, "They're in short supply but I bought this from a trooper that was returning to the States. We'll get you one." He completed his outfit with the light overseas cap and no spats. He wore boots since he didn't know what he would encounter. They walked out of the hospital with Joe's medical records to prove where he had been for two weeks. He put them in his duffle bag that they would lock up at CID headquarters. Joe put a hundred bucks in his wallet and the rest in his money belt. He would wire some home as soon as he got the chance. He said goodbye to the staff and thanked them for their service.

Dennis carried the duffle bag for Joe and put it in the back seat of his staff car. Joe was taken aback, "Where did you find this relic?" It was a prewar Citroen painted desert tan with red and green camouflage stripes randomly sprayed on it, a good choice if you were hiding it in a circus. It had the signature Citroen corporal stripes on the radiator. It rode very low to the ground and had front wheel drive, both completely foreign to him.

Dennis said it is Citroen *Traction 11CV*. "Some German officer didn't need it anymore. It is serviceable and roomier than a Jeep. Plus I don't want that Kraut officer out in the open."

They drove toward the center of the city, past block after block of bombed out houses. Women were gathered in groups hammering the mortar off bricks to reuse them when they rebuild the structures. Some were salvaging lumber that had not been burned. They looked organized and methodical about their work. His memory went back to the WAC barracks that he helped salvage on field day. Back then, it was a lark, something to do other than classes and drill for a day. These people were doing it for their very existence. He could not imagine the meager amount of food or money they got for their effort.

The bombers had clear visibility and a rising full moon the night they attacked Nuremburg. The center of the city, particularly the eastern half, was destroyed. The castle, the Rathaus, most of the churches and many preserved medieval houses went up in flames. The area of destruction also extended into the more modern northeastern and southern city areas. The industrial area in the south, containing the important MAN and Siemens factories, and the railway areas were severely damaged. Most industrial buildings were destroyed. It is said that Joseph Stalin asked that the German churches be destroyed and they were not rebuilt in the eastern portion of the country under Russian rule. Why did we have a maniac as an ally in a war against another maniac. Nürnberg was famous for producing toys and gingerbread cookies, not war materials; it was the ideological center of Nazi Germany and Hitler's favorite city. Nürnberg was regarded as the "most German" of all the cities in Germany, which made it a target for vindictive Allied bombing.

They reached Dennis's headquarters in a small non-descript hotel that survived the bombing. No marquee announced that it was CID headquarters. They parked in the courtyard of the building and Joe struggled into the lobby under the weight of his duffle bag and musette bag. An old German gentleman lounged at the front desk. Dennis retrieved his key and they went up the lift to the third floor. CID occupied the whole floor. First, they went to his room to drop off the luggage and then to an office where three WAC enlisted women sat at typewriters. A teletype squatted in a corner chattering out copy and dinging a bell now and then. The two of them walked into the inner office and saluted the WAC major in charge. "Marjorie," said Dennis, "we've found our man. This is Joe Conrad who fell off the books two weeks ago. He has been recovering from smoke inhalation at Standort Lazerett Kaserne. We didn't know that place was operating."

"Who runs it?" she asked.

"They have a mixed bag of doctors and personnel and an even greater variety of patients. Joe was in a room with two Brits. The 166th General Hospital Unit will be taking it over next week. They are repairing bomb damage now. The roof is nearly covered. Joe and I are going to take a drive to Passau to pick up the SS Sturmbannfuhrer Linus Routenstraut. We need a bunk for PFC Conrad for a couple days. We also need to send a message to his battalion in Munich saying we found him and he will be TDY to our unit for a week. We have to get him off AWOL status."

Marjorie jotted a message with the required information. "What is your unit?"

"It's the 713th MP Battalion, Company C," replied Joe.

She showed it to Captain Williams and then gave it to one of the typists to send on the teletype. "Private, you'll bunk with Sergeant Holland in room 314. He's out on assignment right now. Here is a meal card for our contract restaurant, Der Friesenhaus. I hope you like hasenpfeffer."

"What is hasenpfeffer?" asked Joe.

"We like to think of it as four legged chicken to keep from imagining Bugs Bunny," replied Marjorie.

"Oh!" said Joe. He dispositioned his duffle bag and sorted out his musette bag for an overnight trip. Williams told him that he could put his surplus cash in their safe and draw out 100 marks for snacks or beer on the trip. Williams would take care of food and lodging since he had the expense account. "We will stay here today and leave first thing in the morning. Get some rest today. Tomorrow morning we'll check out our weapons and I'll show you the blue Danube. Oh! Bring your blackjack along. Just keep it out of sight. I'll see you at six and we'll go to Der Friesenhaus for supper."

Chapter 17 – CID

Joe went to Major Marjorie and drew his 100 marks. She said it was around $35, give or take a little bit. He gave her the bulk of his cash and kept $45 for himself and she wrote out a receipt for the money. He walked down Schönweibstrase away from the hotel looking for a light lunch. He went into Pilsstube zur Wurzl Inh and ordered braunschweiger on a kümmelweck roll with sauerkraut on the side and a Heineken beer to top it off. The beer was from Netherlands. That is probably the last they would be seeing of that beer for a while. He put plenty of mustard on the sandwich. The course salt on the roll made him thirsty so he ordered a second beer and took out the letters that Captain Dennis brought him.

The first one he read was from Daisy dated May 5. It was the day after her birthday. She thanked him for the cross that he gave her as a present. She said that she had a wonderful birthday made all the more special by his call in the morning. It weighed on her during the day that he was sailing away. She said that the thought of him being away for so long saddened her. She just plodded along through her classes. Her mother baked a strawberry cake for the occasion. The second letter was dated May 13 after her prom. The dance didn't work out so well as the dance with Joe. Bobby Pavlat picked her up in his truck. She was afraid of getting her dress dirty even though he said he washed it up special for her. The gym looked real pretty for their Evening-in-Paris theme. The engineers club did a swell job of erecting a fourteen-foot Eifel tower in the corner by the bandstand. She wondered where they got all of the empty wine bottles to put on the tables. Each bottle had a candle in it. Maybe the Catholic Church saved them up. The band was good but the seniors weren't playing in it since it was their prom. It was no Thundering Herd or even a First Herd. Anyhow, the asst. principle caught Bobby taking a sip from a half-pint bottle in his pocket and asked him to leave. He said, "Come on Babe. Let's blow this joint." I told him I wasn't going anywhere. "It is my prom and I'm going to enjoy it." So he left. I danced every dance and had a fine time. I called my Dad for a ride home afterward. My parents thought I would be upset but I was glad to be shed of that jerk. The rest was about her family and friends.

The third letter was dated May 20 and she still hadn't received a letter from Joe. He was still sick on the train.

Dear Joe,

I've been crying all day thinking about writing you. My mind is in a muddle. I have been talking to my parents about college. I know I said I wanted to get married as soon as I got out of school but you have shown me that there are better men out there than my choices around here. Bobby showed me that as well. I don't think I can wait a year or two for you to come back and if I go to college, I am committed to four years. We didn't look at the state schools. They are too big. My choices are Stephens College, Fontbonne University and College of the Ozarks. The first two are Catholic and the last is Presbyterian but they're cool. The College of the Ozarks charges no tuition, because of its student work program and donations. They require students to work 15 hours a week on-campus and two weeks during breaks. They call themselves "Hard Work U." That would save Daddy money for Marty's education.

I hope you understand. You've helped me to see there is more to life outside of St. Robert. I hope you won't mind if I keep the cross that you gave me to remember my first real love. I will always love you.

Sincerely,
Daisy

"Well, that takes care of that," thought Joe as he finished his beer. "I expected her to be Mrs. Pavlat by now. No, don't be like that! You have to be magnanimous. I don't often get to use that word. I need to write her back and wish her the best of luck but not now though."

He thought he should be getting back to the hotel but he had three more letters to read so he ordered one more beer. The letters from home were newsy about Erie and the neighborhood. As far as they're concerned, they are still at war while it seems to be over in Europe. There is still plenty of conflict and turmoil to go around. They had a letter from Chuck who seemed to be in the Philippines at the time he wrote it. Parts of the letter were blacked out. He just said he was busy.

He saved Vivian's for last. It was a puzzle how her letter even reached him. He gave someone in the Army Post Office a lot of credit. The waiter offered him another beer. "Nein bier bitte. Danke" One more letter and I'll go.

My Dearest Joe,

Surprise! If you are reading this, my hat is off to the Army Post Office. I got your service number from your dog tag while you were asleep. I just had to tell you what a wonderful time I had with you. I only wish it could have been sooner so I could really have shown you the City. I have been telling all of my friends about the brave soldier who saved me from certain death at the hands of a knife-wielding assassin. ("She could have knocked him on his ass all by herself.") I know I've overblown it but it was exciting to get the best of that thug. My neighbors ask about you and I have nothing to tell. You are a phantom who appeared in my life and then went off to sea but I wouldn't have missed it for the world.

Be sure to contact me when you come to New York again. I'd love to see you and hear about your adventures. You know where to find me or just ask Tony.

Ciao and Amore
Vivian Palermo

"That was refreshing Joe thought. I'll write her again later, Daisy too," he thought. He paid for his meal and needed to get back and take a nap. He had gotten used to that in the hospital.

He walked back on Schönweibstrase to the hotel and up to the third floor. He reported to Major Marjorie and asked if he needed to do anything. She replied that he should rest today and he'd be expected to get into the action tomorrow. "I've heard about your harrowing journey and the time you spent in the nonexistent hospital. You need to have your breakfast and report to me by 06:00."

He went to his room and organized his stuff a little more and thought, "I've got to get back out in the air." He would keep close to the hotel and make sure he got the lay of the land. There was minimum bomb damage in this area but there was some evidence of it. He saw a little girl in a polka dot dress stepping over a pile of rubble. She was wearing loafers or moccasins and white stockings that reached nearly to her bloody knee. She had scraped her right knee on the concrete but she was bright and cheerful. "Guten tag mein Herr! Wie Spat ist es?" she asked while pointing to her wrist.

"Es is drei Uhr," (3:00) replied Joe.

She asked, "Was ist du Namen?"

"Joe, " he replied "Joe Conrad. Was ist du Namen?"

"Hermina. Wie alt sind Sie?"

"Achzehnte," Joe replied that he is eighteen. "Wie alt sind Sie?" he asked her.

"Acht!" She replied. "Ich haben blut en das Knie. Haben sie wasser? Haben sie Schokolade?"

"Nein wasser. Nein Schokolade." Joe motioned for her to walk with him the half block back to the hotel. He sat her down on the curb to wait while he went for his canteen and first aid kit. He returned shortly and washed off her knee and put a clean gauze bandage on it. He also had a Hershey bar for her and told her that she better go home. She put the candy in her coat pocket to share with her mother and sisters.

"Store ich?" she asked. This threw Joe but she finally got across why she was bothering him.

"I've got to walk," he said.

"Ich gehen. I walk!" she said firmly and took his hand. So they walked. Half a block later, they saw an old woman standing on one leg in an alley. She was washing the mud from her shoe with a rag and a pail of water. Her grey hair was pulled straight back in a severe bun. She wore a striped apron to protect her black dress.

"Guten tag, Frau Haberer!" called Hermina.

"Guten tag, Hermina. Wo ist der Soldat?"

"Er ist Joe. Er, ist gut. Er verbinden mein Knie," and she pointed to her knee.

"Das ist gut," said Frau Haberer and they walked on.

Farther on, they saw a group of women loading bricks from a rubble pile onto what he took to be a charcoal powered truck. The women were knocking the mortar off the bricks and piling them on the flat bed of the vintage truck behind the retort that converted the fuel. A carpenter built the cab and bed from wood. The retort was a black iron vessel filled with wood and fired by a pipe that came off the top of the apparatus. Another pipe went through a series of cylinders that may have been filters or coolers. The resulting vapor was piped forward to the engine. Rube Goldberg would have been proud of it. The lettering on the truck proclaimed, "A&M Buchanan – General - Träger."

All of the women wore babushkas and aprons. A woman pointed to the rubble pile and said, "Amerikaner und Briten! Danke! Wem gehort das, Hermina?"

"Er ist Joe. Er, ist gut. Er verbinden mein Knie," replied Hermina cheerily and the women all laughed.

"Guten tag, Herr Joe!" they said.

"Ich muß nach Hause gehen," said Hermina which she indicated by walking her fingers on her arm. "Bis bald Joe!"

He thought that meant goodbye but later found that she meant, "See you soon!" Joe replied, "Auf Wiederschen, Fraulein Hermina!" She crossed the street and disappeared around the corner. He walked up to the window of a camera store. It was like a candy store to him. They were mostly used and vintage Leica cameras along with Ilford, Rolliflex and Leitz. There were even a few prewar Kodak and Argus cameras in the collection. There was a Kodak Autograph camera like his Uncle Carl owned. It had a little flip door in the rear where you could write on the back of the film carrier. He had the money to make a purchase but he would look around more and make his purchase carefully.

He returned to the hotel and lay down on his bunk. He was quickly asleep until he heard a knock on the door. He jumped up and straightened his tie. It was Captain Williams. "Ready for chow, Joe?"

"Yes sir!" Dennis had his officer uniform on again.

"Let's head to Der Friesenhaus." Major Marjorie had left for the day. They walked down the stairs and out to the street. Traffic was minimal this time of day, a Jeep now and then. They crossed the street and walked down the block. Joe told him about his lunch at Pilsstube zur Wurzl Inh. "You should have come here since it's paid for."

"I needed some time alone to read my mail. I hadn't received any mail since I left Missouri. I lost a girlfriend and gained a friend. I told you about Daisy when we passed her house. She has decided to go to college and I don't fit in her plans. I knew it was going to come. It was only a matter of time. I knew she wasn't going to save herself for a year or more after only knowing me three weeks. That would be a lot to ask."

"I applaud you for being realistic," said Dennis. "By the way, we're going to be very close for the next two days. Please call me Dennis as long as no one is around. Tomorrow, I will be a sergeant again and you can call me Sarge."

"How do you see tomorrow going?" asked Joe.

"He'll come quietly enough. He's not a violent man, but I'm told he may have a following. We'll be armed. Do you know your way around a hand grenade?"

"Whoa Captain. The war is over. Let's not start another one," replied Joe.

"I'm looking at smoke and concussion grenades, just as a backup."

"Don't we need more personnel?"

"Don't you see what I had to go through to get you to help me? They told me I could use you, if I could find you. Luckily, I'm a clever detective."

Joe asked, "Why the grenades then? Do you see his compatriots trying to spring him?"

"We have three kinds of threats on this mission. There are those who want to set him free. Then there are two groups who want to see him dead. There are those representing his victims, who want to kill him and there are higher ranking officers, who see him as a witness to their crimes and would happily eliminate him."

"Not a popular guy, huh?"

They reached Der Friesenhaus and were shown a table by the window. Dennis asked for a table further back against the wall. It was best for American military to remain less visible until the country got more used to their presence. It wasn't that long ago that General Patton's tanks were crossing the Oder.

"Have you had a chance to try schnitzel?"

"Isn't that some kind of wiener," said Joe.

"No! It's a cutlet. Could be beef, veal or pork. My favorite is Jaegerschnitzel. It is served with mushrooms in brown gravy. It makes a hearty meal."

"I'll have what you're having," said Joe.

They enjoyed their meal and a couple of beers. They checked out their armament when they got back because they would be leaving around sunrise.

05:00 came early when the duty officer shook him awake. She had a pot of coffee started and had purchased half a dozen pastries from a nearby bakery. She had been on duty since midnight. She was a lieutenant and her name was Kelly. She was very pleasant to see first thing in the morning even though he was sleeping in his skivvies. He shaved and met Dennis in the office for a bite of breakfast. They poured the remainder of their coffee in their canteen cups and took the remaining pastries. Dennis asked Joe, "Do you want to begin driving or should I?"

Joe admitted, that he didn't have a license. His dad never had a car and he hadn't learned to drive.

"Oh fine! As soon as the sun comes up, you're going to learn to drive, fella!"

Joe put the hand grenades in the glove compartment. They had taped sticks to the smoke grenades so he stowed these under his seat. None of it would be needed until tomorrow. Dennis drove to Neumarkt, the first town of any size and when they reached the south side, he turned the wheel over to Joe. "It's all yours, Joe! Let's see what you can do. Have you any driving experience at all?"

"I sat on my Uncle Carl's lap and steered the car back from Presque Isle."

"Well that's a start but you are not sitting on my lap!"

They got out and switched sides of the car.

Dennis instructed Joe to push in the clutch, find the first gear (it was diagrammed on the gearshift nob) and release the parking brake. "Now release the clutch slowly as you press on the gas pedal." The Citroen lurched forward bucking its passengers forward and back. Soon it was moving slowly in a forward direction.

"Stop the car. Push the clutch in as you push on the brake. Now try it again with a little more gas as you let out the clutch." They repeated the maneuver a half dozen times until Joe had it down smoothly. He felt pretty cocky as he put it in second gear until the engine started whining toward maximum RPM. Dennis ordered him to put it in third gear. "Now slow down and shift back to second and then to first gear and stop." Joe soon had that down pretty good too. He eventually got it into fourth gear and thought he had it under control until they came to a steep grade descending into a village. He shifted from fourth to third and slowed down. Then it popped out of third and the car sped up in neutral. "Shift into second!" Dennis yelled. "I can't get it in!" said Joe. "Double clutch it!" "What's that?" "Accelerate in neutral and then shift to second!" It worked. Joe was able to slow down as the engine screamed in second. Joe drove slowly in the village but no one seemed to be around.

They reached Regensburg where they saw a half-a-dozen GIs operating a field kitchen from the back of a deuce-and-a-half. They were using immersion heaters to cook American hot dogs in GI cans and serving them to lines of Germans who were waiting. Dennis and Joe stopped to talk to the mess sergeant and see if coffee was to be had. They found out the Russians took all the food when they fell back to Austria and these people were starving. "You fellas want a hot dog?" asked the mess sergeant. Dennis said, "Okay, why not as long as were not taking food from these people." The Sergeant said, "Sure! We have enough. There is plenty more where these came from and get you some coffee over there." They went to another GI can full of black coffee and filled their canteen cups. "We better be on our way. Thanks Sarge!" The sergeant came to the driver's window. "Where did you get this old clunker? It's French isn't it? Say, the main bridge across the Danube is shutdown. They found it was mined with explosives and the combat engineers are working to clear it now. You'll have to drive up the river road about ten clicks to cross. Good luck to you!"

"Thanks!" said Joe. He started the Citroen and they continued their journey.

"That puts a kink in it," said Dennis. "Oh well! Let's see the beautiful blue Danube." They turned west on the road to Ingolstadt. Joe was driving like a pro now. The river was beautiful but there was evidence of artillery damage along the way. The road was battle-scarred with ruts and craters hastily filled with dirt or sand. It was slow going and Dennis suddenly hollered, "Stop!" He got out of the car and picked up a battered wooden sign that proclaimed, "Minen" in white painted letters. "What do you know about mines, Joe?"

"We didn't have much call for that in MP or radio school but I got a little in basic training. They often mine the sides of the road to force vehicles to stay in line where artillery can pick them off. We also learned to dig them up with a bayonet. Darn, I forgot my bayonet."

"Good! I'm going to walk down the center of the road and see if I can find another sign. They don't usually mine the center of the road. Nobody drives there."

Dennis walked about a hundred meters ahead and found another sign on the same side as the other. This confirmed his thesis that the mines were on the side of the road. They got through the mined area and the road smoothed out a little. They crossed the river and headed back on the other side. They were back in Regensburg but on the other side of the river. They had not gone very far and they spent a lot of time doing it. They found a restaurant, Unter der Linden, and decided to eat while they had the chance. There was a painting of a Linden tree over the door with the branches caressing the door. They had seen grafitti on the side of the building that depicted an America covering a lifeless body and grabbing at fistfulls of dollars. They weren't sure of the significance so soon after occupation. A young boy nearby was wearing a cardboard sandwich board that said, "Du sollst nicht töten." They found out later that it said, "You should not kill." They seemed to be welcome in the restaurant. Anyone with marks or dollars was welcome. They learned that there had been an incident in the town with a few renegade American soldiers.

They ordered their dinner. Nothing adventurous, just pork chops, red cabbage and potato salad. They don't call it German potato salad over here. They were running behind so one beer would do it. Joe continued to drive down the southwest side of the Danube until they had to cross the Isar River at Plattling. Dennis told Joe that a concentration camp was located here. They still haven't relocated the survivors of the camp and the 260th Infantry Regiment was caring for them until they could be repatriated. "There are still plenty of Nazis in this area though they deny it."

Joe continued driving to Passau until they located the Waldwerke Passau-Ilzstadt. It was the second of three concentration camps in the area. This was where they found SS Sturmbannfuhrer Linus Routenstraut in the can, a solitary cell left over from its previous use. Dennis and Joe couldn't be bothered with him, though. They found bunks in the German guard's quarters and went out to locate some vittles. They got their grenades and put them in a small duffle sack. They took them into the restaurant with them. Customers were scarce and they had the manager's full attention. They were still kind of full so they shared a wurst plate and a couple beers. They had to keep their wits about them in a strange town after dark.

Chapter 18 – A Harrowing Journey

It was four when the Sergeant of the Guard awoke them. He had sandwiches and coffee for them so they could eat quickly and be on their way. The SOG took them to the can when they finished their chow. They met Linus Routenstraut there. He was taller than either by an inch or two, slim and muscular. He had light brown hair, not the blond ideal but close. His shoulders were broad with a smallish head mounted on them. He reminded one of a cheetah, built for speed without much between the ears. His eyes were grey and yes, they were piercing, kind of squinting as if he misplaced his glasses. He was dressed as an enlisted man with the rank of Rottenfuhrer (corporal). He didn't get the joke of Rottenfuhrer Routenstraut. He was sullen and uncommunicative. His costume was to keep from arousing attention but there were enough officers pretending to be someone else that everyone was suspicious. His handcuffs were attached to a chain that hooked to his ankle bands. The chain was passed under the driver's seat and bolted to it. He was free to sit up but sat rather hunched over. One of them always sat in the rear to make sure he left his shackles alone. They were leaving before dawn to keep from exciting the locals. They hoped to be many miles up the river when the sun rose. Dennis began driving since it was dark and skillful maneuvering may be needed.

It wasn't too long before Dennis spotted something behind them. It was the absence of light now and then that piqued his curiosity. Without a moon, there was no glint of light from the radiator. It was just, now and then, a distant light would be obscured. He thought it was paranoia but it happened three times. It must have been twenty car lengths back but it was getting bigger. Maybe he could lose it on a curve. He accelerated into the next left turn and told Joe to light off a smoke stick. "Hold it out the window, Joe, and then drop it when I say...now!" Dennis sped away from the curve as fast as his lights would let him. "Oh hell! This is straight enough." Dennis shut the headlights off as they hurtled through the night. He turned right through a curve and turned them on again. Joe said, "Thanks!" The German murmured, "Danke." The horizon glowed red on the other side of the Danube. The sun was rising. He could see the car gaining on him from behind. It was still half a click back but it was gaining. The divided grill looked like a BMW and an open top at that. Their smoke bomb slowed them down but that wouldn't work again, or would it.

There was a right turn ahead at a cross street in a hamlet. Joe hollered, "We turn there!" as Dennis drove through the intersection. Dennis told Joe to drop a smoke stick at the crossroads. As the BMW went through the intersection, Dennis did a combat U-turn and took a left turn at the crossroads. The front wheels of the Citroen *Traction* dug in and pulled them around the turn. Joe dropped two yellow smoke grenades in the middle of the road. The result looked enough like chlorine to scare the locals half to death. Two local drivers and a truck screamed to a stop in the crossing, blocking the road as the drivers ran for safety. Joe spotted the two men as they drove by them. The passenger was waving an old-fashioned broom-handle Mauser pistol at them but not shooting among the civilians. Linus yelled, "Gott im Himmel!"

They got across the bridge at Regensburg without incident. Dennis thought it was time to look for lunch and disappear their clown car somewhere in the old town. They carried K-rations with them but thought they could do better.

Dennis found a greasy spoon restaurant within the medieval walls. He left Joe to guard the prisoner and keep a sharp lookout. Linus began complaining about the toilet. "Nein," said Joe. "Later!" Dennis returned with a sack of rye rolls, three Thüringen sausages and three-liter bottles of the local beer. He also juggled a greasy newspaper full of potato crisps. It rankled him to be buying the enemy a beer but they had to keep him in good condition to stand trial. He got back in and poked around until he found a rubble-filled alley near the bombed Messerschmitt factory. This filled the requirement to relieve their bladders and eat lunch. The sausage was fine. You could taste a bit of caraway and marjoram in it. It was still warm from the charcoal fire used to cook it.

Dennis asked Joe to get out and check out the road before he pulled out. They began their journey again reasonably sure, they had lost their pursuers. Dennis turned the wheel over to Joe when they got north of the city. They knew they weren't out of the woods yet because there was really only one way to get to Nuremburg. There were side roads but there was no guarantee that the bridges would be intact. Dennis thought they could cut their risk of an ambush in half by taking a road to the left that said, "Neumarkt 45 km." It was longer than the thru road but it could be safer. It was rutted and muddy from a recent rain but it didn't have shell craters like the one they drove on yesterday. Linus complained as the bumps jerked him at the end of his shackle. He would have to take it because they weren't going to release him. They encountered a farmer driving a hay wagon toward them. It was pulled by a single ox. It was picturesque but he was in the middle of the road and wasn't yielding. There was a broken sign on the right side of the road. He couldn't see what it said but he thought it might say, "Minen!" Joe backed up a hundred feet to where the cart could go by. It wasn't hay. It was manure. "Dünger!" muttered Linus as they smelled it go by. Joe began to drive again and slowed down for the sign. Dennis said it said, "Regensb-." It was the a broken km marker. "That's a relief." After a half hour more on the rough road they came into a side street in Neumarkt close to where he began driving yesterday. Joe took a left onto the main road to finish the last thirty kilometers.

He drove into the courtyard of the Nuremburg headquarters. Dennis said, "The next step is for you to get a driver's license. First let's get this mutt under lock and key." There was an improvised lockup on the first floor of the courtyard. Dennis told Joe to go secure the gate to the courtyard before removing the prisoner from the car. Linus knew he wasn't going anywhere so he waited patiently while his captors made their preparations. Joe had to bend down to free his shackles from the car seat. They moved him to his new cell. His only remark was, "Ich hunger haben." The guards would take care of that shortly. They would have to bring him a plate from Der Friesenhaus. Joe brought him the valise he had in the trunk of the Citroen with his officer's uniform and personal grooming items.

Major Marjorie stayed overtime waiting for their arrival. "Welcome boys. It's good to have you back. Any bullet holes in your circus car?"

"No Mam," said Joe. "The captain outmaneuvered the only bad guys we encountered."

"Trouble is, we don't know if they were bad guys or good guys. We don't know who they were, but they were trying to shoot us with one of those old-fashioned Mauser pistols like they use in the movies. In fact, they looked like they were from Central Casting," said Dennis.

Joe piped up, "The captain here, did a daredevil U-turn and could have shook the drivers hand as we passed them and disappeared in a cloud of smoke."

"Well put it all in your report Dennis. It's time to eat now," said the Major. "Let's go to Der Friesenhaus after you wash up. You both are in need of a shave."

"We left awfully early, Sir...Mam," said Joe.

They met back at Marjorie's desk in twenty minutes and the three of them walked across the street to the restaurant. Joe felt uncomfortable with the two officers but after a beer with them, he felt more at ease. They ordered their food. Joe thought he'd have some more schnitzel, like the meal he had the other night. That seemed so long ago. Then Marjorie dropped it on him.

"Joe, have you considered a career in the CID?" she asked.

"No, Mam! I've been in training for a year now and I haven't even reached my unit. I have no experience. I have guarded a couple school crossings but I did that in eighth grade. I have escorted a couple prisoners and that is the sum of my military career."

She went on, "Well think about it. I'll give you travel orders to take the train to your unit in Munich. You can travel tomorrow. I will also give you an application for the CID school that they are putting together in Chelles, France. I don't know when yet."

"You have more experience than you think," said Dennis. "I have been on two missions with you. I have heard about your conduct on the train and the way you subdued a thief in the New York Subway. You can think on your feet and take action as required. What's more, we need agents. You would have the temporary rank of corporal while going to school with a promotion to sergeant after you complete the eight weeks of training. You can fill out the application and leave it with us. Go to your unit and if you want to join our merry band, just give us a call."

Major Dempsey seconded his invitation, "You can contact either of us. What is this about the subway thief?"

Joe told her about the incident and also about the complaint filed against him by the humiliated mugger.

She said, "We can make that complaint go away just so it never jumps up and bites you in the butt."

They ended the evening with a glass of cognac. Joe thought it felt like an employment interview and he was being wooed.

Joe got up early in the morning and went to Der Friesenhaus for breakfast. Dennis was already there with two other officers. Joe started for a table alone but Dennis waved him over. Joe hesitated and then joined them. Dennis introduced him to his associates as a potential recruit. They were discussing some recent hijackings of medical supplies destined for DP camps. He said that Joe is considering joining their division as if it was a done deal. Joe thought, "This is going too fast for me."

Lieutenant Kelly had a handful of forms for Joe to fill out when he returned to the office. The biggest one was for his security clearance. He hadn't considered that. He had no skeletons in his closet. It was just an awful lot of information that he would have to dig up. Others were applications for a passport and the application for the CID school itself, which begins August 6, 1945. She also prepared travel orders for him to take the train to Munich to join his unit. The orders also covered his time in the hospital and his TDY assignment to Passau. "Boy that's a lot of papers. Some of it, I don't even know about myself."

Lt. Kelly said, "Put down as much as you can. It will make the investigator's job easier. They like to have the investigation complete before you begin your second month of training. I will have a runner pick up your train ticket for tomorrow. You will need most of the day to complete the paperwork, take an entrance test and sit for a couple of interviews." Joe worked at it until around 10:00 hrs. Kelly gave him a ten page test to complete in two hours. Joe paged through it. There wasn't much about crime fighting. There was mathmatics and reading comprehension, some rudimentary science and grammer. It looked like what he thought a college entrance test might look like. He finished by 11:15 and went back over it to check his answers. He gave the test back to Lt. Kelly at 11:30. "One more thing Private and then you can go to lunch. Sign this statement."

It was a loyalty oath that stated that Joe was not now nor has ever been a member of the Communist Party. Joe saw no point in it, but what's the harm in it. He went ahead and signed it. He didn't even know what the Communist Party was all about. Then he went to lunch and joined Captain Dennis at his table at Der Friesenhaus. "That test was easy. You wouldn't believe what Lt. Kelly made me sign."

The captain said, "A loyalty oath? Yeah, everyone has to do that now. The government sees a communist behind every tree and bush. Waiter, a menu, bitte! Have you made your decision yet?"

"I think I ought to report for duty first and see what it is like."

"What is there to think about? Two promotions in two months? Small team operations? Working on your own initiative. I think you ought to make up your mind."

Joe considered the choices. He thought of the last week since Dennis bailed him out of the hospital versus standing guard at the gate, breaking up bar fights, chasing speeders on base and watching schoolchildren as they crossed the street. Dennis won.

"Private Conrad reporting for duty sir! Go ahead and make it happen, sir!"

Glossary

Achzehnte (Ge.) – Eighteen

Auf Wiedersehen (Ge.) – Good bye

Au Revoir (Fr.) – Good bye

AWOL (AM.) – Absent Without Official Leave

Bis bald (Ge.) – see you soon

Bitte (Ge.) – please

Bitte seher (Ge.) –

Bon jour amis (Fr.) – Good day my friend

Bonsoir (Fr.) – Good night

Café noir (Fr.) – black coffee

C'est combine? (Fr.) – How much is it?

C'est trop cher! (Fr.) – Too expensive!

Œuf (Fr.) – eggs

Chevaux (Fr.) – horses

Danke (Ge.) – Thank you

Danke shön (Ge.) – Thank you very much.

Dreh dich um. (Ge.) – Roll over

du (Ge.) – you

Du haben (Ge.) – You have

Er verbinden mein Knie (Ge.) – He bandaged my knee.

Es is drei Uhr – It is three o'clock.

Frühstücken (Ge.) – breakfast

Gehen (Ge.) – go, walk

Gern gschenhen (Ge.) – Glad to do it.

Gott im Himmel! (Ge.) – God in heaven!

Guten morgen. (Ge.) – Good morning.

Guten Tag. (Ge.) – Good day.

Hasenpfeffer (Ge.) – rabbit

Homme (Fr.) – men

Ich (Ge.) – I

Ich hunger haben (Ge.) – I have hunger.

Je voudrais acheter le pot. (Fr.) – I'd like to by your pot.

Kommen sie (Ge.) – Come here.

La Moulin Rouge (Fr.) – The Red Mill

Lazerett (Ge.) – hospital

Le Bosche (Fr.) – German soldiers

Le Maureva (Fr.) – Le Maureva

I' ai plus le pots. (Fr.) – I have more pots.

die Lungenentzündung (Ge.) – the pneumonia

Milch (Ge.) – Milk

Mittwoch (Ge.) – Midweek, Wednesday

Musette bag (Fr.) – haversack

Muß (Ge.) – must

Nein (Ge.) – No

Neveu (Fr.) – nephew

Nicht berühen (Ge.) – Don't touch!

Oncle (Fr.) – uncle

Pain m grille (Fr.) – grilled bread

Parlez vouz anglais? (Fr.) – Do you speak English?

Per boite (Fr.) – per box

Per bouteille (Fr.) – per bottle

Rasieren (Ge.) – razor, shave

Rottenfuhrer (Ge.) – corporal

Schokolade (Ge.) – chocolate

Sehr gut (Ge.) – very good

Selbstverständlich – Right!

S'il vous plait (Fr.) – if you please, please

Soldat (Ge.) – soldier

Strandort (Ge.) – garrison

Sturmbannfuhrer (Ge.) – Major

Schön (Ge.) – beautiful

Strasse (Ge.) – street

Stuhlgang (Ge.) – bowel movement

Vous pouvez bassier le prix? (Fr.) – Can you lower the price?

Was ist du Name? (Ge.) – What is your name?

Was ist los? (Ge.) – What's happening?

Was ist tag? (Ge.) – What day is it?

Wasser (Ge.) – water

Weib (Ge.) – woman

Wie alt sind Sie? (Ge.) – How old are you?

Wie Spat ist es? (Ge.) – What time is it?

Wo bin ich? (Ge.) – Where am I?